A Lady's Guide to Mischief and Murder

Center Point
Large Print

Also by Dianne Freeman and available from Center Point Large Print:

A Lady's Guide to Etiquette and Murder
A Lady's Guide to Gossip and Murder

This Large Print Book carries the Seal of Approval of N.A.V.H.

A Lady's Guide to Mischief and Murder

Dianne Freeman

CENTER POINT LARGE PRINT
THORNDIKE, MAINE

For my mom and dad, Lottie and Hank Halicki.
Love and miss you!

- - - - -

This Center Point Large Print edition
is published in the year 2021 by arrangement with
Kensington Publishing Corp.

The text of this Large Print edition is unabridged.
In other aspects, this book may vary
from the original edition.
Printed in the United States of America
on permanent paper.
Set in 16-point Times New Roman type.

ISBN: 978-1-64358-811-7

The Library of Congress has cataloged this record
under Library of Congress Control Number: 2020948316

Chapter 1

October 1899

Why does it always happen that just when I begin to feel life simply couldn't get any better, fate drops a disaster into my path to prove me right?

While I have no idea how common this phenomenon may be among people in general, it happens to me with rather exasperating frequency. For example, a little over ten years ago, when I was merely Miss Frances Price, I married the man of my mother's dreams and became Frances, Countess of Harleigh. A joyous occasion. I'd done my family proud. My husband was dashing and handsome. I learned too late he was also feckless and philandering. After making me miserable for nine years, he had the audacity to die in the bed of his lover. Once I'd emerged from mourning, I found myself similarly buoyant and optimistic. That period also ended in death, or more precisely, murder.

This cycle of highs and lows weighed on my mind because my life, at the moment, was purely idyllic and I couldn't help but wonder if disaster loomed right around the corner. Regardless, I carried on as usual, taking breakfast in the nursery with my eight-year-old daughter, Rose, while we made plans for an upcoming visit to the country. When the time came for her lessons, I slipped downstairs to my library, where Mrs. Thompson, my housekeeper, had left a pot of coffee next to the morning mail on my desk, and waxwings trilled outside the window looking out over the garden. While enjoying my first sip, I learned that was the moment fate would drop the other shoe.

Aunt Hetty and my sister, Lily, slipped into the room, both looking far too distressed for such a fine morning. Lily was soon to be married, and she'd been floating through the past two months as the happiest of brides-to-be. But with her blue eyes red-rimmed and watery, her complexion blotchy, and her golden hair spilling from its coiffure, she looked rather like a ghoulish version of her usual, sunny self.

The first twinges of apprehension tickled the back of my neck like icy fingers. "Dearest, is something amiss?"

She burst into tears.

Hetty wrapped her arms around Lily and cast a scowl my way. "Now look what you've done."

I must admit the exchange left me baffled. And concerned. I swept around the desk and leaned over my sister. "Lily, please, tell me what happened."

As her tears continued to flow, Hetty settled her in a chair and gave me the news. Lily was with child. I reeled back against the desk and uttered the first word that came to mind.

"Disaster!"

This brought on renewed wailing and a fresh bout of tears from Lily, and a peevish huff from Aunt Hetty.

"Honestly, Frances, you are no help at all. Lily turns to you with her troubles, and this is your reaction?"

I gave her a slow-burning glare, intended to make her cringe, or at least take her criticism elsewhere. It didn't work. Hetty was immune to glares, mine or anyone else's. As my father's sister, she shared his pragmatic nature, dark hair and eyes, and the uncanny ability to make money from anything. Hetty had survived the loss of a beloved husband, made and lost several fortunes, and held her own with businessmen and society matrons alike. She was not to be intimidated by the likes of me.

Instead, she sidled up to Lily and placed a protective arm around her shoulders. As if I were going to harm her in some way. For her part, Lily struggled to fight back her tears and mopped her eyes with a handkerchief.

"Of course I'll help. You just took me by

surprise." I glanced at my sister and sighed. "Your wedding is only eight weeks away. Couldn't you have waited?"

Lily, with the face of an innocent babe, raised her handkerchief to her watery eyes. "That's exactly the point, Franny. We saw no reason to wait." As she waved the handkerchief dismissively, Hetty drew back and took her own seat. "After all, we'll be married so soon. I had no idea it could happen this quickly. You and Reggie were married for some time before Rose came along. And Aunt Hetty was married for years and never had children. How should I have known?"

How should I have known was not likely to pass muster as an excuse for our mother. I could just imagine her reaction had I made such an announcement *before* my wedding. Though now I think about it, it wasn't as if there'd been time. My mother had singled Reggie out as a possible husband for me before we even left New York. A mutual friend introduced us soon after we'd arrived in London. Reggie and I danced a few times, he and my mother came to terms, and we were married without ever having a chance to become acquainted.

Have I mentioned the marriage was a disaster? Is it any wonder I wanted Lily and Leo to have a long engagement period? To take some time and come to know one another?

Clearly, they came to know one another all too well. Now what were we to do?

"Leo suggested we elope," Lily said, almost in a whisper.

Her words pulled me from my thoughts. "Oh, no, dear. That will never do."

She balled the handkerchief in her fist. "Well, we can't wait eight weeks as we'd planned. How on earth will I explain giving birth so soon? It would be less than six months."

"You wouldn't be the first, dear." Hetty patted her hand.

"No, you wouldn't, but if it can be avoided, so much the better. However, an elopement is almost a proclamation that one is with child. I agree the original wedding date is out of the question, but an elopement is not a satisfactory alternative." So where did that leave us?

Since Lily seemed to have recovered herself, I ventured to ask another tricky question. "What does Leo's mother say?"

She gawked at me as if I'd just asked her to set herself on fire. "Mrs. Kendrick says nothing as she has absolutely no idea of our situation." Her voice had become a shriek. "You cannot seriously think I'd tell her? Frances, I'd die first." She stared and clutched at her throat as if choking. "I'd simply die."

"Well, we can't have that, but how do you intend to keep this from her?"

"That was the point of the elopement."

I was relieved to see Hetty narrow her eyes in confusion. "Were you planning to elope and stay away for nine months?" she asked.

Lily took a breath to speak then stopped herself, sinking against the back of the chair. "Bother. I suppose we'd have to, wouldn't we?"

"Leo couldn't do that, dear, at least not without giving his father a very good reason. Unless he can come up with a plausible lie, you will still have to tell them the truth. Mr. Kendrick isn't likely to allow him a nine-month wedding trip."

Leo Kendrick was a businessman. In fact, he was a partner in his father's business. I wasn't entirely cognizant of what he did, except a portion of the business involved mining and part, manufacture. His grandfather had started the company, and his father expanded it and made it quite profitable. Enough to raise his daughters as gently bred ladies and send his son to the best schools and raise him as a gentleman. Though he planned for Leo to take over the running of their enterprise eventually, all four of the children were expected to make advantageous marriages.

Leo's oldest sister, Eliza, had done just that, and Leo's choice of Lily also met with his father's approval. Thank goodness, as the two were hopelessly in love. They'd have married months ago if I hadn't urged them to wait. I pulled my thoughts up short. I was not about to take responsibility for Lily's pregnancy.

But looking at her now, lost in her misery, I felt compelled to come up with a solution—as did Hetty, it seemed. Since she'd come in here to support Lily, she must have known about her condition at least a bit longer than I.

"Have you any ideas, Aunt Hetty?"

She shook her head. "I thought an elopement was their best option."

"It's not a horrible option, but it should be considered only as a last resort. Surely, we can think of something better."

"You're right." Hetty squared her jaw in determination. "We are three intelligent women. What would we do if we had every possible option to hand?"

"If Graham weren't selling Harleigh Manor, we could arrange a wedding there in under a week," I said. "Just have the closest family members in attendance. As long as we're not in town, no one will feel snubbed if they aren't invited."

I sighed and leaned against the desk behind me. Selling the old family home was the best idea my brother-in-law ever had. The behemoth of a mansion had sucked several fortunes into its very walls, including mine. That fortune was the only reason Reggie had married me. Not that I didn't have other redeeming qualities. I was a consummate hostess, an intelligent conversationalist, and knew how to dress and act in society. While I was taller than the average woman, the rest of me was indeed average—fair skin, as society required, dark hair, blue eyes—nothing off-putting, but nothing to inspire my late husband to hold me in higher regard than my dowry.

Reggie's brother, Graham, was now Earl of Harleigh, and he just couldn't afford to keep Harleigh Manor going. Fortunately, the house itself was built by his great-grandfather on an unentailed part of the property, and he was free to sell.

But it would be lovely to have use of that house now.

"A wedding in less than a week might be a bit too soon," Hetty said. "Your mother will only just be arriving, and Lily can't get married without her."

"Can't I?" Lily's lip trembled. I sympathized with her plight, but she could not marry before our mother arrived then leave me to deal with her fits of temper. Not that she wouldn't be justified after traveling all the way from New York to attend her youngest daughter's wedding.

"No, dear, you can't." I turned to consult the calendar on my desk. "Her ship arrives on Tuesday. It would be wise to marry as soon as possible after her arrival so as to leave her less time to fuss about the change in plans."

"That's why the elopement was such an

attractive idea," Lily said. "Leo's parents are away from town this week. Mother won't be here. We could marry and present them with a fait accompli."

In fact, they'd be presenting nothing. I'd be stuck with the dirty work. "That's not fair to Patricia Kendrick. Leo is her only son. She'd want to be at his wedding." I crossed my arms in front of me and gave her a long, hard look. "And the two of you will have to tell her about the baby at some point, don't you think?"

"Not until after the honeymoon. But you are right. I expect her to be disappointed in us, but if we marry quickly, at least she'll see we took some action to mitigate the gossip." She gave me a pleading look. "That should help, don't you think?"

"Only if we find a country house in which to hold this small family wedding. So far, we only know what isn't available."

Hetty cocked her head as she turned to me. "Don't some families ever lease their homes?"

"Not for such short a time." Hetty and Lily had only been living in London since April when Lily made her debut. They still had much to learn about the ways of society. Aristocratic society, that is. One could lease one's manor out for a year or longer, and though everyone would know the family was having financial trouble, taking this step would seem like a sensible way out of those troubles. Renting one's family home out for a week, however, would give the appearance of running a hotel and would reek of middle-class business. It simply wasn't done.

"What of Leo's sister and her husband?" I ran through a mental list of distant acquaintance names. "The Durants, if I remember correctly? I know they keep a house in town, but where is Mr. Durant's family seat?"

Lily wrinkled her nose. "I'm not sure where they're from, but Leo would know better than I. Let me fetch him."

She rose and crossed the room as if Leo were waiting just outside in the hall. She opened the door and reached out.

Heavens, he was just outside in the hall.

I cast a glance at Hetty, who shrugged. "We all thought it better if he waited while Lily gave you her news."

Leo, usually friendly and gregarious, shuffled into the room, his head down. He darted nervous glances at me while Lily tugged him along behind her—a sight in itself. Leo was not a tall man, but he had a square, sturdy build, and Lily was so petite it looked as though she were guiding a repentant Goliath to a chair.

Good. He couldn't be any more uncomfortable than I, and he'd been a party to bringing this situation upon us. I invited him to sit while I searched for the right words to begin.

Hetty had no such problem. "We've been discussing your situation, Mr. Kendrick, and Lady Harleigh seems to think an elopement might give rise to a great deal of gossip."

Leo chewed on his lip while he studied me, his warm brown eyes wary. "I rather think the gossip would be less vicious over an elopement than if we wait for the proper wedding date."

"Perhaps," I said. "But not by much. Since the wedding invitations have not yet gone out, is it possible for you and Lily to change your venue and date? Somewhere in the country in a week or so, with only family in attendance."

He contemplated the idea then blew out a breath. "I can see the advantage to a quick, simple ceremony, but where exactly in the country did you intend the wedding to take place?"

"Would it be possible to hold it at Mr. Durant's family home?"

His eyes grew wide. "In Northumberland?"

I slumped back against the desk and let out a *tsk*. "That far away?"

He bobbed his head. "And I'm not certain they'd be agreeable to the idea. Durant's not very close to his family. Don't know if he'd be willing to ask them."

"Well, that settles it," Lily said. "We will have to elope." She perched on the arm of Leo's chair. "And we should do it quickly while your parents are away."

I hated the idea, but before I could comment, a knock sounded at the door and Mrs. Thompson poked her gray head inside.

"Mr. Hazelton is here for you, my lady."

"Is he?" I couldn't stop the smile that slipped across my lips. No matter what problems bore down on me, just the thought of George Hazelton drove them from my mind.

"Must you see him now?" Lily flashed me a look of impatience.

I rose to my feet. "Yes, I must. He's on his way to Risings, so he won't be here long, dear. Besides, you and Leo have a great deal of planning to do." I shot her a warning look as I followed Mrs. Thompson out. "Don't you dare leave before I return."

The second I stepped through the drawing room door, George pulled me into his arms. I made no protest. On the contrary, I thoroughly approved of his actions. George Hazelton and I were to be wed, though we kept that lovely secret to ourselves, so as not to steal Lily's thunder. Once she and Leo married, we could make our announcement.

I released a small sigh at the thought of Lily's wedding.

George pulled back and gave me a penetrating look. "That sounded nothing like a sigh of pleasure, Frances. Is something wrong?"

Dearest George. Still in his arms, I reached up

16

to brush back a dark lock of hair. I loved that I had to tip my head back to look into his eyes, but was close enough to see the dark rim surrounding the paler green iris, so full of mystery. It could take years to unravel the mystery of this man, and I would treasure every one.

Slipping my hand into his, I led him over to the cozy conversation area of a large tea table surrounded by plump sofas and chairs, upholstered in a blue and white print. We settled into one of the sofas. "Just a little trouble with Lily and Leo's wedding plans. Nothing so terrible, I suppose."

He frowned, making two vertical lines appear between his brows. "Please tell me it won't keep you from joining me at my brother's home next week. A romantic rendezvous requires the presence of both parties. I can't do it without you, you know."

I placed a hand over my heart. "Ah, yes. You, me, and the dozen people who make up your shooting party. The ambiance leaves me breathless."

"I've only invited the Evingdons, my sister, and her husband. The rest are neighbors who won't be staying at the house so I believe I can arrange the ambiance you seek." His voice dropped to a low growl, sending shivers across my shoulders.

George was the youngest brother to the Earl of Hartfield, who was currently traveling on the continent with his wife, a second honeymoon of sorts. They set out on their trip a month ago and planned to continue their travels for another. As this was quite some time spent away from the estate, the earl had asked George to check on Risings, to ensure everything continued running smoothly. He agreed, of course, and would be leaving today for a stay of two weeks. And what would two autumn weeks in the country be without a shooting party?

The prospect of such an event left him as excited as a child with a new puppy. He'd asked me several times to join him, and I finally conceded. Though with Lily's wedding coming up, I thought I could only spare a week.

"Actually, this spot of trouble means I may be able to join you even sooner."

His brow smoothed as he grinned. "Have they decided to elope then? Wise choice."

I shrugged. "As it happens, it's their only choice."

"You're serious." He leaned back and took me in with a glance. "Truly? After all their plans they intend to elope?"

"They must marry soon." I gave him a meaningful look.

He responded with a blank stare. "They are marrying soon."

Clearly, I needed to work on my facial expressions. "No. I mean they must marry immediately."

His raised brows told me he finally understood. "Isn't your mother on her way as we speak? She'll be terribly disappointed if she misses the wedding."

"As will Leo's mother, but we couldn't think of another option. I suggested we put together a small family ceremony in the country, but Harleigh Manor is for sale and thus, unavailable." I shrugged. "As Leo's parents have no country home, there is nowhere to gather even a small family party."

"They could come to Risings. Plenty of room there."

"That's lovely of you to offer, but your brother is no relation to any of us. We cannot ask him to host a wedding, even a small one. It's far too much of an imposition."

"Correction." He held up his index finger. "You are soon to be my brother's sister, a very close relation indeed." A second finger joined the first. "He is not in residence, thus no imposition at all. And finally"—his ring finger joined the others—"I am already hosting a shooting party as Hartfield has given me leave to entertain as I wish. Another dozen people or so will make no difference." He gave me a nudge with his shoulder. "Bring them to Risings."

I bit my lip, hardly believing my good fortune, or Lily's good fortune as it were. Perhaps this could work after all. Risings was in Hampshire.

Not far at all. We could gather the immediate family quickly. My mother would arrive in just a few days, and both she and Mrs. Kendrick could attend their children's wedding. This could work. A quick but proper wedding. No disappointed parents. Society none the wiser.

"If you are in earnest, and you really don't mind." I paused, giving him a chance to reconsider, but he merely cocked his head, awaiting my answer.

I leaned my head against his shoulder, relieved to have a solution. "Thank you, George. That would take care of everything."

"I am always happy to help you in any endeavor. And I'd also hate to exclude a mother from her child's wedding."

A grimace twisted my lips as I gazed up at him. "I confess, the thought of telling my mother she missed the wedding is largely what motivates me." I shuddered at the thought.

He nodded. "Yes, I've met your mother. I would not want to be the bearer of bad news either."

"Well, now neither of us has that onerous task." I pressed his hand to my cheek. "Thank you, George. You always manage to have the solution to my problems."

"You offer the best rewards." He twined his fingers with mine and brought us both to our feet.

"I don't recall offering a reward."

"You'll be joining me at Risings at least a

week before I expected you. I'd call that a reward."

He pulled his watch from his pocket, unaware he'd removed a letter at the same time. It fell to the floor while he checked the time.

"Do you leave right now?" I asked.

"Almost, I have a stop to make first, so I should be off."

As he headed toward the entry hall, I picked up his letter and trailed behind him. "Is your stop at Newgate Prison?"

"What?" He snapped around so quickly I almost ran into him. "No. Why would you ask such a thing?"

I pulled back in surprise, the letter dangling from my fingers as I handed it to him. "This fell from your pocket." The lines of tension around his mouth faded as he relaxed his jaw. He took the envelope and shoved it back into his coat.

"I couldn't help noticing it came from Newgate. Are you corresponding with a prisoner?"

He let out a sharp laugh. "Hardly that, but it does relate to my errand. I'm taking it to the Home Office." He rested a finger against my lips. "Don't even ask. You know I can't tell you."

"I'm marrying a very mysterious man," I said, the words distorted by the pressure of his finger on my lips. With a smile, he replaced the finger with his own lips, and I was reminded how much I loved him.

A few minutes later, I'd seen him out the

door and leaned back against it, considering the morning's events. I'd been presented with a somewhat sticky problem, and with George's help, managed to work through it. Holding the wedding at Risings was the perfect solution.

Fiona, George's sister and my best friend, would be there as her husband, Sir Robert, would be joining the shoot. She'd be a great help. Once I determined how to transport my mother to the country when she arrived, this should be a relatively simple operation. One small wedding to plan. How difficult could that be? Perhaps I'd broken my cycle of highs and lows.

Chapter 2

‿‿⁀ᗓ

After seeing George out, I returned to the library to share the good news and was surprised to find Lily less than thrilled.

"I can't believe you told Mr. Hazelton."

Even Leo's cheeks reddened, and once again he refused to meet my eye.

Dear, perhaps I shouldn't have told him. Though I considered George as almost my husband, these three were unaware of our engagement and understandably did not see him as family. I sat down on the window seat, facing my sister and her fiancé.

And lied.

"I told him nothing, Lily. I simply stated the two of you were unwilling to wait another eight weeks and were threatening elopement." I made a mental note to ask George to forget he knew anything about Lily's condition.

"So he offered his family home for our wedding ceremony?" Leo looked unconvinced.

"Well, I did mention my objections to the elopement." I shrugged. "And then he offered."

Lily nodded and seemed to accept the idea, but Leo watched me with suspicion. "It's possible he just guessed there might be more to your decision than impatience," I added. "But since he made the offer of hosting the ceremony, and your family, at his brother's home, he does not appear to be either judging nor condemning your behavior."

At this Leo turned an even brighter red, something I hadn't thought possible.

"Why do you hesitate?" I spread my hands. "Does this not provide the perfect solution?"

"I would say it does," Hetty said from her perch against my desk. "But this is rather a large favor, Frances, don't you think? I'm just a little surprised at your willingness to accept it." She eyed me suspiciously. "This is the type of favor a close family member might offer."

A hint of a smirk played at the corner of her lips. Aunt Hetty saw George as the perfect match for me and had hopes of a marriage between us. Knowing I had the power to send her into transports of delight tempted me sorely to tell her the truth, but with Lily and Leo in this awkward position, it was perhaps not the right time.

"Mr. Hazelton is such a close friend to us all, he feels part of the family. And for Lily and Leo's sake, or more for their mothers' sake, I chose not to look too closely at the propriety of accepting his offer." I raised a brow. "Call me a coward if you must, but I'd rather not have to explain to them why their children eloped."

Hetty's smile gave way to a look of horror at the prospect of such a task. "No, I cannot blame you for that. But it brings to mind another bit of trouble. Daisy will be arriving with your brother in only three days. If we are all gone to Hampshire, how is she to know where to find us?"

Daisy was my mother. Though she'd been christened Marguerite, her father, an amateur botanist, quickly dubbed her Daisy, a name that bothered her not a whit until we all moved to New York, and Mother tried to break into the Knickerbocker society. To her, the name Daisy seemed too indicative of the lower classes. But her secret slipped out, and much to her disappointment, once she was known as Daisy, the name stuck.

"Leo's parents won't know either," Lily said. She'd perked up a bit as if she was just beginning to realize this plan might actually work.

"Can you send a message to your parents, Leo?" I asked. "I understand they have gone to visit one of your father's factories."

"I'd rather not give them too much warning," he said. "My mother would likely drag my father back home so she could orchestrate the proceedings or attempt to change our minds." His lips twitched upward on one side. "Now it is my turn to be called cowardly, but I'd prefer to leave instructions with the butler and have them come to Risings upon their return home."

Lily nodded her agreement, and I suppose I understood. Armed with a plan, they wanted nothing to interfere with it. Even a well-intentioned mother.

Which left only our mother to worry about.

"I suppose I can do my part and take care of Daisy," Hetty said.

I turned to see her taking a deep breath as if bracing herself against the onslaught of my mother's ire.

"Define *'take care of,'*" I said. Visions of Hetty locking Mother in a spare guest room passed through my mind.

"I'll stay behind to meet them, tell them about the change in plans, and escort them to Risings the following day."

"That's very kind of you, Mrs. Chesney." Leo looked doubtful. "Though I don't know how else we'd manage it, are you certain you don't mind?"

"I'm sure, my dear boy." She leaned forward and patted his hand. "Lily's brother, Alonzo, is accompanying Daisy on this trip. He'll be a great help to me."

"What about Leo's sisters?" Lily asked. "And Mr. Treadwell." She turned to Leo. "He's to be your best man, is he not?"

Leo had not yet caught Lily's excitement. His brow furrowed when he turned to me. "As long as you're confident Mr. Hazelton won't consider it an intrusion, I can see this is a much better solution than eloping." The taut line of his jaw relaxed as he squeezed Lily's hand. "And I would very much like to have my family at our wedding."

"They were all included in Mr. Hazelton's invitation, so you can be assured they'll be welcome." I glanced around at my partners in intrigue. "Are we all agreed to this plan?"

"Agreed," Leo said with authority. "And thank you, Lady Harleigh."

I received nods from Lily and Hetty, and that was that. I left it to Leo to take care of the travel arrangements and round up his siblings. We had our own arrangements to make, and we'd best see to our packing.

Leo shared my love of organization, and between the two of us, we managed to shuttle a mass of luggage, five maids, a valet, one nanny, and one eight-year-old to Victoria Station in time to board the train to the town of Harroway early the following morning. The adult guests, we assumed, could manage their own transport to the station.

Yet, as the time drew near to depart, six of us found ourselves on the platform, tapping our toes as we waited for Leo's elder sister, Eliza, and her husband, Arthur.

Leo craned his neck, hoping to spot his sister in the stream of fellow travelers. "Are you certain

Eliza said they'd meet us?" This was the third time Leo had asked the question of Anne, his younger sister, and each time she answered with an increasing level of heat.

"They are adults, Leo. If they don't arrive in time, I'm confident they can find their way to Risings without us."

All the Kendrick siblings, at least the ones I'd met, resembled one another. The sisters both had a softer version of Leo's chiseled features. All three had a downward tip to their noses, brown wavy hair, and the same eye color—coffee with a dollop of cream, yet I'd never say their eyes were alike. Leo's were round and wide and the proverbial window to his soul. One had only to look into his eyes to know his mind and heart. Clara, the youngest had half-moon-shaped eyes that sparkled and tipped upward at the corners as if they were smiling even before she did.

At the moment, Anne's could only be described as impatient, and I didn't think it was all due to her sister's tardiness.

"Miss Kendrick's right, old man. I think we should board." The suggestion came from Ernest Treadwell, another member of our party. We had a slight acquaintance as we moved in the same social circles. In his mid-twenties, he was tall, lean, fair, and wore an air of entitlement, hardly unusual among the young men of his class. The second son of a viscount, he would neither inherit the title nor ever want for money, as the family was enormously wealthy and his allowance generous. Nothing was expected of him but charm and good manners. He could meet those expectations when he chose to do so. He struck me as an odd friend for Leo, but they'd been close since their school days, so there must be something to Treadwell I didn't quite see.

Leo finally agreed we should wait no longer, but as Treadwell assisted the misses Kendrick into the train car, someone hailed Leo from farther down the platform. The Durants had finally arrived.

"Just in time," Leo said. He took my arm and assisted me up the step to the train, then turned to provide the same service for his sister.

Once inside, Arthur Durant slipped across the compartment with a nod to acknowledge the group, while Eliza stood in the doorway blocking Leo's entrance. Shifting her to the side, he moved around her and introduced the two of us.

Eliza had her mother's good looks—a flawless complexion, rounded cheeks, pointed chin, and golden-brown hair—combined with the same wide, brown eyes as Leo. Hers narrowed upon spotting Treadwell.

"Good morning, Mrs. Durant." Treadwell touched the brim of his hat and gave her a crooked smile. "So pleased you could join us."

With a sniff, Eliza took a seat next to me. "Forgive us for being so tardy," she said. "I had such a difficult time convincing Durant to accompany me. He was most determined to stay at home and see to business."

"Right. Seems as though someone ought to." Durant had removed his hat and overcoat and balanced a document case on his knees. The lines between his dark brows led me to believe the scowl he wore was of a permanent nature. It made him look older than I suspected him to be, but with a beard covering his jawline and chin, and spectacles blurring his eyes, I found it difficult to venture a guess at his age, though his disposition was easy to read. I might pity Eliza if she did not look equally irritable.

As Leo hadn't known how many of his siblings would be traveling with us, he'd taken a first-class compartment in a Pullman car. This was fortunate since we were eight now that the Durants had arrived. There was plenty of room inside for all of us, but I was still pleased I'd decided to have Rose travel with Nanny, Bridget, and the other maids. Rose's manners were good, but I didn't know if they'd stretch to accommodate the two-hour trip.

I needn't have concerned myself. The train was barely underway when the bickering began between Leo's younger sisters.

I'd met Clara and Anne at my first dinner

with Leo's parents. Anne had impressed me as an intelligent young woman, not yet married at the age of twenty-three. I felt certain she'd love nothing more than to join her father in the world of business. As that was not an option, she occupied herself with lectures, committees, and reading. Leo's youngest sister, Clara, not yet eighteen, wanted nothing more than parties, balls, and fetes. Hardly uncommon pursuits at her age. Though they had their differences, they had seemed well-mannered and got on as well as any two sisters might. I now suspected that amity was due to the presence of their parents.

Within fifteen minutes of our departure, I was to find out what they were like without the watchful eye of their mother. The compartment we occupied was spacious and fitted out with comfortably upholstered chairs situated against both the forward and rear walls, carpet, curtains, and a table along the side, all of which made it feel like a smallish sitting room. Leo and Durant took two seats along one side of the compartment and made a makeshift desk between them, leaving not quite two seats beside them. Regardless, Anne and Clara chose to squeeze into the space. The result was explosive.

"You are sitting on my dress!"

Anne looked up from her book and rearranged the skirts between them. Peace reigned for less than thirty seconds.

"Stop reading over my shoulder," Anne said, never lifting her eyes from the book.

"I am not reading over your shoulder. Who but you would want to read such boring, dusty old tomes? Why didn't you bring a novel to read?"

"If I did, you would read over my shoulder."

"Aha! So you admit I am not now reading over your shoulder."

"If you weren't, you would not know what I was reading. And why didn't you bring a novel of your own if you wish to read so badly?"

The bickering continued for a quarter of an hour at least. I cast a glance at Lily sitting next to Mr. Treadwell a seat away from me. Though they were directly across from the girls, they seemed not to notice and maintained a conversation that had Lily smiling. I began to wonder if I was the only one bothered by the argument.

"The two of you are behaving like children." The outburst came from Eliza. Her fine brows were drawn together, her dark eyes narrowed. As she leaned in toward her sisters, her profile to me, she looked for all the world like a hawk poised to attack her younger siblings. "I'd expect you to behave better in company than you do at home."

Her rebuke seemed rather harsh. The two sisters jerked back in surprise, but in the space of time it took to draw a breath, they joined forces against Eliza, and the worst kind of caterwauling ensued.

Through it all, Leo and his brother-in-law remained oblivious. The two men busied themselves with some documents, though how they were able to concentrate at all amazed me. I could take it no longer.

"Anne."

All three young ladies turned their gazes on me, surprised to hear someone else speak.

"Why don't you trade seats with me? I believe the light is better here for your reading." I stood before she could answer, giving her no choice but to comply. With the exchange made, I sat on the bench next to Clara, with Lily and Treadwell now across from me. Eliza pulled out some needlework and Anne returned to her book.

Perhaps this new configuration would allow us some peace. I gave Clara a smile. Dressed in a tailored traveling suit of plum wool, her warm brown curls upswept and supporting a tiny hat with a matching plum feather, she looked very grown up. I had to remind myself she was still only seventeen and not yet "out." "Have you spent much time in the country, Miss Kendrick?" I asked.

She shook her head. "I really haven't traveled much outside of London. Once to Oxford when Leo was at school there. My parents travel for business of course, but they leave us at home."

"Then this should be rather exciting for you."

But I'd already lost her attention. I followed

33

her gaze to Lily and Treadwell, who were still in conversation and—heavens! His hand rested atop her hand, which rested atop her knee.

It lasted less than an instant. Lily laughed and moved her hand. Treadwell pulled his back. In the next moment, he leaned forward to say something to Anne.

Lily's expression was perfectly calm—no blush, no glance about to see if anyone had noticed. Surely, my imagination had exaggerated his touch, blown it up into something more intimate than it really was. Lily loved Leo. Of that there could be no doubt.

Treadwell was Leo's closest friend and a gentleman. Not that a gentleman couldn't be a bounder, but Lily had no interest in men who had nothing with which to occupy themselves but their own entertainment. She wanted a man like our father, who worked and made something of himself. I undoubtedly imagined the incident and should put it out of my mind. I glanced around to see if anyone else had noticed and caught Eliza just as she turned away, her lips tightly compressed. Perhaps I hadn't imagined it. Would she say something to Lily? Or worse, to Leo?

"Clara, can't you see you're crowding Lady Harleigh?" Eliza's tone was sharp.

This brought me from my reverie to see the girl leaning almost into my lap and nearly clipping my jaw as she shot back into her seat.

"I am not," she said.

"You were."

The balance of the trip continued in this manner. A short silence, followed by bickering, followed by admonishments, and a full-scale argument. When Eliza snapped at her sisters, I wondered if she was truly annoyed with them, or upset by Treadwell's forward behavior to Lily, and taking her anger out on the girls. By the time we arrived at the Harroway station, I had reached the end of my tether and could not have suffered their company for another mile.

As the train came to a stop, I smoothed a hand over my skirts, chasing the wrinkles, and straightened my hat. Once I felt presentable, I glanced around the compartment and realized everyone waited for me.

"Shall we?"

Leo stepped around me and opened the door. Before my foot hit the first step, George reached up to hand me down. He had never looked better to me. With his homburg in hand, the sunlight cast a sheen on his dark, neatly trimmed hair. His suit was impeccable; a light gray with a darker waistcoat. And there I stood, rumpled from travel. His smile told me however disheveled I might be, he was delighted to see me.

"How lovely you've come to meet us," I said, loathe to release his hand once I'd reached the platform. "I thought you'd be shooting."

Apparently, George didn't want to break the connection either. He brought my hand up to his chest and drew me away from my travel companions. "And miss your arrival? I wouldn't think of it."

We paused at the end of the busy platform to wait for the others. "How was the trip?" he asked.

"Next time, I think I'll sit with Rose and Nanny." I boggled my eyes. "Or perhaps the luggage."

I brightened at the sound of his laugh. "That bad?"

"No, I am just feeling peevish." With a sigh, I returned his hand and clasped my own in front of me. The rest of our group would soon catch up with us. "The Kendrick girls are not quite the traveling companions I'd hoped for, but all will be fine, I'm sure."

"Then you'll be delighted to hear I have two conveyances to take us back to Risings."

"You are my hero," I whispered as Lily and Leo brought the Kendrick party our way.

"We'll have to take the footbridge to cross the tracks to the carriages," George said. "Shall we be on our way?"

George led our little group off the platform toward the stairs with Leo by his side. I turned to see if Lily was nearby as I'd hoped to avoid sharing a carriage with the Kendrick sisters. Of course, she lagged behind. I parted my lips to urge her to keep up just as another train pulled into the station with a screeching of brakes.

I chose to save my breath until the noise subsided, but then a new disturbance caught my attention—a rumble and banging up ahead. I glanced up at the stairway to see a cart full of baggage fairly flying down the steps directly at George and Leo. I gaped in horror as bags and trunks fell off the cart and tumbled down the stairs. In one fluid motion, George clamped a hand on Leo's arm and jumped to the side as the bags and cart landed on the pavement with a crash and a cloud of dust.

Chapter 3

A fter an instant of shocked paralysis, the rest of us rushed forward as one, stumbling over and around the offending luggage. George and Leo climbed to their feet, brushing off their clothes. Certain as I was that we'd find them at the bottom of the heap of bags, I nearly sagged with relief.

I looked George up and down, then turned to assess Leo. "I can't believe neither of you were injured."

"Good thing Hazelton acted so quickly," Leo said, "or that might not be the case. I'll admit when I looked up to see those bags tumbling toward me, I thought that might be the end."

"I shall not be done in by a rogue baggage cart." George drew me aside as Lily bounded past us and threw herself into Leo's arms. I felt quite jealous as I could do no more than touch George's sleeve while we were in such a public space.

Indeed, the rest of our party stood around us, watching with interest. Treadwell stepped up and handed George his homburg. "We should call for the stationmaster, I'd say. Have him explain how the deuce such a thing could happen."

"I find it shocking we would have to call him," Eliza said with a sniff. "He should already be here to see what caused all this racket."

Anne gave her sister a look of scorn. "The train was arriving at the same time. I doubt anyone on the platform heard a thing."

"Unless you've a mind to call for him, Hazelton," Leo said, "I'd rather we just move on. Obviously, someone left the cart unattended."

"And at the top of a stairway." Treadwell clucked his tongue. "Someone should lose his position for such a careless act."

"I do believe we should call for the station-master," I said. "I'd like to give him a piece of my mind."

George grazed my fingers with his own. "While I dislike denying you the satisfaction, Lady Harleigh, I'm of the same mind as Kendrick. We are off to a rather sticky beginning, but both of us are fit, so I say we head to Risings and enjoy the rest of our week."

"Hear, hear," Leo added.

With the two of them determined to brush off the incident and get on with the week's entertainment, it would be churlish for any of the rest of us to kick up a fuss. One by one, we nodded or shrugged, and our little party climbed the stairs and set out for the carriages.

The accident had delayed us long enough to meet up with the servants outside the station. A few footmen and another man in a suit, probably an upper servant, were directing the loading of our luggage onto a cart. I spotted Rose holding Nanny's hand and took her into my custody, while George quickly dispersed our party into the two carriages. Leo, Lily, and Rose rode with us, and Mr. Treadwell, Mr. Durant, and Leo's sisters climbed into the second carriage. The servants would follow us to Risings with our bags.

The drive took less than an hour but was long enough to calm my nerves. George and Leo were fine after all, and while the accident had been quite bizarre, no venture was without its stumbling blocks. I stole a glance at George through the corner of my eye. He appeared unscathed.

"I am fine, Lady Harleigh." His lips twitched into a smirk. "Stop worrying about me and enjoy the scenery."

I leaned forward to see we were approaching a bridge that crossed a lake. "Are we close to the estate?"

"We're on the property now," he said. "Change seats with me so you can see it from the window."

"I'd like to see, too," Rose said, wriggling forward in her seat opposite us.

"Excellent. Step right up to the window, young lady. Your mother and I can easily see over your head."

George took Rose's hand to steady her as the three of us exchanged our seats. Lily and Leo, on the opposite seat with their heads together, were oblivious to our activity. "Is that your lake, Mr. Hazelton?" Rose asked.

"Not mine, but it belongs to the estate, yes."

I absorbed the fact that the Hazeltons owned this lovely lake, and while we crossed at the narrows, I could see it widened to our right and reflected the gold-tinged meadowland surrounding it, as well as an enormous edifice. Pushing my head closer to the window, I let out a gasp as the house came into view. The meadow gave way to a manicured lawn, which in turn gave way to a graveled drive along the front of the house which seemed to stretch on forever in pure grandeur.

The carriage stopped in front of a grand stone stairway leading to a great hall at the center of the house. It was framed by two wings, three stories high, with balconied porches on the second floor leading to what must be state apartments. The house was apparently designed to accommodate royal visits. It was the fantasy of any young girl who ever dreamt of becoming a princess.

As we climbed down from the carriage, Rose stared in awe, reminding me to close my mouth and stop gawking. "My goodness, Mr. Hazelton, your sister has described Risings to me, and indeed I've heard of its beauty, but nothing prepared me for its sheer size."

"Is this your first visit?" George looked surprised. "I'd thought surely you'd been here with Fiona."

I took his arm as we all headed for the entrance, gravel crunching under our shoes. "The first time I visited your sister, she was already a married woman with a country home of her own."

"Then you must allow me to give you a tour," he said as a gray-haired, painfully thin butler bowed us inside.

We entered a great hall, as large as a ballroom, walled with carved oak panels, and topped with windows that reached up to the two-story ceiling where three chandeliers were suspended. The housekeeper, Mrs. Ansel, waited in the entry to take everyone up to their rooms. Once they'd freshened up, tea would be served in the drawing room.

George held my arm when I would have joined the group heading up the stairs and sent Mrs. Ansel on without me. "Lady Nash will be joining us shortly. She wished to greet Lady Harleigh."

"I am here now." Fiona's voice rang through the hall as she entered from a door at the opposite end. Her shoes tapped on the marble floor as she sailed across the room, holding out her hands to take mine. Fiona was one of only a few ladies of my acquaintance taller than I, and as she looked down her narrow nose and into my eyes, I could see true happiness glowing in hers. She was the only person I'd informed of the understanding between George and me, and this was our first meeting since I'd sent that letter, so I could well understand her enthusiasm.

She nearly burst with joy, bouncing on the balls of her feet until her chestnut coiffure threatened to come tumbling around her shoulders. Once Nanny arrived to take Rose to her room up in the nursery, and only the three of us remained in the hall, she caught my hands in hers.

"Frances, I cannot properly convey my delight that you and George are to be married." She gave my hands one final squeeze and released me in favor of her brother, declaring he had made her the happiest of sisters.

"Your happiness was uppermost in our minds, Fi," George replied, earning him a poke in the chest.

"Now, I suppose I should leave the two of you alone. I know George plans to keep you to himself and show you the house." She kissed the air near my cheek. "Welcome to Risings, Frances. I planned a meeting with the vicar this afternoon, so come find me when you are through with George."

With that, she was off and George and I were finally alone.

"I missed you," he said. Taking my hand he lead me across the hall and through ornate double doors to the drawing room.

"I saw you just yesterday," I said, though I was thrilled to hear I'd been missed.

"That's one day too long." As he whispered the words his breath tickled my ear and his arm encircled my waist.

I turned around within the enclosure of his arms. "Well, I'm here now."

"There you are!"

George and I leaped apart as Lottie Evingdon came bounding into the room like a puppy, her flailing arms disturbing an arrangement of framed photographs on a nearby table. Though several of them wobbled, none hit the floor. For Lottie, I'd count that as a triumphant entrance.

She took my hands and spread them wide as if looking me over. There was likely no more change in me over the last two months than I saw in her. Her dark ginger hair still refused to stay where her maid pinned it, a smudge of ink marred one creamy cheek, and a shawl had fallen from her shoulders and now lay on the floor. "I was so excited to hear you were all to join us. This is the first I've seen of you since my wedding."

Lottie Evingdon, formerly Deaver, was a friend of Lily's from New York. She'd come to stay with us last summer and met my cousin, and George's friend, Charles Evingdon. They fell in love while we were all trying to prove him innocent of murder. Perhaps the fact that I'd allowed her near an accused murderer means I'm not the best of chaperones, but given the fact that they married, it all worked out in the end.

Except she'd just interrupted what might have been a tender moment between George and me. I supposed I'd better get used to it. This was a house party, so it was likely to happen more often than not.

We chatted for a moment and I sent her off to find Lily. Once she departed, I turned to George. "Is there perhaps a more secluded part of the house you could show me?"

"An excellent idea." With a smile, he took my arm and led me out of the drawing room and into a gallery that ran behind the great hall and connected the two wings. He drew me outside to a formal garden in the courtyard at the back of the house.

"There's something I want to show you," he said, pausing in the middle of the courtyard between a fountain and a tall spray of asters.

"Indeed? Is it a flower?"

He removed a small box from his pocket and held it between his finger and thumb. "It's a ring." His lips quirked into a crooked smile. "A betrothal ring."

My hands fluttered before my chest until I clasped them together and brought them to my lips to cover a squeak of excitement. I couldn't help but laugh at myself. "Forgive me, George. I'm as giddy as a schoolgirl."

"I can't recall the last time I was this nervous." He held the box before me and opened the lid to reveal a single round diamond in a setting of intricate gold latticework, studded with more tiny diamonds.

I gasped. "It's beautiful!"

"Then you like it?"

I tore my gaze away from the ring to look at his face. His brows were drawn down in concern. An uneasy smile played on his lips. "You truly are nervous," I said.

"I had it commissioned the very day after you agreed to marry me. Then we decided to wait to make a public announcement until after your sister's wedding. I've had it for over a month and each time I look at it, I worry you won't like it."

"It's perfect." I reached up to caress his cheek. "I can't imagine anything more beautiful."

He blew out a breath of relief and, taking my hand, dropped a kiss into my palm, and another on my lips, then moved to return the ring to his pocket.

I stilled his hand. "Wait. May I not try it on?"

"No, you may not." The box disappeared into his coat. "I know you can't wear it yet, and I refuse to put it on your finger only to take it off again."

I stared in disbelief, my mouth drooped open. "What was the point of showing it to me only to put it back in your pocket?"

"What is the point of a betrothal that must be kept secret?"

I went numb. Had he torn off his clothes and jumped into the fountain, I couldn't have been more stunned. "What do you mean?"

He turned his face to the sky and let out a groan. "I shouldn't have said that." Taking my arm, he led me back to the house. "Let's continue our tour. I think better when I'm moving."

We stepped back into the gallery and headed toward the north wing, side by side, our hands behind our backs. I was still too shocked to speak. After a few minutes of nothing but the sound of our heels clicking on the marble floor, he took a deep breath.

"I well and truly mucked that up." He snuck a glance at my face. "Since I have no idea when our betrothal can become public or when our wedding will take place, I've become somewhat anxious."

I cannot describe the relief I felt in that moment. Though he'd just presented a ring, I'd been almost certain I'd lost him. With relief, came anger. "Don't ever frighten me like that again. If you objected to keeping our engagement secret, why didn't you say so when I suggested it?"

He pretended to grimace at my sharp tone as he opened a door and we entered a library. "I don't mind keeping the news between us, but we've made no plans, we've set no date. I fear you'd be content to stay betrothed indefinitely. I, on the other hand, wish to marry you."

His words struck home. I'd been so caught up in Lily's wedding plans, that I failed to make any of my own. But he spoke another truth, one I didn't care to admit—I might very well be content to stay betrothed indefinitely.

We left the library and moved throughout the house, but I have little memory of anything he showed me. We discussed how we'd tell Rose, (together), how we'd tell my mother, (I'd handle that), and how soon we'd marry (as soon as the banns were read). But we never touched on the topic that concerned me the most. What role would I play in this partnership? Before I could bring that up, Fiona arrived to collect me for our visit to the vicar.

"Are you showing Frances where to find you, brother dear?" She rested her arm on the railing of an elegant staircase.

I glance up its length. "Where does this lead? I thought we were in the working part of the house."

"On this floor, yes," George said. "But upstairs is the bachelors' wing. It's an addition to the second floor, running over the kitchens and alongside the old nursery and schoolroom. It's to keep the unmarried ladies of the house safe from those lecherous bachelor visitors. There's a second staircase farther down the hall." He waggled his brows. "In case you do need to find me."

"I see, but as family, why are you staying here? Surely your brother keeps a guest room for you in this house?"

He smiled. "I usually stay in a large and beautifully appointed room at the back of the south wing, looking out over the maze and gardens. When I realized your mother would be joining us, I put her in that room."

Fiona rolled her eyes as I sighed and, I'm certain, took on the look of a lovesick puppy. "How kind of you." Honestly, the man thought of everything.

"That's all very nice," Fiona said. "But we really should be off, Frances, or we may miss the vicar."

"Where is Lily? Is she not coming with us?"

"I believe she and Mr. Kendrick are exploring the grounds." Fiona gave my arm a tug, but I kept my feet firmly planted.

"What do you mean she's exploring the grounds? She should be coming with us. It's her wedding after all."

Fiona waved away my protest. "I suggested as much, but she feels you will make the right choices. It seems she's happy for a few moments alone with her fiancé and doesn't wish to go."

I heaved a sigh and considered dragging Lily

off with us, but from the set of Fiona's jaw I could tell she wanted no interference in the wedding plans, even from someone as consequential as the bride. Ultimately, I gave in.

Our visit with the vicar proceeded splendidly. The church was perfectly picturesque, seventeenth-century stonework, placed in a bucolic setting and enclosed by a stone wall covered in vines. Fiona assured me the greenhouse at Risings could provide flowers in abundance. Lily was sure to be thrilled with it.

Once we showed the vicar the license, he became most accommodating and set the date for Saturday morning, six days hence. He was also helpful with his suggestions for decorating the church and where to find assistance for that task.

I was confident our decisions would please my sister, but I decided to bring her out here before the wedding so she could see everything for herself and give her stamp of approval. Within two hours, Fiona and I had settled everything and were on the wooded path for the short walk back to the manor. The sun, shining through the trees, dappled the ground before us and dry leaves crunched underfoot.

"You and George might consider holding your ceremony here," Fiona said. "Have you discussed a venue for your wedding?"

"We haven't considered a venue, but we were

making plans for the wedding just this morning." I chuckled. "It was the first time we've discussed any details. George was worried that I planned to put off the wedding."

She examined me through narrowed eyes. "Do you?"

"Of course not."

She placed a hand on my arm and came to a stop. "There's something you're not telling me. This should be the happiest time of your life. Something must be wrong, or you would have taken every opportunity to make your plans weeks ago. Now, tell me what it is."

"What could possibly be wrong?" I took a step to move on, but she tightened her grip on my arm and refused to budge.

"Fine, if you must know, I'm a little shy of marriage in general. I'm worried I'll be relegated to the role of wife and mother and deposited in the country to rusticate."

"George has no country home."

"You know what I mean." Though I wasn't entirely certain she did. George's work for the Crown was confidential and I had no idea how much Fiona knew or suspected. Would I be a part of his work, or would I sit at home and worry about him?

"Considering your marriage with Reggie, I think I understand, but George is nothing like Reggie, and you will be a wife and mother. Is there something else you wish to do? Something of which he wouldn't approve?"

How to explain it? "I simply wish for us to be partners. I don't want to take a subservient role in our marriage."

"Ah, I think you'll handle that beautifully, my dear." She gave me a warning look. "But if you're truly worried, you should discuss your fears with George. If he senses your hesitation, he may think it means you've changed your mind—that you no longer wish to marry."

A knot tightened in my chest, recalling my fear of losing him just a few hours ago. "I'd never want him to think that."

"I wouldn't worry, dear. My brother is too cocksure of himself, and far too determined, to allow you to change your mind."

"He is rather confident, isn't he? But you are right. I should talk to him about my concerns."

I turned at the sound of shouts and excited voices farther up the path. We shared a curious glance then hastened our steps. Ahead of us was George and two men I didn't know—estate hands by the look of their dress. One of them held the reins to a skittish horse, who became even more so when Leo rode up and dismounted. As the groom moved both horses to the side of the lane, he revealed another man lying facedown on the ground.

A sense of dread tickled the back of my neck. There must have been an accident.

Chapter 4

Fiona and I covered the remaining yards to where the men gathered around the downed man. One of the estate men, a very young man indeed, assisted George in turning him onto his back. Just as we reached them, the man on the ground howled with pain. I cringed, but at least the cry meant he was alive.

"What happened?"

George steadied the downed man, while his younger assistant wiped the man's head and face with a cloth, looking for signs of a head injury, I assumed. As he was currently covered in dirt, grime, and a jaw full of whiskers, it was impossible to tell if there was also blood.

"None of us were here to see," George said. "But it appears the horse threw him." He turned his gaze to the man's leg, twisted in a frighteningly unnatural position. I winced at the thought of his pain. "And it further appears he's been injured."

George turned to the young man assisting him. "You work with Gibbs, don't you?"

The man bobbed his head, and I recognized him from the train station, helping to organize the servants and bags. "Yes, sir. John Winnie. I'm Mr. Gibbs's assistant."

"Well, Winnie, go check the stables and see if you can find us some sort of litter. Gibbs won't be walking on that leg anytime soon."

"And have someone fetch the doctor as well," Fiona called to Mr. Winnie's retreating back. "He'll need medical attention."

George instructed the other man to go with Mr. Winnie and return Gibbs's horse to the stables. Mr. Gibbs was awake and taking in his surroundings. Aside from a few scratches, and the obviously broken leg, he seemed otherwise intact. He let out a groan.

"Don't try to move," George said.

"Can you tell us what happened, old man?" Leo asked. "Did you take a fall?"

Gibbs released a growl. At first, I thought it was due to his pain, but apparently, anger had taken over. "Haven't taken a fall since I was in short pants. This was no fall. We ran into something in the road. Felt it hit me in the chest just before I went down. Yanked back on the reins. Lucky this beast didn't stomp all over me."

"Lucky indeed," I said. "What a terrible accident."

"No accident." The man tried to turn my way, then grimaced in pain with the movement.

"Lie still," George instructed. "You don't want to move your leg until the doctor has seen to it and set the bone."

The man lay back on the path with a grumble. "No accident," he muttered.

Leo made his way to my side, leading the gray horse behind him.

"He must have run into a low branch," he said. The path looked as though it had been in use for hundreds of years. It was quite spacious and surrounded by trees that appeared very grand and very ancient. I saw no sign of any low-hanging branches, but perhaps this was not the time to point that out.

I jumped as the horse nudged my arm with his nose. "Have you been riding, Leo?"

"No, I was just on my way, when we heard the caterwauling. I rode out this far to see what had happened."

When I looked up the path behind him, I couldn't see the stables, but I knew they were just around a turning. "You didn't get very far, did you? Everything seems to be in hand here if you still wish to ride."

He gave me a grin. "I believe I shall. I don't often have a chance for a good run." He mounted the gray and cast a cautious glance at the steward. "If you're certain I can't be of any use here?"

I waved him on. "The men are returning with a litter now. Go while you still have good light."

As Leo rode off, John Winnie pulled the litter up beside the injured steward and George bent to help lift him. The men decided the steward's cottage was the closest building and arranged to transport him there. As they seemed to have everything under control, Fiona and I made our way back to the house so we could direct the doctor to the patient upon his arrival.

What remained of the afternoon skittered by quickly. I spoke to Lily about the arrangements I'd made with the vicar, broke up an argument between two of Leo's sisters, and changed out of my dusty clothes into something more suitable for dinner, a new aubergine silk with a lace ruffle on the left side running from my shoulder and curving around to meet the short train. By the time Bridget finished my hair, dinner was only an hour away, the gentlemen had returned from the shoot, and I happily chatted with Lottie in the drawing room.

We'd barely finished discussing her wedding when Charles interrupted our little tête-à-tête. "Cousin Frances," he said, seating himself beside his new bride, "I'm delighted you and your family were able to join our little group after all. Hazelton said you'd try to put him off, but he was determined. He does tend to get what he wants, don't you think?"

I parted my lips to answer, but he continued.

"But you definitely have a mind of your own, and if you chose not to come, I was certain you'd stand firm. Still, I didn't know which of you would be victorious."

56

Lottie attempted to stop his loquacious explanation with a jab of her elbow. Unfortunately, she held her teacup in that hand, and as Charles leaned forward, she jabbed only the sofa, sloshing the liquid onto her skirt.

I smiled in contentment. It was comforting to see some things never changed. "Were you successful in the field today, Charles?"

"Yes, indeed." He grinned, revealing two lovely dimples. Charles was more than ten years Lottie's senior. Though the aforementioned dimples and his thick blond hair, coupled with his boyish charm and energy belied his age, this difference was a fact that troubled me when it first became apparent his interest in her was of a romantic nature. Fortunately, my concern was for naught. He and Lottie seemed perfectly happy with one another.

Lottie dabbed at her skirt with her napkin and sighed. "I'm afraid I'll have to take this to my maid right away, before the stain sets."

The dark spot had grown across her skirt. "I'm sure she'll be able to set it to rights," I said "At least I hope so. That color is perfect on you." Indeed, the soft pink brought out the auburn in her hair and emphasized her brown eyes as well.

Charles rose and offered her his hand. "I shall go up with you. Not long before the first gong, so I should change for dinner as well."

"Did you happen to see Mr. Hazelton on your way in, Charles?"

"He was headed to the earl's offices not twenty minutes ago."

I watched the two leave the room and rose to my own feet. I'd taken Fiona's words to heart about discussing my concerns with George. A house party was not likely to allow for much privacy, so if he was alone in his office, now would be the best time to approach him.

Fiona was right. I didn't want to give George the impression I had second thoughts about marrying him. I slowed my steps as I reached the doorway. In a manner of speaking, I did have second thoughts, but it was due to my previous experience of marriage and nothing to do with George or my love for him.

But how on earth could I introduce the subject?

I pushed myself past the doorway, through the hall, and down to the lower gallery. The house was massive, but if I remembered correctly, the offices were in the north wing, toward the back of the house. With every step, I became a little less determined to have this conversation. What if he did believe a wife should stay in the background, and I could no longer play a role in his investigations?

The office loomed ahead of me, the door closed. I gave myself a mental shake. Better to know now.

I knocked.

Leo opened the door.

Leo? Bother. Apparently, there was a meeting taking place. Leo waved away my protests and gestured me inside the room where I found not only George, but Fiona's husband, Sir Robert Nash, Arthur Durant, Mr. Treadwell, and John Winnie. Nash and George were seated in deeply cushioned chairs, Durant and Treadwell leaned against a large mahogany desk, and Winnie stood at attention beside it.

"Forgive the interruption, gentlemen. I only wished to speak to Mr. Hazelton, and I can do so at another time."

"No reason to leave, Lady Harleigh." George stood and, taking my hand, led me over to his vacated chair. "I daresay you wish to know how Mr. Gibbs is faring."

"Of course." In truth, I'd forgotten all about the steward and his accident. Leave it to George to assume the best of me. "His leg looked quite mangled," I said, attempting to sit on the edge of a chair that seemed bent on swallowing me into its depths. "Is it broken? Is he in much pain?"

"Even worse when the doctor set the bone," Nash said, making a twisting motion with his hands. "He's going to have a slow recovery, I'm afraid."

George placed a hand on the back of my chair. "He has a sister in the village. The vicar came by with a wagon to transport him to her cottage. The doctor dosed him with laudanum for the trip, and we cushioned him as much as possible, but I suspect as soon as the drug wears off, he'll be in some significant pain." George grimaced. "But he'll be better off there where he'll have someone looking after him. He'd never be able to manage on his own."

"I'm pleased to hear he has someone to care for him," I said. "But how will you get on without him?"

He nodded at John Winnie. "This young lad has been assisting Gibbs for the past month and seems willing to step in."

Mr. Winnie couldn't be more than twenty. His light brown hair, oiled, combed back, and cut just above his collar was clearly an attempt to look older, but his lanky form and the sparse patches of whiskers on his cheeks and chin proved him to be quite a young lad indeed.

"Gibbs says he's capable and a quick learner," George said. "Between the two of us, I think we'll keep the estate running."

"And keep the shoot going," Nash added. "Don't forget the shoot."

The newly promoted steward had been staring at George and seemed to pull himself from a trance, before tipping his head at an older man I hadn't noticed before, standing off in the corner. "The shoot is in the hands of your very capable gamekeeper, sir. I don't presume to have those skills."

In an elegant motion George stood and gestured toward the man, who took a reluctant step forward as if he'd prefer to remain in the shadows. "Never fear, Nash," George said. "Winnie is right. My brother is fortunate enough to have the best gamekeeper in the county in his employ. Tuttle here will ensure the shoot proceeds without a hitch."

"Aye, you'll have woodcock, grouse, and partridges aplenty, don't you worry."

"You'll just have to worry about your aim," George said with a grin.

"It sounds as though all will be fine," I said. "Mr. Gibbs has a home to recover in, Mr. Winnie will take over his responsibilities, the shoot will proceed, and by week's end, Mr. Kendrick will be a married man."

Leo blinked in surprise before excitement lit his eyes. "Then I take it we have a date. I say that calls for a toast, don't you think?"

"Indeed, I do," George said amid a round of huzzahs. "Durant, will you see what my brother has in that cabinet?"

Durant and Treadwell both pushed off the desk and stepped around it to open a glass-fronted cabinet. "Looks like sherry," Durant said as he set about pulling glasses from the cabinet.

George shrugged. "I suppose it will have to do."

Durant poured rather generous portions while Treadwell and Winnie passed the glasses of sherry around, including one for me, which Treadwell handed off with a flourish.

"To Lily and Leo," George said, giving me a wink. "May they have many happy years."

"Remember, one's wife is always right," Nash added.

Everyone laughed and drank.

Nash drained his glass and made a noise of distaste. "We'll have to do that again with a good whiskey, don't you think?"

"Before the week is out, there will be plenty of opportunities," Leo said.

The dinner gong sounded in the distance, reminding us all of the hour. George glanced around the room. "I believe we've settled everything, so I'm for dinner. Tuttle, we'll see you in the morning, ready to shoot. Winnie, if you find it easier to take up residence in Gibbs's cottage have his belongings stored for now."

The young man acknowledged this with a glazed blink, and I wondered if he would soon come to idolize George. He and Tuttle returned their glasses to a tray on the desk. The gentlemen came to their feet and made as if to leave. Leo stood next to me, and I noted he hadn't taken so much as a sip from his glass.

"You won't drink to your own happiness, Leo?" I asked him.

"Never could stand sherry." He curled his lip in disgust as he set the glass on the tray. "That's not bad luck, is it—not drinking a toast to my wedding?"

He reached out to retrieve the sherry, but I stilled his hand with a touch of my own. "I'm certain it will have no effect on your happiness."

George stepped up as everyone departed. "Was there something in particular you wanted, Frances? I need to dress for dinner, but if it's urgent, I'll risk being late."

I leapt at the chance to forgo our discussion. Indeed, he had so much on his plate at the moment, I hated to burden him further. "No, I'd just wanted to check on the status of Mr. Gibbs, that's all."

He raised a brow. "That's all?"

"And of course, I missed you." It surprised me how much truth the statement held.

George tucked my hand in the crook of his arm. "Then walk me to the stairs?"

I happily complied. "Do you think Mr. Gibbs will be distressed when he hears Mr. Winnie has taken over his lodgings?"

We slowed our steps as we reached a stairway I hadn't noticed earlier. "This is the back way to the bachelors' wing," George said. "Closer to my end of the hall. As for Gibbs, I hadn't thought of that. The steward's office and living quarters are both housed in the cottage. I just thought it would be easier for Winnie to move his belongings since he'd be working there anyway. Gibbs will be away for a month or more after all."

"As long as that? Do you find Mr. Winnie up to the task?"

"More so than anyone else, I'd say. With Gibbs nearby we can always consult him if we run into any problems. My brother and his steward have the estate running like clockwork however, so it should just be a matter of keeping the gears turning. I don't anticipate any trouble."

"But there will be trouble if you are late for dinner. Go up and change. I'll meet you in the drawing room."

Everyone but George and Leo had already gathered in the drawing room by the time I found my way back to the south wing. The double doors from the hall stood wide open as did the doors to the south terrace. The final rays of the sun cut across the patterned carpet on the diagonal, leaving one side awash in a yellowish glow while the other remained a deep red. Arthur and Eliza Durant stood together right on the dividing line and the light cut across them as well. Eliza's left arm and shoulder shimmered in silver while the rest of her gown turned a dark gray. Half of Arthur's face appeared warm and inviting, while the other half looked shadowed and cold.

I shook off the strange observation and ventured inside the room, one of the most elaborate, and large, I'd seen outside a royal palace. The paneled walls were a warm ivory with the detailed plasterwork surrounding the high ceiling tipped in gold leaf. The portraits of Hazelton ancestors lined the walls, fitted right into the panels with frames built around them. The furnishings were a mix of Jacobean and Restoration, old and beautifully maintained.

Fiona met me at the door and drew me toward the empty side of the room. "Were you able to locate my brother?" She slipped her gloved arm through mine, leaving us close enough for discreet confidences.

"I did find him, but he was not alone."

She let out a *tsk*.

"He was in conference with two of his staff, Kendrick, Durant, Treadwell, and Nash, discussing plans for their hunt and a replacement for Mr. Gibbs."

I gritted my teeth as I remembered the poor man's condition. "His leg is indeed broken, and he'll require quite a bit of time to heal properly."

"That's unfortunate," she replied absently. I couldn't tell if she referred to the steward's situation or the fact that I hadn't been able to speak with George privately.

We wandered to a sofa, and she pulled me down near her side. "Tell me about Mr. Kendrick's sisters," she whispered. "Are they always so disagreeable?"

"Only when they are together, I think, or away

from the supervision of their parents. Otherwise, they are quite pleasant."

"So, if the rest of us are to enjoy ourselves, we must attempt to keep them apart. Is that it? Send one on a mission to find bluebells in the woods, lock another in the attic, that sort of thing? That could be entertaining."

"I believe you can find a better source of amusement than tormenting Leo's sisters, but you do make a good point. Perhaps we should each take charge of one sister."

"That still leaves one remaining."

"What is she to do, argue with herself? Besides, Leo and Charles will be shooting during the day, Lily and Lottie can play their part in keeping the sisters amiable."

"Lottie, perhaps, but Lily seems to have her hands full." Fiona cast her gaze across the room to where Ernest Treadwell held Lily in captive conversation. "What is that all about?" she asked. "Is he setting himself up as a rival to Kendrick in the very days before the wedding?"

"I can't say what he's thinking. I noticed how attentive he was to her on the train from London and so did Eliza Durant. I don't know why Lily hasn't put a stop to it. Or Leo, for that matter. Treadwell is supposed to be Leo's best man, but he gives all the appearance of trying to win Lily's favor."

As I came to my feet, Lily placed a hand on Mr. Treadwell's arm. It was a far too familiar gesture.

Was she leading him on? I stepped over to the pair and took my sister's hand. "Dearest, Fiona and I must talk to you about the preparations for the church. As we have a few minutes before dinner, why don't we do that now?" I turned to the young man who pursed his lips in annoyance. "You'll excuse us, won't you, Mr. Treadwell?"

"Of course," he replied, his voice a rich baritone, his smile clearly for Lily alone. The man was a practiced flirt but his expression seemed to hold more than mere flirtation.

"Of course," I repeated, hauling Lily away. He'd probably excuse her anything.

"Frances, you've already told me about the arrangements for the church. Is there something else I should know?"

"No, dear." We paused by the open doors. I smiled at George, who'd just walked in, a sight to behold in his evening tails. Fiona shooed him away, and I returned my attention to Lily. "There's something I need to know—specifically why you are encouraging that young man's attentions."

Lily turned a shocked expression on Fiona, who merely raised a brow. Seeing she'd find no quarter there, she glanced back at me. I waited, not so patiently. Finally, she let out a breath in a huff. "I am not encouraging his attentions. How can you say such a thing?"

"You are at the very least allowing them, which, he may well be taking as encouragement. Mr. Treadwell is your fiancé's good friend. You will cause yourself no end of misery if you allow this to continue."

She lifted her chin in defiance. "I am allowing nothing. He is simply being kind."

Fiona looked doubtful, and I held up a hand to stop Lily's protests.

"You are both against me," she said.

"If the man were *simply* being polite or kind, I would find nothing wrong with his actions, or yours, but I'm beginning to think his feelings are engaged. To lead him on is not only cruel to him but unfair to Leo. Can you not see that?"

Lily appeared to be sincerely surprised. "You think his feelings are engaged?"

"I do. Are you telling me you've never noticed?"

"No." She frowned as if she were trying to decipher a puzzle. "I wanted to be friends with him since he is so close to Leo. We are thrown together quite often, and I find him a good companion when Leo is not available." She shook her head and backed off a step. "I promise you, I never saw him as anything more than a friend, but he has become more attentive since we came away from London."

"I think he may see you differently," Fiona said.

Biting my lip, I nodded my agreement. "I'm relieved to learn you aren't playing with his affections or teasing Leo, but I'd advise you to take care with Mr. Treadwell if you don't want to damage your relationship with Leo."

At that moment the object of our conversation crossed the room with George and the second gong sounded for dinner. Lily sent her fiancé a smile. I knew her love for Leo was true and felt certain she'd take my caution to heart. But what of Mr. Treadwell? If he was such a great friend to Leo, why did he pursue the man's intended?

Chapter 5

In the interest of keeping the Kendrick sisters apart, I invited Anne to join Rose and me on our morning ride the following day. She and I were just about to stop in the breakfast room for tea and toast when a footman handed me a note.

"Mr. Hazelton asked you to meet him in the stables, my lady."

In the stables? I unfolded the note as the footman bowed and stepped away. *Lady Rose and I are choosing a suitable mount. Won't you join us?* The warmth that radiated between one heartbeat and the next told me I was completely besotted with the man and delighted he was trying to win my daughter's favor.

Anne eagerly agreed to postpone breakfast in favor of joining Rose and George. I felt light and carefree, enjoying the crisp morning air, as we tripped along the path to the stables, entering through wide, open doors in the center, just in time to see George assist Rose into the side saddle—on the back of the same gray horse Leo had ridden yesterday. The creature looked entirely too big for her. She'd only just graduated from a pony a little more than a month ago.

Rose spotted me and waved. Once George had her settled, he turned to me with a smile. I hated to ruin the moment, but as a mother, my nerves rather forced me to it. "She'll be safe on that horse, won't she, Mr. Hazelton?"

His smile slipped. "Of course not, Lady Harleigh. I've found her the wildest stallion in the stable. No man in the county has managed to ride him, but Rose wanted to try her hand, and I thought, why not let her have a go?"

He said this with such a calm demeanor, I might have believed him if not for Rose's giggles. "She's not a stallion, Mummy, she's a mare."

I gave George a tight smile. "Laugh if you must, but I worried you might overestimate the level of Rose's skill."

"I'm a good rider." Rose's red cheeks told me I'd embarrassed her. Anne quietly stepped off with a groom to select a horse of her own. I was making a complete hash of this.

"I know you are dear. Perhaps I'm over-reacting."

George stopped me with a hand on my shoulder. "Paloma is as gentle and obedient as a horse can be. I would have chosen her as your mount had Rose not developed a fondness for her." He shrugged. "I can have the wild stallion saddled for you."

This time I laughed along with him and Rose

joined in. "If Paloma has a mild-mannered sibling," I said, "that would be preferable."

"I'll see what we can do."

While the groom assisted Anne, George found a quiet, reliable mount for me, and the three of us set off within a few minutes. As we guided our mounts out of the stables, I reminded myself Rose knew how to handle both herself and her horse and decided simply to enjoy the ride. The sun was just breaking through the trees to the east, and we walked on toward the path George suggested we'd enjoy. It wound through a cool section of wood before opening up to a road where we could let the horses have their heads. Not that I was likely to do anything of the kind. New to riding, I found anything faster than a trot caused palpitations.

My horse, a roan gelding named Hercules, had a different idea. As soon as we broke from the trees, Rose and Anne gave each other a nod and set off into a canter. Hercules clearly felt left out. Without bothering to consult me, he bolted. Granted, it was only a matter of a few hundred feet before we caught up and settled into a speed and rhythm I could manage, but it was enough to rattle my bones and confidence, whipping off my hat for good measure.

Rose and Anne never even noticed. The road led to a neighboring estate, and they turned back upon reaching its drive, slowing down to a walk. Fortunately, Hercules followed suit.

"Well, that blew off the cobwebs," Anne said, her cheeks flushed from the exertion.

"And my hat." I reached a tentative hand to my hair to find it had fallen from its smart knot into a tangled mess.

"We'll keep an eye out for it on our way back," Anne said as the two sidled up beside me. Anne looked me up and down with some concern. Rose leaned over and touched my arm. "Are you all right, Mummy?"

"Of course, dear," I said in as breezy a manner as I could muster. "You are clearly a horsewoman, Anne. I think Rose did well to keep up with you."

"I've been riding since I was about Rose's age. There's some good riding just north of London, but I wish I had more opportunities to visit the country and ride like this." She gave my daughter a nod. "And the fact that you did keep up with me tells me you will be a far better horsewoman than I. If you keep at it, that is."

Rose beamed at the compliment. She and I had both been taking riding lessons for the last two months. It was my present for her eighth birthday. Rose had already been a good rider, but she longed to jump. She even injured herself trying to take her fat pony over a fence not long ago. Her determination made me decide it was in both our best interests to have proper lessons and a proper mount. Taking the lessons with her was more of an afterthought and a gift to myself for my twenty-eighth birthday. I'd never been much of a rider, but this was something we could enjoy together, and it was never too late to learn, was it?

We urged the horses forward in a walk and headed back three abreast with Rose at the center. The groom followed behind.

"Mother and I plan to ride every morning while we're here," Rose said. "You'd be welcome to join us, Miss Kendrick."

"We plan to ride as long as it doesn't interfere with Lady Fiona's schedule," I added. "I hope you will join us, Anne." Apart from my assignment, I was coming to enjoy her company. Moreover, she gave Rose a far greater challenge than I did.

"There's nothing I'd like better." Anne cleared her throat as she leaned forward to pat her horse on the neck. "I should warn you, my sisters don't ride much, but they may ask to join us when they learn I'm riding with you."

That would completely defeat the purpose. "Do the three of you enjoy spending time together?"

She raised her shoulders in a shudder. "Not at all, but Eliza is terribly jealous. If she thinks I am receiving any sort of preference from you, she will want her due. Clara cannot bear to be left out of any activity."

Rose watched Anne with interest, perhaps giving thanks for her status as an only child.

"I doubt you need worry about your sisters, at least not Mrs. Durant. It seems to me Lady Fiona has taken a liking to her, and if I know anything about Fiona, your sister will not have a moment to spare for you."

Anne seemed to brighten. "I am glad to hear that. Clara's prattling I can manage, but Eliza is often cruel."

She gave me a sharp glance. "Perhaps *cruel* is too strong a word, but she does like to have her way. She is quite jealous of everyone, even Leo. She thinks my father should make her husband a partner in the company, as Leo is."

This was, perhaps, more information than she ought to discuss outside her own family circle. "I'm certain your father knows his business and has good reasons for his decisions." I gave her a firm nod, intending to end the discussion.

"Of course. He expects Arthur to quit working as soon as he inherits his father's title. Why should he invest the time to train him, and give him a position of responsibility, if he's just going to leave the company?"

That reasoning made perfect sense except for one crucial detail and good manners aside—I had to inquire. "He does realize Arthur Durant's father is not yet fifty, does he not?"

Anne nodded and bit her lip, clearly trying to hold back her laughter, which ultimately snickered its way out. Rose and I joined in though I wasn't sure Rose understood why we were laughing. It was a fine morning, she was riding with two companions, and that was reason enough.

"I do hope Lord Durant is not aware my father expects his demise to come at any moment." Anne barely choked out the words through her laughter and tears.

"I promise never to breathe a word of it." I leaned forward to give Rose a conspiratorial smile. "Rose, we must ask you to keep this secret as well."

She drew a cross over her heart with her finger, and I was much relieved.

"I'm glad Aunt Lily and Mr. Kendrick decided to hold their wedding here rather than at a big church in London. The country is so much better."

Anne nodded her agreement. "A society wedding is just for show, don't you think?"

Rose looked a bit undecided, but I could attest my own wedding had been entirely for show. I'd been utterly embarrassed by the pomp and ceremony my mother had insisted upon. I hoped I'd be able to console her when she learned Lily was to have such a simple affair.

"I do prefer an intimate, family ceremony over a lavish public display." I smiled at the girl. "And I love being in the country, so for me, I must agree with Rose, this is much better."

"There's your hat, Mummy."

I glanced around, expecting to see it stuck to an unreachable branch or attached to a hedgerow, but instead saw it in the hands of an elegant gentleman dressed in tweeds and a homburg, walking toward us with a friendly smile.

We stopped as he approached. "I suspect this must belong to you, madam?" He held out the chic top hat with its now-torn veil. He had a gentleman's hands, his nails neatly trimmed and buffed.

I took the hat and returned his smile. "Sir, if you are implying I should cover my bedraggled hair, well, I can only agree with you."

He removed his own hat and gave us a courtly bow. A shock of blond hair fell over his dark eyes, and he swept it back in a reflexive motion that suggested habit. "I would never imply any such thing. I only noted it seemed to match your habit. Are you ladies riding out from Risings?"

"We are. And you, sir? This seems a strange place for a man on foot."

"Ah, perhaps it does to you now, but if you go forward just a few steps"—he gestured behind him—"you will see the lane leading to Fairview. I'm visiting my aunt there at present."

I searched my memory for the owners of Fairview. "That would be Lady Esther, would it not? You are her nephew?"

"Great-nephew." He grinned, deepening the

lines around his eyes. "Percy Bradmore at your service. You know my aunt?"

"You have indeed done me a service, Mr. Bradmore. I thank you for rescuing my hat. As to your aunt, we have met many times in town. How does she fare?"

"Not well at all, I'm afraid. She's recuperating from an illness, and while she's much improved, she has some way to go before she can claim good health."

I had a sudden rush of guilt for having always thought of Lady Esther as a crotchety old woman. Though I had never wished her any ill, I had often wished her out of my sight. Or better yet, my hearing. Considering this man was her relation, and George's neighbor, it seemed churlish to refrain from introducing ourselves.

I gave Mr. Bradmore our names and leaning over as far as the saddle, and my stays, would allow, shook his hand. "I'm glad to hear someone is in residence at Risings," he said. "I'd heard the earl is traveling on the continent."

"You heard correctly. His brother, Mr. Hazelton, is in residence, and he is hosting both a shooting party and a wedding."

"Is Hazelton to marry then?"

His question sent heat rushing to my cheeks, but I was quick to clarify my statement. "He is not the groom. Are you acquainted with the Hazelton family?" I waved a dismissive hand.

"Of course, you are. How foolish of me. You are neighbors after all."

"Actually, we are not acquainted, at least not as adults. The last time I visited here I was a child of six. I recall something of children in the neighborhood at the time, but not enough to know who they were." He shrugged. "Neither do I spend much time in London, which explains why we have never met, my lady. I hope while my aunt recovers, I may call on her neighbors and have a bit of conversation. I only arrived yesterday and already the quiet of this house has become rather gloomy."

Poor man. I knew well what that was like. During most of my marriage, I'd been left alone at Harleigh Manor. Too much solitude can be depressing to the spirit.

"You do seem to be a man who prefers society," I said. "I hope you will call on us when you have some idle time." I made a mental note to tell Fiona I'd met her neighbor. No doubt she would send over a message inviting him to join us. And perhaps the gentlemen would welcome another gun.

"Thank you, I shall. The shooting party is after woodcock, I'd wager." His broad grin faded as he turned serious. "Is that how the earl's steward was injured? I'd heard he was recuperating with his sister."

Word certainly traveled fast in the country.

"He took a fall from his horse," Anne said.

Bradmore cocked his head. "Truly? The talk around the village was a bit more extreme. I believe someone said he was set upon by brigands, though I thought that unlikely." He chuckled. Not only did word travel fast, it escalated.

"Nothing so dramatic as an attack, I'm afraid. Simply an accident."

He nodded. "Accidents can be every bit as dangerous. I hope you'll all take care, especially those in the shooting party."

"Most of them are quite experienced, and I'm certain they'll keep a sharp eye on the novices."

Bradmore gave me an expansive bow. "It was a great pleasure meeting you, ladies. I look forward to furthering our acquaintance in the coming days."

As Rose grew restless, I thought it best to move on. We bid Mr. Bradmore good day and set off back to the estate. The sound of gunfire warned me we were approaching the open meadows, and I motioned for the groom who trailed behind to move ahead and lead us back to the estate. He guided us back to a path through the wood which would take us around the grounds to the far side of the house and on to the stables.

We walked on companionably, chatting when we could ride abreast, and lost in our own thoughts where the path narrowed. The day had turned from bracing to brisk and it was a pleasure to be on the sun-spattered trail. As we took a turning, I realized this was the path Fiona and I had taken to the village. Just up ahead was where the steward had fallen.

I wondered if Mr. Gibbs's insistence he hadn't fallen but was knocked from his seat had any basis in fact, or if the man was trying to divert attention from an embarrassing fall. The path grew narrow here, but as I'd noted yesterday, the trees were mature, with branches closing in overhead—well overhead. Mr. Gibbs was surely taller than I, but he'd have to be a good three feet taller to come into contact with any of these branches.

While we passed through the area, I looked around for any broken branches and gashes in the trees where a limb might have broken off. I don't know what I expected to see. Did it matter whether Mr. Gibbs fell off his horse or was knocked off?

Then my gaze lighted on something that didn't belong. A length of line tangled among some leaves. I urged my mount closer to the branch. It looked like a braided fishing line, tangled about shoulder height, but the branch sprouted from the tree about six inches lower. Try as I might, I could not disengage the hopelessly tangled mess.

"Would you like me to get that for you, my lady?"

The groom had stopped at my side, and my two companions waited patiently behind him, giving me curious looks. "What would this be doing here, I wonder?"

"Couldn't say, my lady. Maybe someone swinging a fishing pole got the line caught. At least that'd be my guess." The young man looked as if he couldn't imagine what interest this bit of line could hold.

"I suppose that's possible." I set my horse back on the path. "No need to remove it. It just stuck out amid the greenery and caught my attention." I smiled at Anne and Rose. "Excuse the delay. I expect you're as hungry as I am. Shall we head in for breakfast?"

They agreed readily, and we headed past the stables and across the lawn bordering the maze. My stomach growled, pushing the thought of the fishing line from my mind. It might have been tangled there for years.

The three of us dismounted in the drive and headed to the house, leaving the horses in the care of the groom though Rose wanted to stay to help.

"Nanny will be waiting for you, dear," I told her. Passing through the great hall, I sent her upstairs and turned to Anne. "Do you suppose if we take the time to change out of our riding gear and freshen up first, there will still be some breakfast left?"

She looked doubtful. "Lady Fiona planned an outing for this morning, and I suspect the group left early. I'll go and check the breakfast room. If the chafing dishes are still out, I'll ensure they stay there until you come back down."

"Thank you, dear." Anne was off, but before I could place a foot on the stairs, the housekeeper, Mrs. Ansel, pushed through the baize door at the end of the hall and called out to me. She rushed forward with some urgency.

"Yes, Mrs. Ansel? Is something wrong?"

"My lady, there's a terrible ruckus below stairs, and I'm afraid I just can't settle everyone down. Mr. Hazelton has been gone since dawn, and Lady Fiona took the rest of the guests on a jaunt early this morning, so there's been no one about while all the staff is screaming bloody murder."

How strange. The staff had seemed so disciplined, it must be quite a crisis to have set them all off. I turned and walked with her toward the service door. "Of course, I'll do what I can, Mrs. Ansel. What exactly happened?"

She raised troubled eyes to mine and heaved a sigh. "One of our footmen died during the night, and some are saying it's murder."

Chapter 6

~~~

Murder? Good heavens!

Mrs. Ansel set a brisk pace through the gallery back to the north wing, and through the service door to the kitchen and the servants' hall. It did indeed appear to be in chaos despite the sharp words from the butler who stood with his back to us. Two young maids, probably from the kitchen, huddled together in the corner, while tears streamed down their faces. An older woman sat at the table, her face buried in her hands, while two footmen argued over her head. Several of the other staff muttered among themselves. The butler looked on in horror, clapping his hands in a fruitless bid for order.

I raised my voice to speak above the din. "I understand you've suffered a tragedy." The butler, Crocker, swung around, and upon recognizing me, a wave of relief cleared the displeasure from his expression. Everyone scrambled to their feet and silence fell on the room.

"Is it true one of your footmen has passed away?"

He nodded. "Yes, my lady. It appears he died in his room last night or early this morning."

"Has someone sent for a doctor? And Mr. Hazelton?"

"We have sent for the doctor, but not Mr. Hazelton as yet. He did not leave word where the shoot was taking place today. I was just about to have someone inquire of Mr. Tuttle."

One of the footmen who'd been in the shouting match approached us. "I heard one of the gentlemen at breakfast this morning say where they were shooting. Shall I run and fetch Mr. Hazelton?"

"Go to the stables and send one of the grooms for him," Crocker said. "Make sure the groom tells him what has happened and that we are in need of his assistance."

The young man bobbed his head and made off. I wondered how distorted the story would be by the time George received it. I motioned for Mr. Crocker and Mrs. Ansel to join me off to the side of the room. "Now tell me, why is the staff in such a state? Who called it murder and can it be true?"

Mrs. Ansel cast a worried glance at the butler. "Mr. Crocker," I prompted. "Did the footman not die peacefully in his sleep?"

"No, ma'am." The lines in his forehead deepened. "The lad was clearly ill, violently ill even. We are short one footman, so he did not share a room with anyone. Mores the pity, for then we could have called a doctor in sooner."

"I see. This is a somber event. I can understand why the staff is so distressed, but why the uproar? Why did someone call it murder?"

Mrs. Ansel made a grunt of disgust. "They're saying he must have eaten something that made him so sick. Some are pointing a finger at our cook, saying she poisoned his food."

Her remark left me speechless. Someone dies, and members of the household are prepared to suspect one of their own of murder? I couldn't imagine my staff acting in such a manner. "Have they any reason to believe she'd do such a thing? It sounds rather foolish to me since all evidence would point directly back to her."

"No reason at all, ma'am." Mrs. Ansel spoke up when the butler remained silent. "I don't know why they'd make such foolish claims. It all seemed to grow out of nothing. First, three of the maids left the house, shouting about Russian influenza. The under-butler called that a convenient excuse, a way to cover poisoning." She fluttered her hands helplessly. "Someone suggested one of the maids poisoned him. The next thing I know, everyone's looking at the cook with a suspicious eye."

What an odd group. "I'm sorry you've had to bear this burden. Once the doctor has arrived and given his verdict, send word to those maids that they should return to their duties."

Crocker gasped and looked at me in horror.

"After abandoning their posts, you'd bring them back?"

"Lady Fiona may feel differently, but once the doctor can assure them there's no fear of contagion, we should allow them back. I can understand the girls' concern after all. Do you recall how quickly the Russian flu spread? I can hardly blame them for running off. As for Cook, well, accidents do happen, but it would seem unlikely a bad bit of meat would affect only one of you."

I took in the handful of staff in the common room. "Has everyone else returned to their duties?"

"Most of us were already going about our business when we heard the news." Mrs. Ansel fidgeted with her cuffs. "Mr. Crocker set everyone else back to work. Mrs. Humphries's girls are at a loss without her guidance." She nodded at the cook. "And I can't say why the footmen are still milling about." She raised her voice, causing the two footmen to look up, then scramble to the door. I'd have stopped them, but what was the point? If someone on the staff had caused the footman's death, he'd had plenty of time to cover his tracks by now.

Mrs. Humphries drew a shuddering breath. "Try to calm her, Mrs. Ansel. I daresay, the doctor will be here soon and will likely exonerate her of all wrongdoing."

In fact, it was the doctor I expected to see when I turned at the sound of boots on the stairs. Instead, it was George who rounded the corner, his face full of alarm. His gaze took me in.

"Frances, er, Lady Harleigh, have I heard right? Has someone died?"

"I'm so sorry, Mr. Hazelton, but yes, you did hear correctly." I explained the whole of my knowledge of the matter in a few short sentences. "The doctor should be here soon."

He nodded. "I'll check on the lad in the meantime."

Crocker made as if to lead the way, but I placed a hand on George's arm. "Do you think that's wise? What if it was influenza?"

He shook his head. "I've heard nothing of influenza in the county, and I'd like to see for myself what happened to the young man."

"Fine. I'll go with you."

He stopped and gave me a quizzical look. "I thought you were concerned about influenza?"

"But you've just said that's not possible."

His brows drew together as he turned and placed a hand on his hip in a show of impatience. "I didn't call it impossible, just highly unlikely."

"If highly unlikely will do for you, it will do for me." I gave him a look that dared him to say no.

"It won't be a pretty sight, Lady Harleigh."

"We have cleaned up the room, sir."

George threw a glance at the butler. "Have you removed the body?"

Crocker took a step back. "No, sir."

George pursed his lips and turned to me, leaning in close. "I think you had better stay down here."

By no means did I wish to be in a small room with a dead body, but I truly hated to be coddled. I gave George a look of deepest disdain. "It's not as if I haven't seen a dead body before. I'm coming with you."

I caught a glimpse of Crocker's horrified expression as I swished past him and followed George through the servants' hall and up the enclosed staircase to their quarters. The tap of our shoes on the wooden steps echoed and sounded overly loud in the close confines.

"Crocker, what is the lad's name?"

"His name is Michael, ma'am," he said, following us up the stairs. "Michael O'Brien."

"Thank you. It feels rather cold to continue referring to him as *the footman*." George had already reached the second-floor landing and turned left into a hallway. I hurried to catch up with him.

"It's the last door on the left, sir." Crocker spoke at my shoulder. George gave me one more warning look before pushing the door open and stepping inside. I followed.

The two small windows near the ceiling did

little to illuminate the room, which was just large enough to hold a cabinet, two beds, one bedside table, a cane-backed chair, and a trunk at the end of the bed nearest to the door. The bedside lamp was dark. It would have been gloomy even without the smell of death, and vomit, and the body lying in the bed. Perhaps I should have allowed George to coddle me this time.

He'd pulled the straight-backed chair next to the bed and bent forward, examining the boy's eyes. He glanced up when I walked in and gave me a look that said, *I warned you.* I squared my shoulders and advanced to his side.

"What are you looking for?" I asked.

He shrugged. "Signs of what might have killed him."

"He obviously had some sort of stomach distress."

George wrinkled his nose and nodded in agreement before turning back to the body and lifting Michael O'Brien's hand. "I was annoyed when Crocker said the room had been cleaned, but as I can still smell the aftermath, I can only be relieved that he did so."

Crocker poked his head around the door. "It was just a cursory cleaning, sir, as no one wanted to spend much time in here."

"When you had the room cleaned, Crocker, did you remove anything—food, drink, perhaps a pitcher of water?"

"No, sir. Nothing was removed."

"When did he first mention his illness?"

"From what I understand, he was perfectly healthy yesterday, sir." Crocker maintained his post at the doorway. "He didn't fall ill until evening."

The poor footman had been young, and it looked as though his death had not been easy. His face was still drawn in a grimace as if he'd been in pain. Otherwise, he'd been a handsome young man, tall and well built, as a footman ought to be, with fair skin and dark hair.

George interrupted my assessment. "What was his complaint?"

"A stomach ailment, sir. His face looked rather red, and with guests in the house, I worried he might have something catching, so I relieved him of his duties for the rest of the night and he retired to his room."

"Did no one check on him? Or call for the doctor?" I couldn't believe the poor man had been left to die alone.

"Of course, my lady, but I must remind you with the guests, the staff were run off their feet, and it was quite late to send for the doctor. I knocked at his door before I retired for the night. When he didn't answer, I assumed he was sleeping."

"He might well have been gone already, Crocker." George rose from his examination and faced us. "The doctor will be able to tell us for sure, but from the description of his symptoms, and since the young man went from healthy to sick, to dead in such a short time, I'd suspect arsenic."

I heard an intake of breath and glanced at Crocker, who backed away from the doorway, his lips moving soundlessly. Turning back to George, I found the words the butler could not. "Are you saying someone murdered him?"

He blinked and jerked his head back. "Of course not. At least I have no reason to believe so." He narrowed his eyes. "Do you? What have you heard?"

"Nothing. The entire hall was in an uproar when Mrs. Ansel brought me there. I'd only just settled them down when you arrived."

"I suppose we should inquire if anyone had a score to settle with poor O'Brien, but I'd imagine he ingested it accidentally."

"How does one ingest arsenic accidentally?"

"Arsenic, you say?"

I started at the sound of a new voice from the hallway, then stepped around the second bed to allow the man to enter. The doctor, I presumed. A large man with a mix of sandy and gray hair, and a bit more bulk than brawn, though I could imagine twenty years earlier that would have been reversed.

George presented the man as Dr. Woodrow and shook his hand. He moved aside to allow the doctor access to the body. "It's more that I suspect arsenic, Woodrow. I'll leave it to you to make the determination."

Dr. Woodrow bent to examine the body, muttering to himself while George pulled me aside. "I'm going to look around the room for anything that might contain arsenic. Why don't you return to the hall and see what you can learn about O'Brien?"

I'll admit, it was a relief to be out of the room. Crocker looked positively green as I passed him in the hallway. I found Mrs. Ansel waiting at the bottom of the stairwell and pulled her aside, suggesting she and I have a cup of tea in her parlor. She seemed reluctant to leave her post but agreed.

In the few minutes I waited in Mrs. Ansel's cozy parlor, while she prepared the tea in the kitchen, I devised some questions that might lead me to a better understanding of the late Mr. O'Brien. Unfortunately, Mrs. Ansel was anything but loquacious, rarely answering with more than a single word. I learned Mr. O'Brien, though of Irish descent, hailed from no farther than London, and had only twice returned to visit his family. He'd worked at this house for a little more than a year. He performed his duties well enough to become second footman, and to the best of her knowledge, rubbed along with the rest of the staff.

"Did he spend much time in the village?" I asked, wondering if perhaps someone outside of the staff might have had a disagreement with the young man.

She frowned and considered the question. "I suppose he did, at least this past month. With the master gone, the footmen's duties would be over by early evening. There'd be no dinners to serve after all. As long as they didn't come back with gin on their breath, they could visit the village until Mr. Crocker locked up the house. That would be about ten."

"And did he ever return with gin on his breath?"

She raised her brows. "Not that I ever heard, and I think I would have as Mr. Crocker's not one to tolerate the footmen drinking."

I wondered if there was someone else I could talk to about O'Brien. If Crocker was a strict taskmaster and had no tolerance for drink, it was possible the footmen covered for one another. Now might not be the right time, but if need be, I should talk to one or two of the lower servants. Meanwhile, I confirmed that after serving our dinner, O'Brien had dined with the rest of the staff, and claiming illness, went to bed shortly after, as Crocker had said.

"The outside servants had only just arrived, so we all stayed in the hall to visit with them a bit and swap stories."

The visiting servants. How could I have forgotten? I'd brought my own maid with me. Most of the guests would have brought a valet or lady's maid. Perhaps Bridget could give me her impressions of Mr. O'Brien. Though her acquaintance would have been very short, she was keenly observant. I filed the thought away for later.

"About what time did the evening end and everyone go off to bed?"

"Well, the lady's maids and the valets left to see to their people about ten o'clock. Peter, the under-butler, and Ben, the other footman, left about the same time to pick up in the dining room. To collect glasses and such." Mrs. Ansel laced her fingers around her cup and gazed up at the ceiling as if to recreate the scene in her mind.

"Cook and her girls retired to their rooms first. I'm not sure exactly who left when, but by the time I went off to bed, about half-past ten, it was just Ben and Peter who were still about, and they hadn't come back to the hall yet."

"O'Brien remained in his room?"

"Yes, ma'am."

"Who found him this morning?"

"Mr. Crocker. That was about six o'clock."

I had no idea how quickly arsenic would work on a person's body. If, in fact, George was correct, and arsenic was the culprit. At any rate, it would be good to know if the cook could be eliminated as a suspect. "All the staff were present for dinner?"

She nodded, then guessed my next question. "We all ate the same food."

I could think of nothing else to ask, so I thanked her for her time and returned to O'Brien's room to see how George and the doctor were faring. There was no sign of Crocker in the hall. When I peeked inside the room, it was to see the two men rooting through O'Brien's things—Dr. Woodrow digging through the drawers in a bureau, and George practically crawling under the bed.

"I think I have it," he said, lifting his head too soon and banging it on the slats beneath the mattress. "Argh! Bloody hell!"

"What on earth are you doing? Mr. O'Brien deserves more respect than this."

Dr. Woodrow started and spun around, O'Brien's small clothes still in his hand.

I shot a scowl at George. "What is wrong with the two of you? Why are you going through his things?"

"Apologies, Frances." George had crawled out from under the bed and sat on the floor with his back against it, a green glass bottle in his hand.

I crossed my arms over my chest and shook my head. "I am not the one who requires your apology."

With his free hand, he pushed himself to his feet. "I meant for my language. As for O'Brien,

I believe he'd understand we are looking for evidence." He held up the bottle by the neck. "And I think I've found it."

Woodrow crossed the tiny room in two steps and took the bottle from George. Pulling out the cork, he gave it a sniff. "Ah, ginger beer."

I had no idea why this revelation so excited them. "Are you saying he died from too much ginger beer?"

George pursed his lips. "In a manner of speaking, I suppose we are. That is if this ginger beer contains arsenic."

"How is that possible?"

"If the water it was made from contained arsenic. Woodrow says there's been a well or two closed down nearby, due to contamination. This particular beverage is not distilled. If the water was tainted, so would the drink be."

Woodrow eagerly took up the explanation. "If O'Brien felt unwell when he retired to his room, he might have had a healthy sip of this. Ginger beer is often used to treat stomach upsets. However, if this were tainted, the more he drank, the worse he'd feel as he consumed the arsenic."

I understood all too well. "And the worse he felt, the more he'd drink. Is that it?"

George nodded. "Until he'd taken in far too much arsenic to survive."

Though both men appeared confident in their theory, it seemed far too simple to me. "But you don't actually know the ginger beer is tainted."

"No, we don't, but I'll take it with me for testing." Woodrow packed the bottle into the leather bag he'd brought. "I'll have to conduct some tests on the body, but I'm quite confident he died from ingesting arsenic, poor boy."

I blinked. Something about this situation disturbed me. Perhaps because to my mind, Mr. O'Brien had been the victim of foul play. In less than a minute, George and the doctor had turned my theory upside down. Theirs was an entirely plausible explanation. Why didn't it sit right with me?

Chapter 7

~~∾

The doctor agreed to take custody of the body and arrange to have it prepared for burial. I informed Mrs. Ansel and requested information on the boy's family. In the countess's absence, I was certain Fiona or George would want to write them.

As I'd yet to eat anything this morning, and last night's dinner felt like a distant memory, I peeked into the breakfast room only to find the table and breakfront cleared, and the room empty. A glance at the clock told me it was already half-past noon. Hoping Fiona had planned something for luncheon, and she and the other guests would be home from their morning outing soon, I trudged up to my room where Bridget waited to help me change out of my riding habit and into a suitable gown.

She assisted me with the dozen tiny buttons on my jacket, her brow furrowed with concern. "Can you believe that poor footman dying last night, my lady?" She shook her head and let out a few *tsk*s.

"A tragedy indeed," I said. "Did you have a chance to meet him yesterday?"

"Yes, ma'am. He seemed a nice enough fellow and quite handsome, too. Such a shame."

She moved behind me and peeled off my jacket, a process that would be far easier if my arms could be detached from my shoulders. I stumbled forward as my hands freed themselves from the now-turned-out sleeves. Why on earth were those garments made so tight?

"How did he act with the rest of the staff? Could you tell if he got on with them?"

I tried to keep my tone casual, but after an automatic shrug, Bridget's eyes widened, and a slight gasp escaped her lips. "Are you thinking someone murdered him? Will you be investigating?"

The question was not entirely surprising. If I did suspect murder, and if I were investigating, well, it wouldn't be the first time. Nor would it be the first time I'd enlisted Bridget in my surreptitious sleuthing.

If I suspected murder that is.

And I shouldn't. At least not yet. George and Woodrow could be correct; the poor boy may have brought on his own death quite by accident.

Bridget watched me with raised brows, waiting for an answer. "No, on both counts." I worked to unfasten my skirt as she righted the sleeves of the jacket. "Mr. Hazelton and the doctor both believe Michael nursed an ailing stomach with ginger beer made from contaminated water. If their theory proves to be true, then it will certainly be an accidental death."

"But you don't believe that, do you?"

I nearly tripped as I stepped out of the skirt. Bridget placed a hand on my shoulder to steady me. The woman knew me far too well. "I have no reason not to believe them." I might have been trying to convince myself as well as her. "At any rate, the doctor will test the drink, so we'll soon find out if his theory is correct."

"Hmph." She examined my face for the truth before retrieving the skirt from the floor.

"Honestly, Bridget. I'm telling you everything I know. You have no reason to suspect anyone here of murder."

"Glad to hear that, ma'am."

She ducked into the dressing room and returned with a blue, wool walking dress, stopping short upon seeing my confusion. "I understand the ladies will all be walking to the village this afternoon. I just assumed you'd be going, too."

"Ah, I'd wondered what Lady Fiona had planned. Please tell me we're to have luncheon first."

She bit her lip. "That I couldn't say, but if you're hungry, I could nip down to the kitchen and have tea and cakes or sandwiches for you in just a moment."

"That's kind of you, but I can hold out until I'm dressed."

While she helped me step into the fresh gown, my mind wandered back to the footman. "You never answered my question, Bridget. Could you tell if Michael got on with the rest of the staff?"

She turned me around and began working up the buttons. "It's hard to say if any of the staff had a problem with him, but I wouldn't be too surprised if he got on better with the females than the males."

"Truly? Why do you say that?"

"A handsome face and a flirtatious manner." She tugged at the fabric between my shoulders until I straightened my posture. "That's likely to earn him more lady friends than men. Though I suppose if he flirted too much, it could earn him more lady enemies as well." She shrugged and finished doing up the buttons. "I only spent an hour or so in his company, so I can't claim to understand his character all so well. He might get on with everyone just fine. It's only my impression."

An impression about a man from Bridget was as good as a fact from anyone else. She had a pretty face, a fine figure, golden-blond hair, and an engaging personality. Bridget had been attracting men since she came to Harleigh Manor at the age of fifteen. In the intervening ten years, she'd gained a thorough understanding of them. I was fortunate she intended to retain her single status until she met one willing to go into business with her. Sadly, I knew it would happen one day.

"I'll keep that in mind, Bridget, and please understand this is just idle curiosity on my part. I'm certain the boy's death will be determined to be an accident."

A knock sounded at the door. Bridget stepped away to open it, only to jump back as Fiona launched herself in the room with her usual energy.

"Frances, how can I ever thank you for stepping in for me this morning?"

"Think nothing of it, dear. I take it you've met with Mrs. Ansel, and she's given you the details."

"Indeed, such a horrible accident." She frowned and perched on the bench at the end of the bed. "I hear the staff was in quite a tizzy before you settled them down." She gave me a curious stare.

"What is wrong?"

Raising her hands to her head, she pulled a face. "Your hair, dear. What on earth happened to it?"

Remembering the loss of my hat this morning, I reached up to touch the tangled mess as I moved to the dressing table. When I caught a glimpse of myself in the mirror, I let out a shriek. It looked as if I had a bird's nest on my head, and the nest seemed to have suffered from a windstorm. Lovely. Not only had I presented myself to the servants thus, but to George and Dr. Woodrow as well.

Bridget came up behind me, comb in hand. "I'll have you fixed up in a jiffy, ma'am."

I eyed the instrument of torture in her hand, seating myself in front of the glass. Needs must, I suppose.

"What do you think happened?" Fiona asked.

I waved her question aside. "I know what happened. I lost my hat on our ride this morning and didn't retrieve it until we were on our way back to the manor. Which reminds me, we met one of your neighbors today. That is to say, the nephew of your neighbor, Lady Esther."

Fiona raised her brows. "I was actually inquiring about the footman's death, but now that you mention it, who is Lady Esther's nephew?"

"Percy Bradmore. Are you acquainted with him?"

She tapped her fingers against her lips for a moment, then shook her head. "I don't believe I am."

I raised my hand again only to have Bridget fill it with hairpins. Perhaps I was gesturing too much. "He said he hasn't visited her here since he was a child, but it seems she is recovering from some illness." I shrugged and handed Bridget a pin. "Apparently his presence is required while she does so. I must confess, I invited him to call on us."

"Of course. Hmm, I'll have to see if I can learn what is wrong with Lady Esther, and if we should visit her, or simply send our best wishes for her recovery. I recall her as a rather crotchety old woman even while I was growing up. I can't imagine what she's like now."

"Still crotchety when I last saw her." My teeth clacked together as Bridget yanked the comb through a section of my hair, bouncing my head about.

"Speaking of family, I suppose I should find out whom to contact about the footman. I don't know what to do about a funeral either." She raised her hands. "I've never had anyone on my staff die before."

"I suspect Mrs. Ansel or Crocker might be able to give you some guidance there. I have the direction for his closest family so you can write them. They can tell you their wishes. In the meantime, the doctor is doing some tests, and I have no idea how long that will take."

"What type of tests?"

"To determine if Michael died from arsenic poisoning."

"I thought he already decided that."

I shrugged. "He's relatively confident, but wants to be certain."

"Well, I certainly hope he's right. Otherwise, we'll be back to chaos in the servants' hall again, with everyone suspecting one of them murdered the boy, and no one willing to eat for fear of Mrs. Humphries's cooking."

I too would be relieved to know for certain if Michael's death was accidental, but even with my doubts, I'd be willing to sample Mrs. Humphries's cooking. "Please say we are to have luncheon soon, Fiona."

"Absolutely. We meet the gentlemen for a picnic lunch then we walk to the village this afternoon."

Apparently, the shoot was going well. The gentlemen were all in good spirits when they broke for a quick luncheon with us. Today they were hunting on the grounds of Greenbriars, a neighboring estate to the south of Risings, belonging to a Mr. Easton. He and his brother-in-law had joined the shooting party today. Fiona made arrangements for the two gentlemen and Mrs. Easton to dine with us later in the week.

We chatted for an hour or so, but the guns were calling to the men, and as soon as the last bite was eaten, they returned to the fields. One of them, with great reluctance.

Ernest Treadwell stood by Lily's side and called out to Leo. "The ladies are to have an outing this afternoon, old man. If you choose not to accompany your fiancée, perhaps I should."

The sunlight shone on Treadwell's fair head, casting a reflection almost like a halo, though I didn't believe his motive to be angelic. "Suit yourself, Treadwell." Leo was already moving away. "You escort the ladies to the shops, and I'll bring home dinner." He turned to wink at the group of us. "We'll see which of us makes the better impression."

Heavens, Lily really must put an end to this. The younger Kendrick girls were involved in another of their endless arguments, but Eliza Durant stared daggers at Lily and Treadwell. I came to my feet with the intention of sending the man on his way when Fiona spoke up.

"Take yourself off, Treadwell," she said, making a shooing motion with her hands as she approached the pair. "This outing is for ladies only. I've been walking to the village since I was a child and there is no need for male protection. Go back to your shoot. Mr. Kendrick is correct. We need the birds for dinner, and I expect you to shoot a brace of them."

Mr. Treadwell hesitated, as if he might just refuse to leave, but ultimately, he grinned, made Fiona a courtly bow, and headed after the departing gentlemen. Lily stood, staring at her shoes until I took her arm and led her toward the lane, neglecting my duty of keeping Anne Kendrick in my care. Right now, my own sister required my attention.

"What are you doing?" I hissed as soon as we were far enough away from the group.

She pulled herself from her stupor and gave me an angry glare. "What do you mean?"

"We discussed this. I thought you agreed to discourage Mr. Treadwell?"

Her look of shock seemed a bit forced, but mine was quite genuine. I'd expected anything but this. "Tell me the truth. Are the two of you carrying on?"

This time I'd truly surprised her. "No, no. Nothing like that. Goodness, Franny, you know I love Leo more than anything."

"Of course, I do. I would have wagered money on it."

"Well, there you have it then."

I opened my mouth but found no words. The rest of our group gathered their belongings and made ready for the walk to the village. Clara Kendrick came to a dead stop in front of Anne. "Who gave you permission to wear my shoes?"

I tugged Lily over to the lane and headed in the direction of the village, grateful the argument about to ensue would cover our conversation.

"There I have what? You have given me nothing, least of all an explanation for why you are allowing Treadwell to—to—" I waved my hands, struggling for the right words. "Why are you encouraging him?"

"I'm not. He is just—" She let off with a sigh. "It is nice to have someone paying me some attention."

I stared. "When did Leo stop attending to you?"

"From the moment we set out for Risings." Her

eyes glistened with tears. She gave them a swipe with the back of her hand. "Either he's talking business with Durant, or he's following Mr. Hazelton around like a puppy. He's completely caught up with the shooting party and having such a lovely time with the other gentlemen, I might as well be invisible."

I suppressed a smile. "These are the final days before he becomes a married man, dearest. I suspect he is planning to enjoy them before he buckles down to become the model husband."

She made a rude noise with her lips. "I suppose I should be grateful he is willing to saddle himself with a wife."

"Lily, where is this coming from?" And then I remembered. "You are worried about the added pressure of the baby. Is that it? That you will be starting your family so quickly?"

We walked on a bit before she answered. "To be honest, I don't know. There is just so much happening. Changing the wedding without consulting his parents. Keeping the baby a secret from them. Getting married in the first place. It's all so overwhelming, and I suppose I want Leo to be at my side, telling me everything will be fine."

"Is he aware of your concerns?"

Lily shook her head. "I know. How can he reassure me when he has no idea I'm troubled?" She spread her arms out in a helpless gesture. "I realize it makes no sense and I can't explain what I don't understand myself."

The poor dear. I wrapped an arm around her waist and pulled her to my side. "One thing that may help to explain it is that pregnancy is an emotional time for the mother. You're well, then you're unwell, bouts of exhaustion and bursts of energy, neither of which make any sense or follow any pattern. It also becomes more difficult to keep any sort of control over one's emotions. And in your case, you must keep your condition a secret, at least for a while, which only increases your distress. Add to that your change in wedding plans, and who could blame you for feeling overwhelmed?"

"Yes! Yes." She seemed to sag with relief. "I'm so glad you understand, but why doesn't Leo? Why, when I need him so much, is he off having fun with the gentlemen?"

"Because he doesn't know, Lily. You could tell him. Leo's devoted to you. He would immediately glue himself to your side for the remainder of your pregnancy."

Lily chewed on her lip, her gaze fixed on the ground in front of us.

"Or you can unburden yourself to me. Let me take care of you and allow Leo to enjoy this week. The poor man works hard. He doesn't have as much leisure as these other gentlemen. That might explain why you fell in with Treadwell in the first place. Leo is always attending to business. Treadwell is at leisure."

She made a noise that might have been agreement, so I pushed forward. "This is a treat for Leo. By the end of the week, it will be just the two of you. The wedding will be over, and you will have him all to yourself."

She blew her breath out in a sigh. "You are right. He deserves to enjoy himself. He doesn't have many opportunities to do so."

"You deserve to enjoy yourself as well. But you must do something to discourage Mr. Treadwell. I'm concerned he believes he could win you away from Leo."

She angled a glance my way. "But he can't."

I widened my eyes. "Then isn't it unfair to allow him to believe it?"

"Hmm. I will miss him."

"Not as much as you would miss Leo."

She threw me a sharp glance. "You think Leo would abandon me because of Mr. Treadwell's attentions?"

"I'm not entirely certain Leo has even noticed. He sees nothing but good in everyone. But I have no doubt others have noticed, Eliza Durant for one. She might very well mention it to her brother. How would you feel if the situation were reversed? What if Leo and Lottie were forever flirting with one another, or if Leo were encouraging her interest?"

"Yes, I see what you mean. All right, Frances. I shall do my best to discourage him, but he is Leo's friend so I cannot avoid him altogether."

"The men will be out shooting most mornings this week so it shouldn't be that difficult."

We had reached the edge of the village and paused to let the others catch up with us. "The church is just off to our left, Lily. Would you like to see it?"

"Yes, that would be lovely. Would it be rude to separate ourselves from the rest of the group?"

"As long as we don't take long. Fiona and Lottie cannot keep the Kendrick girls apart by themselves."

She tipped her head to the side. "Why do you wish to keep them apart?"

"The constant bickering. Haven't you noticed?"

Lily chuckled. "I suppose I've become used to it. It never occurred to me to divide them. I'll try to help with that."

When the ladies caught up with us, we told Fiona of our plans for a short visit to the church and received her blessing to meet them in the village. We turned our steps to the east. I'd found the church beautifully picturesque on my first visit, and as we walked up the gravel path with a small cemetery to one side and a peaceful garden on the other, I hoped Lily would find herself equally enchanted with the vine-covered stone building. I was rewarded when I heard her sigh.

"It's simply beautiful," she said.

I took her hand and pulled her along. "Wait until you see the interior. The steep roof you see results in an impressive vaulted ceiling on the inside."

We were surprised to find a woman in the church. She was perhaps a decade older than I, with brown hair pulled into a low knot, wearing spectacles and a serviceable blue dress. She carried a stack of hymnals in her arms. "Good day, ladies. May I be of service to you?"

I introduced ourselves and learned she was the vicar's wife, Mrs. Carruthers. Once she learned Lily was to be married at this very church on Saturday, she divested herself of the books and set about showing her every detail of the church. Afterward, she insisted we retire to the vicarage for tea.

Mrs. Carruthers seemed so eager for our company I determined we could spare her the fifteen or twenty minutes to indulge in a nice coze. We declined any food and chatted about church business as she made the tea.

"I almost forgot," she said. "You'll be glad to know Mr. Gibbs is comfortably installed at his sister's cottage now. I took over some provisions to her since she's not used to having a man about the house. Her own husband's been passed these ten years, and she's happy as a lark to be fussing over her brother."

"I'm pleased he has someone to care for him. It was such a terrible accident, and he was so badly injured, he couldn't possibly get by on his own. Is his pain any more bearable?"

With a tilt of her head, she slanted a look over the top of her spectacles. "If his humor is anything to judge by, I'd say not. I was as polite and pleasant as I could be, and it's only natural I should ask what happened. But the moment I suggested he fell from his horse, well, I thought he was about to have some sort of fit. Tells me he never fell. Someone knocked him off that horse."

"Yes, he made mention of that yesterday, too. But I don't know how that could have happened."

"Chances are the poor man just fell and doesn't want to admit it. He's getting on in years, and he doesn't ride as much as he did back in his day. Mostly he sits behind a desk, from what I understand." She chuckled. "But don't tell him that or he may threaten to remove his shirt."

"Remove his shirt?" Lily wrinkled her nose. "Why ever would he do that?"

She gave us a knowing nod. "He claims he has the welt across his chest that proves something whacked him right good, and that's what knocked him to the ground."

Lily harrumphed. "More likely he ran into something."

I thought of the bit of line I found this morning, stuck in the branches of a tree. It was right about where Gibbs fell. "Perhaps he did run into something," I said. "Did he say what hit him?"

"Not to me. All I heard from him was bellowing and barking." Mrs. Carruthers shrugged. "A branch maybe. That would leave a mark."

"You don't know of anyone who would want to hurt him, do you?"

She waved a dismissive hand. "Don't pay his complaints any mind, my lady. He's just a man who doesn't want to admit to a failing. No one around here would want to do him any harm. He fell off his horse, and now he's embarrassed. Mark my words, that's the long and short of it."

If one rides enough, at some point one will take a spill—hardly cause for embarrassment. But then I wasn't a man, and I didn't take a fall in front of my employer, or his proxy, that is. Which, by the way, was something Gibbs and Michael O'Brien had in common—they both worked for the Earl of Hartfield. Perhaps no one had a grudge against either of the men in question, but might someone have a grudge against the earl? Mrs. Carruthers might be right, but with two so-called accidents happening, one after the other, I wasn't ready to mark her words just yet.

Chapter 8

"How did I allow us to be thirteen at the table?" Fiona clucked her tongue. "How very unlucky."

I smiled to myself as a footman leaned in beside me to fill my bowl with creamy chestnut soup. Fiona looked more surprised by the number than distressed.

"Shall I leave, my dear?" Sir Robert rose to his feet, his bowl in hand and mischief in his eyes. "We can't allow bad luck to interfere with the shoot, and I'm likely the one you are most willing to lose."

Fiona scowled at him from across the table. As George's hostess, she sat at the head, while her husband dined at the other end with George, Lottie, Durant, and myself. "Do sit down, Nash, before you spill that soup and cause more trouble."

"You needn't leave, Nash." I gave him a wink. "I can simply fetch Rose down to join us."

"Well, now that would do." A few of us chuckled, but Fiona looked quite serious.

"Fiona, she's eight years of age. She dined hours ago."

She released a little huff before dipping her spoon into her soup. "I suppose we shall have to cross our fingers or find some other way to restore our luck."

"Perhaps tomorrow you can invite Mr. Bradmore to join us for dinner."

"Bother, I completely forgot to inquire about Lady Esther today." She cut her gaze to George. "Do you remember Lady Esther, George? Frances tells me she is in the country and not in good health. If she is well enough to receive us, do you wish to call on her with me?"

George suddenly became very interested in his soup, keeping his gaze directed there. "You should not plan on me, Fi. I have the shoot to organize, you know."

I saw a slight grimace before she pasted on a smile and turned to me. "At any rate, you are right, Frances. I'll invite him for tomorrow, and we'll be back to a more fortuitous number."

"I'd say our luck has been jolly good." Charles Evingdon, seated on Fiona's right, bobbed his head vigorously in her direction. "Never had such a good day's shooting, not that I've ever shot woodcock before, mind you, but I should think this would go down as a good day's shooting in anyone's estimation. I might just make a record of this day. Something to recall in my old age. Tell my grandchildren and all that. An excellent day, I'd say."

He flashed his dimples at Anne Kendrick, seated on his right, who seemed at a loss for words and turned quickly to Leo on her other side. Following suit, I turned to George, seated on my left. "Cousin Charles appears to have enjoyed himself today," I said in a low voice.

"You know Charles, he always seems to enjoy himself. Though I may need to ask him to bridle his enthusiasm in the future." George lowered his voice to a whisper. "His constant chatter had the birds flying off far ahead of us. Thus, our count was rather low today." He shrugged. "I don't mind, but the Easton men were keen to bag a larger number."

"Where will you shoot tomorrow?" Lottie sat opposite me on George's left. Her bright smile led me to believe she hadn't heard us speaking of her husband.

"On the other side of the village. William Stafford's property. So that will mean an early call for all of us. Stafford likes an early start."

As George had turned to Lottie, I engaged Mr. Durant on the topic. "Are you enjoying the shooting party?" He lowered his spoon and gave my question more consideration than I thought it should warrant. Durant was an interesting man. The oldest son in the family, he could expect to inherit a title, but not much fortune or property. As I had married a fortune hunter, I wondered if he was of the same ilk.

While the footman removed our now-empty bowls, he peered at me through the lenses of his spectacles, which magnified his small, brown eyes. "Shooting. Right. Excellent diversion if one has the time. I rarely indulge in such pastimes."

His gaze dropped to his place setting, and he appeared surprised to find his soup gone. He set down his spoon and returned his attention to me. "I don't think it wise for Mr. Kendrick, Leo, and me to be away from the business at the same time. Who's minding the shop, so to speak?"

"If a man can't take time away from his employment for his own wedding, when can he?"

"Leo may take all the time he wishes, but when all three of us are gone for five days, or six days, all manner of ill can happen to the business. They shouldn't have changed their wedding plans. I hope Kendrick doesn't plan to make a habit of this once he's married."

"Changing his plans?"

"Neglecting his work."

While I wasn't pleased with his criticism of Leo, these were the first full sentences I'd heard from Durant. He certainly had strong feelings about his employment. A footman leaned in between us with a dish of lobster curry. I took a serving and waited patiently while Durant did the same. When the footman moved down the table, I asked him about it.

"The business world is fascinating, Lady Harleigh, simply fascinating. And what's more, I find it rewarding to do something worthwhile with my life." He grinned and released a quiet laugh. "Turns out, I like being useful, much to my father's dismay. Father-in-law's, too. He wanted a gentleman for his daughter."

"Surely he knew you would not inherit for some time."

"You'd think so, wouldn't you? Not a day goes by that he fails to ask how my father does."

This was so close to the joke Anne and I shared this morning that I nearly choked on a bit of lobster.

His lips spread into a smile, twisted with bitterness. "Every day I tell him my father does quite well, and I hope he will continue to do so for the next forty years or more." He shook his head. "Don't wish to be the country gentleman. I enjoy the business world, and what's more, I'm good at it. I find it irksome my father-in-law can't appreciate that and anticipates the day I inherit and leave his employ."

It did seem a shame for him to be ousted from the business in such a way. "I'm sure Mr. Kendrick appreciates your talents and dedication."

"Not so sure. If hard work and innovation don't win him over, I may be forced to resort to more extreme measures." He pushed the curry into his rice, his lips turning down. "Won't help matters when he learns I'm spending nearly a week at a shooting party."

"And a wedding. Don't forget the wedding."

"Of course not. Still seems foolish to me to upend all their plans."

"They simply decided they didn't want a large society affair. Since Mr. Hazelton had invited us to join his party, it was an opportunity they couldn't resist."

He compressed his lips.

"You don't suppose Mr. and Mrs. Kendrick will mind, do you?"

His expression changed instantly to astonishment as if he couldn't believe I needed to ask the question. "The Kendricks mind nothing Leo does. Darling of the family, you know. He can do no wrong."

"Come now, Mr. Durant. You are the eldest son in your family. Tell me your father treats you any differently than Mr. Kendrick treats Leo. I'm certain you are the apple of his eye."

Durant took a sip from his wineglass and smiled, though it didn't reach his eyes. "Right. With the exception of my career, I suspect that's true. Just thought the business world would be different."

I tipped my head to the side. "Leo is still the heir, even if it is to a business rather than a title."

"He most certainly is." This time his smile took the form of a grimace.

A footman leaned in with a tray of vegetables, and I served myself. Durant had turned to speak to his sister-in-law, Clara, and as the footman moved down the table, I found myself back in conversation with George.

"Have you heard anything from Dr. Woodrow yet?" I asked.

"Not yet. Country doctors have busy schedules. He'll send along his findings as soon as he has the time."

"Yes, I suppose his hands are full at the moment, and we have provided him with two additional patients."

George raised his brows, and I grimaced at my choice of words. "I suppose that is not the correct word to describe Michael, is it? Poor man. As for Mr. Gibbs, I heard he is somewhat less than a congenial patient for his sister."

"Gibbs is less than congenial at the best of times, I doubt his injury has made him any more so, but his sister must have been aware of that before she volunteered to nurse him." He gave me a quizzical glance. "Did you pay him a visit?"

I shook my head. "Lily and I stopped by the church and met the vicar's wife. She had visited Gibbs earlier and took along some provisions for his sister. She says he is still claiming he was knocked from his horse."

"Stubborn man. More likely he just needs spectacles."

"Mrs. Carruthers suggested he's grown unused to riding."

He narrowed his eyes. "That's also possible. Are you leading to something?"

"It's likely nothing, but when I went riding this morning with Rose and Anne, we rode past the lane where he fell, or was knocked off." I made a circular motion with my fork. "Whatever happened. I found a length of what looks like braided fishing line tangled in some branches. It seemed out of place."

"What are you suggesting?"

What was I suggesting? "I'm not certain. Mr. Gibbs insists something knocked him off the horse. If the line were stretched across the lane from one tree to another, it would be difficult to see it if one were in motion. The braided line looked quite sturdy. It might easily have swept a rider from his horse, or at least startle him enough to lose his balance and fall."

He lowered his fork and stared. "Why would anyone do that?"

"I don't know that anyone would, but those trees are well trimmed to keep the lane clear. Where would the line have come from?"

His expression told me he was about to list all the possibilities. "The path is well used. Anyone could have dropped it there."

Not a list then. "But the way it curled about the tree in a tangle bothered me. As if it had been stretched taut then snapped."

"Was it long enough to stretch across the lane?"

"No, it appears as though it were cut. Or it broke when Gibbs barreled into it. I should have checked the other side of the lane."

He gave me a curious look. His lips slowly turned upward as he leaned toward me. "It may be possible you have been involved in too many mysteries lately, Frances. Are you seeing plots where there is only a discarded length of line?" He raised a brow. "A bird may have dropped it in the tree."

If so, it would have been a very large bird. But it was possible. And I felt ridiculous. I looked down at my plate, ready to admit he may be correct. Until he touched my hand under the table.

"Why do you think Gibbs suffered more than a simple accident?"

"I don't know. I'm most likely jumping to conclusions."

"Perhaps, but I have a healthy respect for your instincts, and I'd like to know what has your antennae twitching. What makes you suspicious?"

I should have known George wouldn't brush my concerns aside without a thought. But to answer his question—what was making me suspicious?

"First of all, Gibbs himself. He claims he was knocked off the horse by a blow to the chest. He also claims to have a mark across his chest to prove it."

"Has anyone seen this mark?"

I released a gurgle of laughter. "The vicar's wife passed on that information. He certainly didn't show it to her, but why would he lie?"

George shrugged. "The man felt foolish and wanted to save face."

"And you know that because?"

"He's a man?"

I released a *tsk*.

"He's an older man who doesn't want to appear old or worse, clumsy in the eyes of his employer."

"But you aren't his employer. You don't know Mr. Gibbs at all. He may be as honest as the day is long. You really have no basis for making such a judgment."

"So, what should I do? Ask him to show me the marks on his chest?"

I grinned. "According to Mrs. Carruthers, he would be more than willing to do so, but Dr. Woodrow examined him. If there were such marks on his chest, the doctor would have seen them."

"Woodrow was focused on the broken leg. Gibbs didn't mention having pain anywhere else."

"Then the only option is to check with the man himself." I picked up my wineglass and took a sip. "It would be an easy way to determine if I am jumping to conclusions or not. And I would like to know."

"Well, I can't allow you to walk into Gibbs's sick room and demand to see his naked chest, so I suppose I must take on that task."

"Thank you, George. You indulge me so."

He gave me a crooked smile. "Why do I have the feeling I've just lost a game of chess?"

"Chess? I can't imagine what you mean." I gave his hand a squeeze before returning mine to my lap. "You agreed to help me clear up some suspicions, and I'm very grateful."

"Well, anything to make you happy, my dear." His eyes sparkled as he whispered the endearment, and I must admit I tingled with pleasure upon hearing the words. "However, it will have to wait a bit longer. I won't be able to get away tomorrow. By the way, what's your second reason?"

I gave him a quizzical glance.

"When I asked you what made you suspicious, you said, first of all, then you talked about Gibbs. What is second?"

George waited while I pushed a bit of curry around my plate. If I told him my suspicions, he'd likely think I was insane, but who else could I share them with? "The second is the footman. Two men, employed by the earl, suffered serious accidents one day apart."

Under the weight of George's incredulous stare, I faltered, bit my lip, and persevered. "I know this sounds ridiculous, but what if someone is trying to cause mischief for your brother?"

"By killing a man?"

"Perhaps O'Brien wasn't meant to die, just become ill. Whoever sold him the ginger beer couldn't have known he'd drink almost the entire jug."

"What would be the purpose of such a diabolical plan—chase all the servants off the estate? Hart would simply find new ones."

"I don't know what the motive would be. I just wonder if it's more than a coincidence."

George opened his mouth to speak, then closed it with a sigh, his brows drawn together in a frown. "Perhaps we should avoid speculation until Dr. Woodrow presents his findings on the ginger beer. But in the meantime, I think I'll take a look at that line you found."

It was reassuring to know George didn't believe in coincidences either.

Each day in the country seemed much like the one before. Anne, Rose, and I rode out again on Tuesday, and again we came across Percy Bradmore. This time, with Fiona's permission, I invited him to join us for luncheon that afternoon, which was to take place on the east lawn just beyond the rose gardens, with a surprise event afterward.

The surprise became apparent when I crossed the lawn to join my fellow guests and nearly collided with Mr. Winnie coming around the maze, his arms filled with archery equipment. He pulled up short and dropped his burden, causing the groom who followed him to stumble forward under his heavy load. Ignoring the groom, Winnie put out a hand to steady me.

"Forgive me, Lady Harleigh. I didn't see you there."

"I should think not. You were loaded up to the top of your head in supplies."

He grinned, showing a dimple in one of the bare spots of his beard. "I should have asked for more help or started this task sooner."

"I can guess who requested archery. This must be Lady Fiona's doing."

"Yes, ma'am. She had me searching for the targets and such as soon as she knew more guests were arriving. Spent the better part of a day rooting through every nook and cranny. Finally found them stored away with some old fishing equipment and cricket bats."

"Well, don't let me keep you."

He stooped to gather the arrows and bows. "Thank you, ma'am. I've plenty of work to catch up on once I'm finished with this."

His words reminded me he was the acting steward since Gibbs's accident. "Mr. Winnie, I'm certain Lady Fiona didn't expect you to set up these targets yourself. You are well within your rights to assign these tasks to others if you have obligations elsewhere."

"I'll keep that in mind." He nodded and bent to his task, and I headed over to the tables set up for our luncheon. I eyed the maze as I walked past. I loved a maze but had yet to investigate this one. The yew walls stretched several feet over my head. I wondered if I could lose myself inside while the archery took place. I never took the time to practice and my proficiency could come and go like a summer shower. Sometimes I surprised myself with my skill, often landing quite near the bull's-eye. Other times, something was just off. Whether it was my aim, my balance, or my rhythm I couldn't say, but I've been known to miss the target completely, or worse, send my arrow a mere yard or two in front of me before it fell to the ground, probably in humiliation.

Fiona sidled up beside me, her eyes glowing with delight. "Won't this be fun, dear? Archery is something we can all have a go at, both ladies and gentlemen. I knew the targets were here somewhere and was positively thrilled to bits when Winnie told me he'd found them." She gave me a nudge. "When was the last time you shot an arrow?"

"Far too long. I don't know if it's wise to trust me with a bow and arrow. Someone could be injured."

"Nonsense. I'll team you with George. He can refresh you on the proper stance and technique." She batted her lashes. "Won't that be fun?"

I could hardly argue with her. Anytime George had his arms around me was lovely. But something else she'd said bothered me. "Did you say *team?*"

"Of course. It's to be a competition. A tournament of sorts. There are three targets so we can play in teams of two or three."

"Should we not just shoot for fun, or to hone our skills?"

"What would be the point of that?" She shook her head. "It must be a competition."

"But you have all these men here. And they are so—competitive. They will argue over rules, and the distance to the target, and anything else they can think of. You may end up with a brawl on your hands."

"Oh, pish! We have everything marked out, the distance to the targets will be measured exactly, and I won't stand for any complaints about the rules." She shrugged. "If there's a brawl, so be it. But I can assure you everyone will behave."

"You don't fool me, dear. I happen to recall you are an excellent archer. You only wish to do this because you expect to win." I chuckled as Fiona pursed her lips. "I'm surprised you're willing to give up George as your partner."

She laughed aloud. "George is skillful with a

bow, but Nash has been practicing. I think we have a very good chance. Now, enough of this." She brushed an imaginary wrinkle from her skirt. "Be a good friend and introduce me to Mr. Bradmore. Is that him coming across the lawn?"

Indeed, Mr. Bradmore was almost upon us. I raised my hand to catch his attention and drew him over to present to Fiona.

"I cannot believe we have never met, Mr. Bradmore. Have you never visited your aunt and uncle before?"

"Only as a child, Lady Fiona. I am actually their great-nephew. My father and the baron were not particularly close. Since Father was in the military, I grew up wherever he was sent."

"As someone who rarely left this estate as a child, that sounds quite fascinating. Do you never visit them in London?"

"I rarely find myself in London, but since it's become clear that I'll be heir to the title, and the current Lord de Brook spends more and more time in London, I must visit him there. But those visits are more business than social in nature. I can't remember the last time I attended a soiree in town."

"That's right. I'd forgotten the current baron has no children. No wonder you stay away from London, Mr. Bradmore. All the matchmaking mamas must be eager to introduce you to their daughters."

He tipped his head and flashed an engaging smile. "You have found me out, Lady Nash."

I stood back as the two of them had a good laugh. Single gentlemen had been escaping mothers of daughters for generations. This was nothing new, yet I had the sense Mr. Bradmore was relieved that Fiona provided an excuse for his absence from town, for what must be ten years or more. The man must be at least thirty. I gave myself a shake. Perhaps he was using Fiona's excuse to evade a direct answer. His reasons, if there were reasons, for avoiding London were none of our concern. The man was just the nephew of a neighbor. I didn't need to know everything about him.

Fiona took his arm and offered to make him known to everyone in our group. I followed them back to the table laden with food. A large white canopy shaded the area, and the table linens fluttered in the breeze as the guests stepped up to fill their plates. Assorted chairs and blankets were strewn nearby so we could eat in small groups.

I spied Leo and Lily relaxing on one of the blankets under a tree, with Mr. Treadwell nearby, as usual. He reclined on Lily's other side, leaning back on his elbows. The men had changed out of their sporting gear and into country tweeds. Mr. Treadwell's jacket was open, his long legs stretched out before him, a straw boater tipped over his eyes. The man was young, reasonably good-looking, and insanely wealthy. Did coming from such a fortunate situation lead him to believe he could have anything he wanted? His friend's fiancée for example?

I wandered over to their little group. Treadwell made as if to rise as I approached.

"No need to rise for my benefit, Mr. Treadwell. There is plenty of room here for me."

I slipped down across from Lily, sitting on my hip with my legs folded to the side. "How was the shooting today, gentlemen?"

Leo's smile lit his face. "Capital, Lady Harleigh. I participated in a shooting party back in my school days, but this is still a novel experience for me. Can't say when I've enjoyed myself so well."

"I'm so happy to hear that. And how nice for you to be able to enjoy the experience with an old friend." I turned to Treadwell, now upright and sitting cross-legged. "I understand the two of you are very old friends indeed."

He examined me dispassionately, knowing full well what I was up to. "Not so terribly old, a good ten years or so. Going back to our school days."

"Rather been inseparable since those days wouldn't you say, old man? Done everything together." Leo leaned forward around Lily to grin at Treadwell.

Lily gave Leo a sweet smile. "I believe I see Mr. Treadwell quite as often as I see you."

"How wonderful to have such a strong and lasting friendship." I turned to Treadwell. "And now, here you are, helping Leo to celebrate this big step in his life."

He nodded but said nothing.

"If the two of you do everything together, perhaps marriage is on your horizon as well?"

His gaze sharpened. "Ah, no. I have not been as fortunate in finding love as Kendrick here."

"Perhaps you need to look a little farther afield." I nodded past Leo's head where his two youngest sisters sat alone.

"You will certainly need to look farther than this blanket, Treadwell. Miss Price is most definitely taken." Leo's tone took the sting from the words, but I suspect he didn't know he might be causing his friend pain. It was difficult to know if Treadwell had feelings for Lily or if he was just amusing himself.

Treadwell scrambled to his feet. "You are right, Lady Harleigh. As a house guest, I should be making myself useful to the other ladies in attendance." He brushed off his jacket and sauntered over to Clara and Anne, offering to procure plates for them.

Lily let her gaze follow him across the lawn; then she turned to me, soundlessly mouthing the words *thank you*.

As my work here was done, I rose to my feet. "I think I shall see what Lady Fiona has for our luncheon."

The group became quite jolly as everyone ate and drank, and tales of the morning's shoot grew ever more daring. But when another hour passed, Fiona would be put off no longer, and we all wandered over to the patch of lawn designated for archery. After some argument over partners, it was decided to play in teams of two. Eliza Durant chose not to participate and wandered over to the maze.

Lottie glanced around and counted heads. "That makes our number uneven, so I will also bow out and cheer you on, Charles."

The relief among the group was palpable.

"That leaves us with six teams. We'll all draw straws." Fiona walked amongst us, the straws in her fist. "Those with the long straws will shoot first."

George wore an expression of suffering as he showed me what appeared to be a longish straw. "My sister is quite the tartar with rules."

"She did tell me there would be no arguing amongst the teams. I assume this is how she intends to prevent it."

"Come, come, you two." We both turned at Fiona's command. She had Leo by the arm, leading him to the first of the targets nearest to the maze. Lily trailed behind. "I think she means for us to play against Leo and Lily. We'd better not keep her waiting."

As I'd guessed, the four of us were on the first target about fifty feet from the wall of the maze. Winnie had placed the other targets at least that far apart so one could safely retrieve one's arrows. Cousin Charles, Arthur Durant, and two of Leo's sisters were to the right of us, leaving Fiona and Nash, and Percy Bradmore and Ernest Treadwell at the far end.

George sidled up beside me. "How are your archery skills, my lady?"

Remembering how Fiona had teased me, I gave him a flirtatious smile. "It has been some time since I've picked up a bow. I'm not certain I recall how to hold it."

He fitted the bow into my hands and directed me into the proper stance. With his arms around me and his lips next to my ear, he whispered, "I think you are playing with me, Frances. I must say, I approve."

"And why should you go first?"

The sharp words dragged my mind back from its blissful wanderings. Both George and I glanced past Leo to see Clara Kendrick stamp her foot as she glared at her sister.

Anne lowered her bow. "For heaven's sake, Clara, by all means, please do go first." She handed her sister the bow and stepped away from the mark to stand next to Mr. Bradmore who watched the group in amusement. Clara narrowed her eyes in one moment and turned an innocent smile to Bradmore in the next.

"Mr. Bradmore, could you help me with my arrow?"

Durant was having none of her nonsense. "Bradmore has his own group to attend to." He snatched the bow from her grasp and nocked the arrow himself. "Should have learned how to do this before you insisted on going first."

I turned back to George as Clara blushed a deep scarlet. "I'm quite sure that's not how she planned that scene to play out."

"The girl acts rather like a spoiled child." Fortunately, George stood close enough to whisper. I would hate for Leo to have heard the comment, but he seemed to have heard neither George's comment, nor his sister's antics. Perhaps turning a deaf ear helped him to maintain his cheerful disposition. He simply assumed everything was well with the world and went about his business.

"Why do we have teams if this is to be a proper tournament?" Durant asked the group in general.

"It is not a proper tournament." Fiona stepped between the participants and the targets. "And if you will spare me your attention, I'll explain the rules." Her explanation ran on and on, but the gist of it was the team sharing our targets weren't necessarily our opponents. The two low-scoring teams would be removed from the competition after each round until only two teams remained. Lottie was assigned to blow a whistle after each end, indicating we could approach the targets and collect our arrows. It seemed simple enough.

The competition began. I was to make the first shot of our foursome. I drew a deep breath, wondering which of my selves would show up for me today. Would I be the archer or the fool? I nocked my arrow and looked out at the target. Wasn't it farther away than it ought to be? Taking my stance, I drew back the bowstring, took one more breath, and let it fly.

A cheer erupted from George and my competitors. I stared at the target. Not only had I hit it—huzzah—but from this distance, the arrow looked to be no more than an inch above the bull's-eye. Happy day! Archer Frances had decided to join the competition.

"Well done, Frances." Lily beamed at me as she took the bow. "I had no idea you were so good at this."

"Neither did I," George said, his eyes sparkling. "You never fail to surprise me."

"Believe me, it comes and goes." I waved my hand airily. "Don't count on my every shot hitting its mark, or I shall surprise you again."

We watched as Leo assisted Lily with the handling of the bow and nocking the arrow. We cheered again as she hit the target though well to the left. Lily hung her head, but Leo would have none of it. "This was your first attempt," he said. "You did well just to hit the target."

George went next, besting me by perhaps half an inch. Then Leo took his turn and hit the top of the bull's-eye. Once we'd taken all our shots, Lottie blew her whistle. Slapping each other on the back, the men stepped off to retrieve the arrows. The competition moved on in much the same manner. Aside from one poor shot that missed the target altogether, I was consistently on the mark. Lily improved as we moved on, but the real competition came down to George and Leo. Their shots were so close, the advantage kept moving back and forth between our teams.

We won the first round, and as their team score was the next highest, we played Leo and Lily again. Bradmore and Treadwell were knocked out of the competition, as were Charles and Clara. Some of the former competitors drifted off. Ernest Treadwell moved to the refreshments table, and Clara Kendrick followed him. Some of them stayed to watch, however, and the afternoon became more festive as they chose their champion teams and cheered them on while heckling the others.

This served to fuel our competitive spirits and, as I'd predicted, the men, in particular, became quarrelsome. Spectators started finding faults—

had George stepped over the line? Had someone coughed while Leo took aim? The competitors at the next target fared no better. Either Fiona or Durant consistently called for a review of their shots, and no one waited for Lottie's whistle before approaching the targets, though to be fair, I'm not sure anyone could hear the whistle over the din.

One turn came under a great deal of scrutiny. Neither George nor Leo had hit the bull's-eye, but both arrows were close. Very close—on either side of the bull. While the other set of teams played on, George and Leo approached our target to determine whose arrow was closer. I rolled my eyes when I saw George using his thumbnail to measure the distance between each arrow and the bull's-eye.

Then Charles stepped over to add his opinion. He bent close to the bull's-eye to make his determination.

"That's hardly fair." Lily gestured to the group at the target. "Charles and George are friends. Someone without bias should make the call."

I gave her an incredulous stare. "It's just a game, Lily. I think Charles can judge without bias."

That's when I heard the shout. Followed by a shriek.

I looked toward the targets where the three men were clustered so closely I couldn't see what had happened. As everyone rushed forward, so did I, and as I came closer to the trio, I saw what the fuss was about.

With a groan, Charles slumped to the ground on his stomach. Lottie, having run to his aid, dropped to her knees beside him. Leo stared down at them, looking stunned.

I was stunned myself.

An arrow was buried deep in Charles's backside.

Chapter 9

~~~

"How did this happen?"

Though I shouted, no one seemed to hear me through the confusion. The heightened sense of alarm made our voices louder. Someone barked out orders. No one listened. We jostled one another, both to get closer to Charles, and away from him. The poor man lay stiff on the ground, facedown, obviously afraid to move. Lottie stroked his face and cooed to him as if she were trying to keep him calm, though Charles seemed far more tranquil than the rest of us. Every few seconds another shriek erupted as someone new spied the arrow protruding from his body. I have to admit, it was a rather disturbing sight, but at least it wasn't bleeding profusely.

I finally realized the person barking orders was George. "You," he shouted to a footman. "Find Hancock and bring him here at once. Then send someone for Dr. Woodrow and bring him back, too."

The man nodded once and ran to the house.

Lottie looked up at George with watery eyes. "Can we remove it?" She glanced at the arrow. "It looks so painful."

George pushed her hand aside as he knelt next to Charles. "Not just yet, if you please. I want to make sure moving him, or removing the arrow, won't cause more damage."

"Gad, George. Tell me I didn't just hear you call for Hancock." Charles's words came through gritted teeth.

"Sorry, old man. If you'd rather wait for the doctor to be found and brought here, I'll send Hancock back to the stables."

"Who is Hancock?" Lottie brushed aside her tears and struggled to rise. I placed a hand under her arm to assist her, mentally cursing tight corsets.

George gave her a wry smile. "Farrier, veterinarian, and officially head groom on the estate. He's been doctoring animals and the occasional Hazelton since I was a boy. He'll know how to remove this safely."

Lottie's hands rose to her cheeks, her eyes filled with a horror I completely understood. A veterinarian would be tending to Charles's injury?

George stood as well. "Here he comes." He nodded to a lanky man dressed in rough clothing who rushed, with a limping gait, across the lawn. "And you're in luck, Charles. It looks like he's brought you some whiskey."

"Good man," Charles groaned.

George took my arm and pulled me toward

Leo. "Can the two of you take charge of things here?"

"Of course," I said, as Leo nodded. I opened my mouth to ask where he was going, but he'd already turned and headed toward the maze at a smart clip.

Lottie hovered over Mr. Hancock, determined to protect her husband from further harm. I drew her away from the poor man so he could attend to Charles. "Did you see what happened?"

"No. I was talking to Lady Nash at the time. I didn't even look this way until I heard Charles bellowing."

"Wasn't bellowing," Charles said.

"What about you, Leo?"

He shook his head. "I was right next to Mr. Evingdon examining the targets when he was hit. It never occurred to me to look back and see who was shooting."

It hadn't occurred to me either.

"Anne was shooting. Arrow must have gone astray."

Arthur Durant had just stepped up beside me. Anne, bow still in her hand, stood right behind him, her face red and her jaw squared in outrage. "Don't be ridiculous. My arrow hit our target."

Durant waved his hand to their target. "That's mine. Your shot hit Evingdon."

She stared at her brother-in-law, then turned to me, one hand raised in supplication, her eyes

144

begging me to believe her. "I did not hit him."

"Not intentionally of course." Durant placed a hand on her shoulder. "It was an accident." Anne's lips parted on a gasp before she twisted away from his touch and stalked off.

Durant bent down to talk to Leo and Hancock just as Lily approached. "Who on earth shot an arrow at Mr. Evingdon?" she asked.

"I don't know." But I was beginning to doubt it had been Anne, or that it had been an accident at all. George had disappeared into the maze. Did he think the arrow had come from there? I pushed Lottie into Lily's arms. "Stay with her, Lily. And try to keep everyone away. Charles deserves some privacy."

With that, I made haste to the entrance of the maze. Mr. Winnie, coming around the back, touched his hand to his hat when he spotted me.

"I heard the commotion and came to find out what happened." He tipped his head toward the group of men on the ground near the targets. "Is someone hurt?"

I gave him a quick summary. "If Hancock deems it wise to move Mr. Evingdon, you may be of some help." He nodded and headed toward the men as I entered the maze. At the very first turn, I encountered Mr. Treadwell.

"Ah! I've been looking for the blasted entrance for the last ten minutes." He did appear much relieved to see me. "What's happened out there?

I heard the shouting, but I couldn't find my way out of here."

"Mr. Evingdon was hit with an arrow." I took him in with a glance. No dirt on his clothing, not a hair out of place, and most importantly, no bow in his hand. "How long have you been in here?" The last I'd noticed him, he was at the refreshments table with Clara.

"Far too long." He ran a hand through his hair and replaced his hat. "If you'll excuse me, perhaps I can be of assistance out there."

He moved around me in the narrow passage, and stepped out, leaning back in before he left. "Be careful in here. It's easy to become lost."

I could see it was a distinct possibility. The yew hedges had to be at least eight feet tall and were quite dense. I knew George was in here somewhere, yet I'd had no sight of him. My only path was forward, deeper into the maze. As I moved on, I considered calling out to him, but if he thought someone had shot the arrow from inside the maze, the culprit might still be here.

Not that I had any idea what George thought. I was beginning to feel foolish as I kept taking right-hand turns, which I hoped would lead me to the outside wall of the maze and the corner nearest the targets. Why else would he come here? Surely, he wouldn't leave his friend injured on the ground while he went off for his own amusement. I rounded another corner and walked straight into Clara Kendrick.

We both let out a shriek.

With a hand to her chest, she fell back against the hedge wall. "Lady Harleigh, you nearly startled the life out of me."

I fanned my face with my hand. "Yes, well, I hadn't expected to find so many people in here. I'm looking for Mr. Hazelton. Have you happened to see him?"

She replied in the negative and once more I had to explain what happened at the archery competition.

"That's horrible." She did look horrified but also titillated, and obviously eager to join the crowd. I stepped back against the yews and pointed the way out. To the best of my recollection anyway.

With one more right turn the hum of the guests on the lawn grew louder. I must have reached the outer wall. Their voices grew clearer as I moved forward. Not clear exactly; I couldn't pick out any words, just the sound of them. One final turn and I found George, sitting on his haunches facing the wall of the maze.

He jumped to his feet when he heard me approach, and for the second time today I'd made someone clutch at their chest. I must be very stealthy indeed.

Once he recovered, he let out his breath in a

huff and placed a fist on his hip. With his other hand, he made an impatient, beckoning motion which one might use with a recalcitrant child. How dare he?

I made a show of looking behind me then returned my gaze to him with wide, innocent eyes. "Surely that demeaning gesture isn't meant for me?"

He pressed his lips together and dropped his gaze to the ground where it remained for a moment. Was he counting to ten? He returned his gaze to me with what might have been a smile or just a baring of teeth. "Dearest Frances, would you do me the honor of coming this way?"

"Of course, dearest George." I stepped up beside him. "What are you examining so carefully? And why did you come in here? Do you think the arrow was shot from here?"

He boggled his eyes at the rush of questions and pointed down. "See how the ground's disturbed? It looks like someone stood here for a time."

I followed the direction of his finger. This section of the maze was in deep shade and due to its placement near the woods, would only have sun for the hour or two surrounding midday. As a result, the ground was damp, and while it was not muddy, I could see a light impression of my steps and George's, but the spot in question held a deeper impression of someone who had stood, possibly shuffling his feet, facing the wall of the maze.

As I moved my gaze up the length of the shrubbery wall, I saw something even more surprising. Someone had thinned this side of the yew hedge with sheers or perhaps a knife. It wasn't exactly a hole, but the branches had been cut and stuffed back in elsewhere along the hedge. A few littered the ground.

George waved a hand toward the thin spot. "Take a look," he said.

I had to go up on my toes to peer through the opening, but once I did, I had a side view of the targets through the remaining foliage. "Whoever stood here, had a clear shot at Charles."

"With a pistol perhaps, but the shrubbery is still too dense for a smooth release with a bow and arrow. It could be done, but even this thinned shrubbery would interfere as the arrow passed through, changing its direction somewhat."

I stepped back from the hedge, both confused and horrified. "Are you saying whoever did this was not necessarily aiming for Charles's backside?"

"Shooting through this?" He grazed his hand along the trimmed yews. "It would require a few practice shots to determine just how the arrow would fly. If the culprit was shooting from here, it would be difficult to know exactly what he was aiming for."

"You, Leo, and Charles were all standing in front of those targets. Who would want to injure any of you?"

"That's what I'd hoped to find out when I ran in here, but I wasn't able to catch anyone in the act."

"With this view, whoever it was must have seen you coming."

"Understood, but how did he get out? I know I spent too much time with Charles before coming after the scoundrel, but there is only one entrance and exit to this maze, and we'd have seen someone come out."

"I don't agree. I never noticed Clara Kendrick or Ernest Treadwell enter the maze, but I found both of them wandering around in here while looking for you. You were by the targets tending to Charles. With everyone crowding around, you couldn't have had a clear view of the entrance."

George tipped his head toward me as if unsure he'd heard correctly. "Treadwell and Miss Kendrick were in here? What were they doing?"

"They weren't together, if that's what you mean. I didn't ask either of them why they were here, but I suspect Treadwell became tired of watching the other matches and decided to wander through the maze." I shrugged. "Clara likely noticed him and took the opportunity to follow. She's a bit of a flirt."

George leaned back against the yew barrier and crossed his arms over his chest. "Blast, that makes three people I didn't see coming in here."

"Who else?"

"Percy Bradmore was searching for the exit when I ran in. Claimed he was wandering about and heard all the hubbub. Asked what had happened."

"Bradmore? Heavens, half our party were in here at the time. Did he see anyone else?"

"No, though he offered to help me look, I sent him on his way. I should have just hacked my way through these hedges."

I raised my brows. "How? Do you keep a trusty machete in your boot? Besides, someone in here was shooting arrows at you. I'm glad you didn't attempt it."

We were quiet for a moment, both wondering just what had happened. Someone had released an arrow at the trio of gentlemen. Whoever it was had been standing right here. The cuts in the branches that hollowed out the space were fresh. But there was no bow and no culprit. Three people had been in the maze at the time and claimed they saw nothing. Any, or all of them, could be lying.

"I can't imagine Bradmore, Treadwell, or Miss Kendrick cutting back this shrubbery, but a worker from the estate might have done so. Is it possible nothing more sinister happened here than a worker watching the competition? The arrow that hit Charles might just have been an errant shot from the other match."

George twisted his lips from side to side as

he considered the idea. "It's possible, but while we're here, indulge me if you will, and help me inspect the exterior walls."

"You think the culprit may have cut his way out. An excellent notion." I took George's hand. "Lead the way."

He gave my fingers a squeeze and drew them into the crook of his arm. "Ah, Frances. You always have a way of making me feel I know what I'm doing—that I'm not just thrashing around in the dark, hoping to stumble upon a clue."

We surveyed the area one more time before he led me effortlessly to the exit of the maze. A glance at the vacant archery area told us Charles had somehow been transported to the house and the rest of the guests had found somewhere else to be. We followed the wall of the maze away from the house and toward the stables. It was rather a large structure when seen from the outside.

"How long has this maze been here?"

"This one, perhaps fifty years, but there was another here earlier, and I was told it dated back to Elizabeth's reign."

I feigned a gasp. "Does that make the Hartfield title older than Harleigh? Please never mention that to my brother-in-law."

"Graham need not worry. Both earldoms were granted around the same generation." He glanced at me through narrowed eyes. "Does he care so much about those things?"

I raised my hand, palm up. "He's very proud of the family name. I suppose I might feel that way too if it were mine."

"But it is yours."

"But I wasn't born to it. I am an outsider. At least that's how the family always treated me." I glanced up at him with a flirtatious smile. "Have I mentioned how happy I am you will never inherit your family title?"

He let out a bark of laughter. "So, that is the attraction. Well, you can be no happier than I. Having charge of the estate for a few weeks is one thing, but I was not meant for this kind of life. You know I am too interested in solving puzzles and looking for clues."

"Well, you are about to walk right past your clue." We'd rounded the corner and come along the back side of the maze. I nodded to the hedge where branches had been hacked to pieces, leaving a wide opening between two yews. Stems and needles scattered across the lawn and the fresh cuts indicated this vandalism had only recently taken place.

George dropped down to his knees to examine the wreckage. "I think this gives more weight to our theory. Our culprit had been inside the maze."

"It might be a good idea to check with Mr. Winnie," I said as we made our way back to the manor house. "The steward's cottage looks out on that side of the maze, and when I ran in to follow you, I met him coming from the cottage to see what the commotion was about."

George nodded. "It's worth asking, I suppose, but I'd like to think if he saw someone hacking away at the maze, he'd have done something about it then and there."

"Looking at it that way, I suppose you're right. It can't hurt to ask though."

We moved on in silence for a moment then George took my hand and drew it to his lips. "This week is turning out to be far from what I'd envisioned when I asked you to join me here."

"Then you weren't expecting your steward to be injured, a footman poisoned, and Cousin Charles to be hit with an arrow in his posterior?" I shook my head in mock wonder. "And I was so certain you'd planned these events."

"Actually, what I'd planned were romantic moonlit strolls, time alone with you, and perhaps a chance to plan our wedding." He squeezed my hand. "It may be selfish of me, but I am still glad to have you here. You've been no end of help."

"Truly? In what way have I helped?"

"Your cool head under these circumstances. Look how you managed to bring calm to the servants' hall. And you took note of your surroundings when Evingdon was struck. Your questions keep me from brushing these incidents off as unrelated accidents."

Well. That came as a surprise. "I thought you were inclined to see Gibbs's injury and the footman's poisoning as accidents."

He smiled. "I can't let you know everything I think."

"I beg to differ. You are to have no secrets from me, do you understand? Now kindly explain yourself."

He gave my arm a tug, and we continued our walk. "I'm not entirely certain what to think. It's still quite possible they were accidents, but with you questioning them, and considering what happened to Charles, I'm beginning to see things differently. That arrow was not shot accidentally, so now I must wonder about the nature of the other incidents."

"You should have a conversation with Gibbs."

"Most certainly. And Woodrow may have some information by now about the ginger beer and if it contained arsenic."

I let out my breath in a huff. "Even if it did, that doesn't mean someone didn't add it to the bottle after the fact. Someone in the household may have poisoned it, knowing the man would drink it sooner or later."

"Gad, Frances, your thought process is positively devious. What's worse is you could be right. We need more information, I'm afraid." He gave me a sad smile. "It seems our week of romantic dreaming is not to be. Instead, we'll be working on another investigation together."

While I did love an investigation, I had no idea where to begin with this one. Someone might have deliberately attacked three people on this estate. One was dead. What would happen next?

As we walked up the front steps to the house, George drew me to a stop. "I'd like to check on Charles first and talk with Dr. Woodrow if he's here. But after that, we need an opportunity to devise our plan."

I looked up into his face. "There's nothing I love more than plotting with you, George."

He smiled and leaned in to kiss me. My eyelids fluttered closed.

The door opened with a clatter.

"Frances, there you are. Why are you two lurking about?"

I suppressed a groan upon hearing the voice. I'd wondered what could happen next and now I knew.

My mother had arrived.

Chapter 10

~⊃

B other, I wasn't expecting Mother until tomorrow. She beckoned us from the doorway, and I was struck anew by her resemblance to Lily, who would look exactly like her in twenty or thirty years—if she were very careful, that is. Thanks to her rigorous beauty regime, and her determination to guard her skin from the sun, my mother would never look twenty years older than either of her daughters. Her hair, more flaxen than Lily's gold, was complemented by the strands of silver threaded throughout, and her complexion remained free of even the faintest of lines.

Climbing the remaining steps, I entered the great hall, thankful to have George at my side. I kissed the cheek she presented, inhaling the scent of lilac I'd always associated with her, and turned to greet Hetty and Alonzo.

"Franny, you are every bit as beautiful as I remembered." Alonzo wrapped me in a hug, lifted me off my feet, and swung me around before setting me back down.

"Heavens, Lon. Stop and let me look at you!"

I took a step back and made a show of looking him up and down. When I'd come to England,

Alonzo had been a child of twelve. He'd visited me with Mother as a gangly youth of fourteen. Now, at twenty-two, my little brother had grown into a handsome young man.

He wore a traveling suit of light wool which showed off his broad shoulders without any sort of padding. Like me, he took after my father in height and hair color, but unlike me, he also had my father's brown eyes and long, lean face. If anyone had taken note of the trio as they traveled, I'd wager they would have assumed Alonzo was Aunt Hetty's son.

"I do believe you've grown up, Lon."

"He's grown into the most sought-after man in New York. If I don't have him married to a Goelet or a Rhinelander, it will only be due to his stubbornness."

As Mother stood behind him, Lon took the opportunity to make a face.

During this exchange, George had been instructing Crocker as to the baggage. Once he'd finished, I drew him forward. "You must meet Mr. Hazelton, our host. Risings is his family home." I paused as a scowl crossed my mother's face. It vanished in an instant and I wondered if I'd imagined it. "Actually, you and my mother may well have met, but since that was so many years ago, may I present Mr. Hazelton to you, Mother?" I finished the introduction and presented my brother.

George took Mother's hand and nodded a greeting while she studied him through narrowed eyes. "It's possible we've met though I can't remember the time or place, to be honest."

Alonzo stepped forward and offered his hand. "Good to meet you, Hazelton. And good of you to have us all. I understand in addition to a wedding, we are to hunt." He raised his hand with a flourish and threw back his head. "Tally-ho!"

He glanced around at our astonished faces and grinned. "I've been practicing."

"He has been practicing a great deal." Hetty's fingers dug into my arm as she muttered the words close to my ear. "At home, at the station, on the train."

"The gentlemen are shooting, Lon. This is not a fox hunt," I said. "There will be no cries of *tally-ho*."

"No?" His shoulders slumped as he turned to George. "We don't ride through the woods, blowing a horn, and shouting *tally-ho?*"

To his credit, George didn't laugh. "Not while we're shooting, I'm afraid. You'd surely frighten off the birds. But there's no general prohibition on the phrase if you choose to use it at other times."

Lovely, now I could expect him to be shouting *tally-ho* throughout the house.

"I see." Lon nodded. "I must have misunderstood."

"I still don't understand why we are here," Mother said. "Why did Lily change the venue for the wedding? Hetty was so mysterious about it all."

The way Hetty ground her teeth led me to believe she'd been over this ground more than once. "There is no mystery, Daisy. I explained they wanted a smaller wedding in the country, with just family and close friends. How is that mysterious?"

Hetty sounded as though she'd reached the end of her tether, understandable after a day and a half of Mother's complaints and Alonzo's shouts of *tally-ho*.

After shooting a glare at Hetty, Mother, who couldn't imagine shying away from pomp and circumstance, turned to me in confusion. She waved a hand toward Hetty. "Do you see? Perhaps you can explain it, Frances."

George suggested we all remove ourselves to the drawing room, but Hetty begged off. I let them go while I waited behind to thank her for bringing my mother and brother to Risings.

"Do you need anything before retiring, Aunt Hetty?"

She gave me a weary smile. "Quiet. That's all I need right now. Daisy hasn't stopped talking since she arrived at your house, and right now, all I want is quiet."

Crocker stood at attention by the paneled wall.

I caught his eye. "Once you've escorted my aunt to her room, please have someone bring her a tot of whiskey."

"A bottle would be better," she muttered.

I gave the butler a nod then joined the others in the drawing room where George poured a glass of brandy for Alonzo. Mother, perched on one of the richly brocaded sofas, was still talking.

"I truly don't understand your sister at all, Frances. If she must hold her wedding in the country, why not Harleigh Manor?"

"I told you, Mother." Alonzo joined her on the sofa, a crystal snifter in his hand. "Harleigh Manor is for sale."

"Well, if it isn't sold yet, it seems one could still hold a wedding there. At least it's family."

George joined our little group, sitting across the tea table from me. "Shall I order tea for you, Mrs. Price?"

"I could do with a cup, but if Frances will show me to my room, I'll take it there." She came to her feet, and the three of us followed suit. "Come, Frances. We'll leave these men to their brandy."

I gave George and my brother a look of desperation which they both pointedly ignored. A private consultation with my mother was a daunting prospect. I may as well confess to being just a bit intimidated by her. She'd both instructed and judged me throughout my youth, and the desire to please her always made me anxious.

These little conversations with her rarely ended well, but it had to happen sooner or later.

"Where is Lily?" she asked as we walked side by side up the broad staircase.

"I'm sure she's around somewhere." Hiding most likely, I thought. As we entered her room, I consulted the clock on the bureau. "We'll be dining in just a few hours, and we meet in the drawing room at half past seven. I suspect she's out taking the air, while it's still fine. I'll ensure she stops in to see you before then."

Mother's maid, Emma, was in the dressing room unpacking, but she'd already had tea sent up. I seated myself at a small table near the window and poured each of us a cup while Mother removed her hat and smoothed her hair.

"How was your voyage?" I asked when she joined me at the table.

She waved a hand. "Fine, I suppose. So few people on board worth socializing with that after a few days, every topic of conversation had been worn thin. I must say if not for the rigors of traveling, I'd spend a great deal more time here with you, my dear. Especially now that Lily is here, too."

I silently gave thanks for the long voyage.

"I would have been here for her come out if I hadn't such a busy social calendar in New York." She shook her head regretfully. "And you know I hate to travel without your father."

"Why isn't Father traveling with you? I haven't seen him since my wedding. He's never even met his granddaughter."

Mother focused on stirring her tea, odd when she'd added nothing to it. "I tried to interest him in the trip, but he claimed the demands of business. It's as if he fears the market would crash should he leave for a fortnight."

I caught a glimpse of something in her expression before she pasted on a smile. Regret, perhaps? She had pushed Father to build the family fortune for nearly three decades while she raised the children. Now work had become his life, and her children were busy with their own lives. Where did that leave her?

"You should encourage Father to slow down a bit, take some time to enjoy the fruits of his labor. The two of you could travel, or if he's completely against the idea, at least go out in society more."

Her smile tightened. "Your father and I have managed our lives for over thirty years without your advice, dear." She brushed a bit of imaginary lint from her sleeve. "Now, tell me about Lily's young man."

I took her hint and allowed the change of topic. "I like Leo a great deal. He's thoughtful and kind and has excellent prospects. He'll be the sole heir to his father's business, so Lily will want for nothing. He's quite bright and easygoing. And he loves her. I think he'll make her an excellent husband."

Mother absorbed the information with a sigh. "I'm trying to take this philosophically, but the more I hear, the more I feel you let us down. Does the man have no connections to the aristocracy? You know I would have liked another title in the family."

That rather stung. "Let who down?"

"The family, of course. What is the point of having money if not to improve one's social standing? Lily didn't seem to understand that, but I shouldn't have to explain it to you."

She didn't have to explain it, I knew her credo well. It's just that after my marriage to Reggie, I no longer agreed with it. When Lily arrived in London and began to mix with society, I took great care that she didn't marry a scoundrel simply because he had a title. Of course, Mother didn't need to know that.

"Lily had the opportunity to meet many gentlemen in society, and Leo is the man who won her heart. I'm certain he'll win yours as well if you give him a chance."

"We'll see."

I served her a slice of seedy cake while she sipped her tea. "It's so disappointing the wedding is to take place in such seclusion," she said. "They should have come to New York, where I could have shown them off. London would have been my next choice. Plenty of society there. But this! I can tell you I am not happy about this arrangement at all."

She poked at the cake with her fork as if assessing what she'd have to forgo later if she indulged in this treat now. Mother had always believed too large a bite of anything would surely ruin her figure. Finally, she took just the tiniest crumb, closed her eyes, and savored it. When she opened them, a scowl crossed her lips upon seeing my smile.

She placed her fork on the plate and pushed it away. "A corset can only do so much, you know. You are looking well, dear," she added, taking me in. "Though that gown is a bit outdated."

"It's one from before Reggie died, so it is older, but I've had it refurbished." I looked down at my afternoon dress of the softest emerald green wool. "I thought my dressmaker had made quite a good job of it."

She shrugged, unwilling to part with her approval. "I believe I do remember Hazelton, now I think about it. His sister was a good friend of yours, was she not?"

"She most definitely was and still is. In fact, Fiona and her husband, Sir Robert Nash, are here with us this week. You'll see them at dinner if not before."

"How have you become so friendly with her brother? As a young widow, you must be careful

165

in forming friendships with gentlemen. If you are seen together too often, gossips will begin to link your names."

She watched me intently. I could see her suspicions were aroused, but I really didn't want to tell her about our engagement yet. I'd have to do it sooner or later, but certainly not now.

"Mr. Hazelton is my neighbor in town. When Lily arrived, he very graciously allowed us the use of his carriage and accompanied us to balls and soirees when he could. And you are right. He did become a good friend to all three of us."

"What of your brother-in-law? Why did he not squire you about?"

I almost choked on my tea. Graham lift a finger for someone else? Mother truly had no understanding of the family she'd married me into. "Graham was at Harleigh Manor much of the time. And even when he came to London, he was still quite occupied with estate business."

"And now he is selling it." She frowned and poked the cake with her fork, perhaps trying to flake out another suitable crumb for her consumption.

"Only the house and the property immediately surrounding it. The rest is entailed." I shrugged. "He is fortunate he can sell the house. It takes a great deal of money to maintain these old estates."

"Hmm. I suppose that's true, but it seems such a waste of all your father's money."

Not to mention ten years of my life, I thought sourly.

She went on to inquire about Rose, and I promised once she had a chance to rest, I'd take her up to the nursery to visit with her granddaughter.

"The nursery? Well, you've certainly settled in here nicely. Tell me, is this Mr. Hazelton's home?"

"It's the home of the Earl of Hartfield, Mr. Hazelton's brother. He's on holiday with his family, and Mr. Hazelton graciously agreed to see to things here in his absence."

"The earl's married, is he? That's unfortunate." She came to her feet. "I think I shall rest a bit, Frances, but do send Lily up if you happen to find her."

"Certainly, Mother."

I'd never been so eager to escape a room. It was as if I were eighteen again, striving to please my mother. I'd forgotten how exhausting it could be—or how impossible at times. She did not sound pleased with Leo as a son-in-law, at least not yet. Nor did she seem happy about my friendship with George. I wondered if she really did remember him. He hadn't been in town much during my debut. I'd met him back then of course, and saw him at one event or another, but once Reggie entered the scene, George had vanished.

I shrugged as I closed the door and headed toward my own room. Though she seemed a bit standoffish toward George, it was likely because he had no title. Mother loved nothing more than a British title.

In my musings, I nearly ran into the doctor as he and Lottie stepped out from the room she shared with Charles, bringing me back to the here and now, and the disaster at hand. Goodness, how easily I'd become distracted.

"How is he?" I noted Dr. Woodrow held the arrow in his hand.

"Better," Lottie said.

"Very fortunate," the doctor added.

I raised my brows. "After having been shot with an arrow, I doubt he'd agree with you on that point."

"Understood. But I maintain he couldn't have been hit in a better spot. The arrow entered about two inches, cut through a bit of flesh and tissue, and barely touched the muscle. No tear, just a small puncture, and it missed the nerve completely. He'll be in pain, but I'd say he's very lucky. It would have been much worse if he'd been hit almost anywhere else. Now, all we need concern ourselves with is the possibility of infection."

"The doctor's given me explicit instructions on all aspects of Charles's care. I'll make sure his wound doesn't become infected."

Lottie gave such a determined shake of her

head, her hat flopped to the side, and clinging to a few strands of hair, batted her in the cheek. With a swipe of her hand, she whipped off the hat, striking the doctor in the back of his head. The way he automatically waved off her apology made me think it was not her first strike.

"I've been distracted by the arrival of my mother for the last hour. Has anyone admitted to shooting the arrow?"

"I've been up here with Charles, so I know no more than you, but it was an accident, surely, and who among us hasn't had an accident?"

Charles called out to Lottie from his bed, cutting off our conversation. She excused herself, and I volunteered to walk the doctor to the door.

"I'm not entirely certain it was an accident," I said. "Considering everything else going on here the past few days, I have to wonder."

"You think someone deliberately aimed the arrow at Mr. Evingdon?"

"Not exactly. Mr. Evingdon merely moved into the path of the arrow at the last moment. It happened so quickly, no one would have had a chance to take aim at him, but two other people were standing nearby—Mr. Hazelton and Mr. Kendrick."

Woodrow studied me for a moment, probably wondering if I was hysterical or simply over-reacting. "How is it none of you knows who shot the arrow?"

I raised my hands. "Simple distraction, I suppose. We were all involved in our own little groups, spread out across the lawn. The culprit took advantage of it. By the way, is it possible for you to estimate how far away from Mr. Evingdon the archer would have been standing? It seems the arrows dug farther than two inches into the targets from where we were all lined up."

The doctor smiled. "The targets are made of different material. They are designed for arrows to sink into them. It would also depend on the strength of the archer. A small woman wouldn't pull the bowstring back as far as a larger, stronger man, so her arrow would not fly as quickly or travel as far."

"Of course, if one were trying to get off a shot quickly, one might not use all of his strength."

"True. Unless someone saw who did it, or the culprit confesses, it's likely you'll never learn who shot the arrow."

"Perhaps it was an accident, and I'm seeing mischief where none exists."

We'd reached the door. The doctor paused and turned back to me as he adjusted his hat. "That may well be, but it's also possible someone was acting maliciously."

His mustache twitched as he weighed what he was about to tell me. "I have the results of the tests on the ginger beer. I'd planned to pass them on to Mr. Hazelton. Perhaps you'd be so kind as to do so?"

I leaned toward him, eager to hear his findings. "Of course."

"There was no trace of arsenic."

It took a moment for his words to register. "How could that be? You and Mr. Hazelton both thought the ginger beer was the source of the poison."

"We thought wrong."

"But do you still maintain arsenic poisoning is the cause of the young man's death?"

He gave me a short nod. "I do. The tests I've run indicate a high level of arsenic in his body. Though I can't say how it was introduced to his system, it was arsenic that caused his death, and that's what I'll be reporting to the authorities."

I nodded, numb. The doctor took his leave, and I stood there, staring at the door. Something strange was going on. If the footman didn't take the arsenic knowingly, and it wasn't present in the drink for him to ingest accidentally, then that leaves only one option—someone else poisoned him. But why? And who? And did his murder have anything to do with the steward's so-called accident, or Charles's?

Raised voices from the drawing room broke into my thoughts.

"I don't know why you won't just admit it, Anne. It's not as if anyone thinks you did it deliberately." The needling whine belonged to

Eliza Durant. I eyed the front door, wondering if escape was an option.

"You simply released your arrow too quickly, or your aim was off, or who knows what, but you ought to admit it, or we'll all look suspicious."

"I'm very sorry Mr. Evingdon was injured, but I had nothing to do with it."

Anne's voice sounded as though she were close to tears. I sighed. Escape was not an option. I headed to the drawing room wishing Arthur Durant had never made this accusation in the first place. In fact, hadn't he been shooting right next to Anne? I'd be more inclined to believe him capable of such a malicious act than her. But was it a malicious act or an accident? If it had been an accident, perhaps he really did see her do it. My thoughts were moving in circles. I needed to speak with George, but I wanted to rescue poor Anne first.

Eliza's voice rang out with another nasty accusation when I reached the doorway, but before I could say or do anything in response, I heard another voice.

"Would you care for a stroll in the garden, Miss Kendrick? It seems to be rather heated in here."

I pushed open the door to see the voice had come from my brother. Alonzo strode to Anne's side and held out his hand.

Her lower lip drooped as she stared up at Alonzo with wide eyes. Coming to her feet, she put her hand in his, and I slowly backed out of the room. My mother might cause me no end of grief this week, but I gave silent thanks my brother was on hand.

Chapter 11

❧

It might have taken hours to search for George throughout the house. Fortunately, I found Crocker, who informed me Mr. Hazelton was meeting with Mr. Winnie and Mr. Tuttle. As the afternoon waned, and I was determined to speak with George before dinner, I headed out to the steward's cottage, which also served as his office.

The location of our archery competition looked ominous as I walked past. The equipment had yet to be cleared away and lay scattered across the lawn. I picked up an abandoned arrow and approached one of the targets. With the shaft in my fist, I jabbed it into the bull's-eye. Dr. Woodrow was correct. It sunk in easily. I supposed the target was stuffed with either hay or straw, both far more porous than Charles's poor posterior. It was possible one of the contestants had shot the arrow, making it an accident. At least it would appear so.

Placing the arrow with the others, I headed around the maze. A tinkle of laughter drew me to the entrance where I found Lily and Leo. "There you are," I said.

The two sprang apart looking absurdly guilty. "Were you looking for us?" Lily asked.

"Mother was asking for you."

Lily's hands fluttered. "Mother is here? Already?"

I nodded. "A day early. She, Aunt Hetty, and Alonzo arrived well over an hour ago. If you don't want to disappoint her, you should at least greet her before dinner."

Lily studied the ground where her foot dug into the soil, making perfect little circles. "Yes, I suppose I should."

Both her reluctance and the singular pronoun surprised me. Now that I thought about it, Mother hadn't asked to meet Leo either. Lily and Mother must have been corresponding these past months. Had something passed between them I should be aware of?

Leo glanced expectantly at Lily, who still looked nervous. Though I couldn't blame her, I felt she should buck up for her fiancé's sake. "Aren't you eager to introduce Leo?" I gave him a coy smile. "Mother will simply love you."

"Yes, we should give her a proper greeting," he said, with a nod to Lily. "I'm very eager for the introduction. Lady Harleigh keeps telling me how alike the two of you are."

When had I given him that impression? "They look a great deal alike, but their personalities are quite dissimilar."

Lily chuckled at my awkward explanation. "I'm sure Leo will discover that for himself." She seemed to pull herself up taller. "And yes," she said, her voice determined. "She will love you, Leo. How could she not?" She squared her shoulders and looked at me. "Is she in the drawing room?"

"I left her in her room. She's probably reading or catching up on correspondence before changing for dinner."

"Excellent." Leo extended his arm to his fiancée. "We'll have her to ourselves."

Lily forced a smile, and with an air of "getting on with it," took his arm. "How jolly."

I watched them walk toward the house, arm in arm, pleased they were spending time alone, and more specifically, without Mr. Treadwell.

Now to find George. I crossed the lawn around the maze and headed to the steward's cottage, a picturesque building of wood and stone with a thatched roof. A cobbled path led up to the heavy wooden door. George himself answered my knock.

"Lady Harleigh. I see I've stayed too long with these fine men. Do come in. I won't be much longer."

I took a step inside following the invitation of George's sweeping arm. "I seem to be making a habit of interrupting your meetings, but if you do plan to finish up soon, I'll be content to wait outside."

"Nonsense, you must join us."

"Please do come in, Lady Harleigh," Mr. Winnie added, "so we may change the topic of our conversation."

George laughed as he closed the door behind me and indicated a chair he must have just vacated. I nodded at Winnie, who'd risen from his seat behind a desk, tucked into a corner of the room. Another nod went to Mr. Tuttle, the burly gamekeeper who leaned against the wall beside the desk, next to a shelf laden with papers, files, and books. An open area with two chairs and a small table served as a sitting room next to this small office area. A door stood open beside the gamekeeper, which must lead to the rest of the cottage.

"Tuttle and I were making a little wager on how long it will take before Winnie's beard fills in."

The lad's beard was absurdly sparse and did nothing to hide the scowl he threw at George. "I agree with Mr. Winnie. It's likely time to change the subject."

"As you wish," George said. He leaned one hip against the desk and turned to the men. "Like me, Lady Harleigh is becoming suspicious of the accidents we've been experiencing the past few days."

"The past few days, sir?" Winnie's brow furrowed. "I thought you were only asking about Mr. Evingdon's unfortunate mishap."

"Indeed, that was uppermost in my mind as it was the most recent." He sighed and glanced at me. "I'd hoped one of them might have seen someone sneaking about the maze this afternoon."

"And?" I edged forward in my seat.

"Sadly, no." Both men shook their heads in agreement with George's statement. "Tuttle will check the damage to the maze and determine if it could have been done by an animal and Winnie will check with the gardeners."

"What sort of gardener would create such a mess of the hedges?"

"Mr. Hazelton mentioned some shuffling footprints in the corner where you found the damage," Winnie said. "It might have been a gardener examining the mess and determining how to repair it."

George nodded. "When I mentioned the past few days, I was referring to Gibbs's riding accident and the footman's death." He stopped abruptly and cocked his head. "By the by, did either of you know Michael O'Brien at all?"

"Can't say I know any of the footmen or maids, sir," Tuttle replied. "Got no business with anyone in the house besides Cook and her girls."

Winnie shook his head. "I'm rather too new here to have made the acquaintance of any of the house staff beyond Mr. Crocker. The first I heard of O'Brien was when he'd died." He cocked his head. "Are you saying someone murdered him?"

"Not as of yet, but three accidents in as many days strikes me as more than coincidence and makes me wonder if someone is up to no good."

Tuttle stroked the whiskers on his chin. "Workers get hurt from time to time. It's true we've never had so many mishaps before, but sometimes an accident is just an accident."

"All the same," Winnie added. "We'll keep an eye out for anything or anyone suspicious, sir."

George shrugged. "That's all I can ask." He gave Tuttle a slap on the back then swept a hand out to Winnie, who stared at it through narrowed eyes. For a moment, I thought he might refuse to shake George's hand, but then he came jerkily to his feet and clutched it in a tight grip. George was still flexing his fingers when he stretched his arm out to me. As I allowed him to lead me to the door, I bid the two men a good day.

When the door closed behind us, he turned to me. "That was odd."

I chuckled. "I believe Mr. Winnie might be thinking the same thing right now."

"He didn't want to shake my hand."

"He didn't know what to do with it," I corrected. "I'm sure the earl never shakes his employee's hands."

"I suppose not. Now that I've had my fingers crushed, I won't do it again either. Oh, well, live and learn. Now, tell me, what was your impression?"

Surprised by the abrupt question I blinked. "About what?"

"Did you think they were telling the truth? Winnie and Tuttle?"

"I have no reason to suspect they weren't." I looked at him in confusion. "Do you?"

He looked down and directed our steps to the maze. "No, I suppose I don't. Winnie was in his cottage working on the accounts, and Tuttle was out checking on the coveys near the pond. Neither man would have seen someone skulking about the maze."

"Mr. Winnie told me he heard the ruckus from his cottage when Charles was struck, so he came out to see what had happened. I suppose that means I can vouch for his whereabouts. What about Tuttle?"

"Tuttle was accompanied by one of the farm-hands so his alibi can be verified."

I let him guide me into the maze. "Why are we going in here?"

He shrugged. "It's a quiet place to talk, and we won't be disturbed."

"It sounds as though you're still wondering about the accidental nature of the recent events. Is that true?"

"The first two are yet to be determined, but I don't know how any of the contestants could have accidentally shot an arrow into Evingdon's backside, do you?"

"No. Had it been an errant shot, whoever did it would have let out a shriek, or a shout of warning." George had released my arm and taken my hand. I walked behind him as we snaked our way through the narrow passages, drawing a fresh, woodsy scent from the yews as we brushed past them.

He glanced at me over his shoulder. "If someone is up to mischief, I don't want to see anyone else hurt. And I admit, I don't like the idea of all these accidents happening on my watch. I think they warrant further investigation, don't you?"

"I believe the decision has been taken out of our hands."

"How so?"

Tipping my head to the side, I gave him a satisfied smile. "There was no arsenic in the ginger beer."

His eyes widened. "No? Woodrow told you that?"

"He did. That's also what he will be telling the local authorities. Does Michael's death now sound less like an accident?"

"Perhaps." He retrieved my hand and set off once more. "Come, we'll sit and discuss this."

A few more turns and we reached the center of the maze, a square garden, the size of a small room, or a large closet. Shade-loving plants surrounded a wrought-iron bench where George led me.

"It's a hidden garden. How lovely."

He smiled at my obvious delight. "When I was a child, it was just an open grassy area where we children snuck away to play, but I like what my brother's done with it."

I seated myself on the narrow bench, and he squeezed in beside me. When I turned, his lips were a mere breath away.

"I must say I like this version as well." My voice had grown husky.

George stroked my cheek, leaned closer, and for the next several minutes, accidents and murders were the farthest things from my mind. He pressed a final kiss on my temple, and I rested my head on his shoulder.

"I found Lily and Leo leaving the maze on my way to see you. I wonder if this is what they were up to."

"They're in love, as we are. They'll be married in a few days, so what matter?"

"No matter at all. I think they're acting just as young lovers should, and I heartily approve. But I probably ruined their romantic moment."

George's chin brushed my head as he tipped it to look at me. "What did you do?"

"I sent them both to the house to see my mother. That might put a damper on their ardor."

"Yes, I can see how that might happen." George

sighed. "Will you tell your mother of our plans while she's here?"

I nodded. "After the wedding when you place that beautiful ring on my finger." I leaned back to look him in the eye. "I assume she'll return home with me. She might wish to stay for our wedding."

He pursed his lips. "She might wish to do more than that."

"What do you mean?" His countenance grew clouded for a moment. He covered it with a smile. I pulled away from his shoulder to gaze into his face. "George, is there something between you and my mother? I thought she'd acted strangely when I presented you."

He gave me a look of mock horror. "Something between us? Please, Frances. Your mother is old enough to be, well, my mother. What could possibly be between us?"

I narrowed my eyes and examined him. "That's what I'd like to know. First, she acted as though she couldn't remember you. Then she seemed to remember you vividly and asked how you and I came to be friends. She seemed more than just curious. Did something happen between you two all those years ago?"

"I shouldn't have mentioned it. Let's just say Mrs. Price and I did not get off on the right foot. If you want further details, you must ask her." He held up a hand as I would have pressed for more.

"We should take advantage of this time to discuss the rash of so-called accidents, don't you think? We'll have to return to the house shortly."

While I'd have preferred to use our time alone for something more romantic, I supposed he had a point. "All right then." I filed my curiosity away for the moment. If he wouldn't tell me what transpired, Mother certainly would. "I assume Woodrow will contact the police immediately, but I don't know how quickly they will respond."

"I'd wager someone from the constabulary will pay a call in the morning."

"They'll be investigating the death of Michael O'Brien. What of our two injuries? You thought they wanted further investigation."

"I was so confident the arrow came from the maze. But Tuttle's suggestion that an animal tore up the maze makes me wonder. After all, who here would want to hurt Charles?"

"I don't think the culprit was aiming for Charles."

"No, perhaps not."

"You and Leo were standing by the target for a few minutes at least. Long enough for someone to take aim and draw their bow." I shrugged. "Charles simply stepped around you and into the path of the arrow. The culprit meant that arrow for either you or Leo." I shivered as I said the words.

George grimaced. "Poor Charles. He stepped

up at exactly the wrong time. Much as I dislike the thought, it makes sense, though I still don't know what the motive would be. Who would want to murder either of us?"

"Do you think it was meant to be lethal? After all, the person aimed rather low."

"I don't know if it was meant to be anything. It might well have been an accident. But it isn't necessary to shoot someone through the heart for an arrow to be lethal. Plenty of arteries to hit down lower. Or it could have dug deep enough to cause a deadly infection. Then there's the fact of Charles moving in the way. It might have been enough movement for the archer to jerk and miss his target." He raised his hands in a hopeless gesture. "Or an animal attacked the hedge, and one of the competitors hit Charles by chance."

I relayed the details of my conversation with Dr. Woodrow to George. "I was surprised the arrow hadn't gone very deep into Charles's . . ." I turned away from George's gaze. "His leg."

He let out a hearty laugh. "He was hit right in the arse, Frances. Or backside, if you prefer. Plenty of flesh there, but also a sizeable muscle. Now that you mention it though, target arrows, at least those we used, aren't particularly sharp. It would require the skills of an excellent archer to pull off a lethal hit. He could do some significant damage to bones, or produce an injury that could cause a slow death, but to hit the neck, or an artery somewhere, that would take some skill. Who would attempt such a thing with a target arrow? I am beginning to see this as more of an accident."

"Dr. Woodrow said Charles was very lucky the arrow landed precisely where it did so I'm not so certain he'd agree with you." I worried my lower lip between my teeth. "I'm not certain I agree either. If someone were trying to murder Leo, they might not realize target arrows were dull, and simply used what was at hand."

George raised his brows. "Leo? Does someone have a grudge against Leo?"

"Perhaps. I don't know the men well, so I can't say this would push either to murder, but Mr. Durant is very covetous of Leo's position with his father's company. He'd love to become a partner himself, but Mr. Kendrick is only interested in promoting his son, no matter how hard his son-in-law works."

"I don't know the man well either, but I agree he seems to enjoy his work much more so than Leo." He gave me an encouraging nod. "Who else?"

"His best man, Ernest Treadwell. The man is clearly infatuated with Lily and doesn't attempt to hide the fact. What kind of friend is that?"

"Yes, I'd noticed it, too. Why doesn't Lily stop him?"

"I wish I knew. She has no interest in the man,

186

but I suppose she was flattered by his attentions. She and I have discussed the matter, and she intends to rebuff him the next time he flirts with her." I paused as a thought occurred to me. "Maybe she already has rebuffed him, and he chose to take it out on Leo."

George's brows drew downward as he considered my information.

"I'm being absurd, aren't I? No one would kill for such reasons."

"I would never underestimate matters of the heart as a motive for murder," he said. "Nor would I discount power and money, as might be the case for Durant. But while they each might have a motive to murder Leo, I can't conceive any likely reason for either of them to want to harm my steward or my footman. Perhaps everything is as it seems—mere accidents."

"Your steward says differently."

"That's right, I still need to pay him a call."

"As soon as possible."

He flashed me a grin. "Yes, ma'am."

"And be serious."

"I am quite serious, Frances. You are making good sense. Here's what I propose; we'll wait to hear the verdict from Tuttle about the hedges in the maze, and what Winnie has to say of the gardeners. Meanwhile, I'll visit Gibbs, see how he does, and get him to show me that welt on his chest."

I gave him a shove for his impertinence, but it only made him chuckle. "I shall also pay close attention to Treadwell and Durant and see if either has homicidal thoughts about Leo."

"That's a start, but I have yet another suspect. Mr. Bradmore. He was in the maze when the arrow was shot."

"As was Treadwell."

I nodded. "And Clara. And I know we're no longer certain the arrow came from the maze, but let me focus on Bradmore for a moment. He is staying at the estate whose border is quite near the path where Gibbs was injured. He claims to be related to the family, yet neither you nor Fiona have ever met him."

"That makes him a suspect?"

"*Suspect* may be too strong, but he is an unknown quantity who arrived in the country just a few days ago. Strange accidents have been happening since his arrival. That's enough to make me wonder if the accidents and Mr. Bradmore are somehow related."

"Anything is possible." He pursed his lips before blowing out a breath. "The police may well call tomorrow while I'm gone. If they do, can you insinuate yourself into their investigation? They're likely to interview the servants, and it would be helpful to know what they have to say."

"I'll do my best. Once we learn how Michael

came by the arsenic, it may give us greater insight into all these accidents."

"Then tomorrow we investigate."

I gave him a cheeky grin. "We could begin tonight. Fiona's invited Bradmore to dine with us. I shall ask her to seat him next to me so I can quiz him."

"I'll sit with Bradmore if you please." George came to his feet and extended a hand to assist me. "The man's single and might interpret your inquiries as interest. And if he doesn't, I daresay your mother will."

Chapter 12

I stepped into the breakfast room the following morning, surprised to see George, and only George, at the table, leaning back from a now-empty plate.

"Good morning, George. How lovely you're still here." I trailed my hand across his shoulder as I passed behind him. He caught hold of it as he stood, and with a mischievous glint in his eye, brought it to his lips.

"I'd be flattered by that comment, my dear, but I'm aware you're only happy to have someone with whom to discuss murder." He winked and squeezed my hand. "I suspect you only wish to marry me because I indulge your sense of the macabre—and supply you with your favorite beverage."

I caught sight of a footman entering the room with a fresh pot of coffee, not something I'd expect in any home but my own. George gave me a smile. "With all the Americans in the house, I thought it best to have it on hand."

Retrieving my hand, I leaned in close to George. "You are so thoughtful. An excellent trait for a husband, but you must know I'm marrying you because you can't possibly get on without me. Don't you remember?"

"You are correct, as always. I can't imagine how I've managed all these years without your influence." He laughed as I pushed him back toward his chair.

"You need not stand on ceremony with me. I can serve myself."

With a gesture from George, the footman brought a cup from the sideboard and poured coffee for me, while I perused the breakfast offerings, plate in hand. Finally deciding on toast, a bit of sausage, and a boiled egg still hot from the chafing dish, I joined George at the table. He signaled for the servant to leave.

"I take it the gentlemen are already out in the field?" I reached for a cup of raspberry preserves and spooned some onto my plate.

"They left almost an hour ago. I was worried we might not have a chance to speak alone this morning, but I've seen neither hide nor hair of the other female guests yet."

"Mother is having a tray sent to her room, and Rose will be joining her. Lily has not been feeling up to breakfast lately, the poor dear. And the Kendrick ladies are decidedly late sleepers."

George leaned closer until his lips brushed against my ear. "Then we have the room to ourselves with no one likely to interrupt us. An island of privacy in the midst of a busy house party."

"Isn't it lovely?" A turn of my head brought us nose to nose. "We can finally talk about our suspects without them overhearing."

He moved back slightly and cocked his head. "Really? I was only teasing about your sense of the macabre. Are you sure this is how you wish to make use of our lovely privacy?"

I placed my hand on his cheek. "Don't frown, George. It has nothing to do with my wishes, but our safety and that of our guests."

"Fine." He settled back in his chair, and I returned my attention to my plate. "Who in particular did you wish to discuss?"

I spread the preserves across my toast. "Did you learn anything about Mr. Bradmore last night at dinner?"

"Not as much as I'd expected." He took a sip of coffee and pushed his empty plate to the side.

"Odd. He didn't strike me as the reserved sort."

"I don't know that I'd call him reserved so much as cagey. I opened the conversation with generalities—hunting, shooting, how he liked the country, social life in town."

"Yes?"

"Usually, that will elicit some sort of declarative statement—I like hunting, or I don't. I prefer some other activity. When in town I usually visit

this club or attend the opera, et cetera, et cetera."
He raised a brow. "You get the idea?"

"Indeed. I daresay he made no such statements?"

"Not a one, yet he chatted on genially, revealing nothing about himself."

"What did you do then?"

"I moved on to direct questions—When did you last visit your aunt? What clubs do you belong to? Where do you go when you're not in town?"

"Where were you when Mr. Evingdon was felled by an arrow?"

George pulled a face. "I doubt I could have acquired an answer for that one either."

"You mean he refused to answer your questions?" I bit into my toast and savored the tangy sweetness of the berries.

"Not exactly. He responded, but he talked all around the questions without ever answering them." George scowled and gave a shake of his head. "I did learn he arrived in the country on the same day as you and your party."

"I wonder if he was on our train."

"It would depend on where he was traveling from, and I wasn't able to weasel that information from him either." George tossed his napkin on the table. "The man's as evasive a devil as I've ever met. Forgive me, my dear."

I waved the apology aside. "He sounds quite mysterious."

"It's been my experience that mysterious gentlemen are usually up to something."

"Actually, it reminds me of trying to gain information from you. You can be quite evasive yourself."

"Exactly my point, as I am usually up to something."

"Hmm, I can't argue with that. What will you do?"

"Keep an eye on him certainly. Fiona mentioned paying a call on Lady Esther. That might be a good idea."

"Perhaps later in the day. This morning she'll be taking the other ladies and Rose on a ride to see the ruins of some ancient castle."

"You are not going?"

I feigned regret. "No, I'll forgo that pleasure in order to be on hand when the police call."

"I'll be eager to hear what you learn." He came to his feet. "And I should be off to see what I can learn from Gibbs. I hope to be back before the gentlemen return from the field. We can compare notes then."

Fiona, looking fresh and chipper in a blue wool morning gown, entered the room and stopped in her tracks upon seeing George. "Good morning, brother dear. What a surprise to find you still at home. Why are you not out shooting?"

"Sadly, I have an errand to take care of this

morning, and I should be off. I leave you in Lady Harleigh's care."

I caught his hand before I left. "Please take care, Mr. Hazelton."

He brought my hand to his lips before releasing it. "Always. Promise me you'll exercise all due caution yourself."

"Of course."

Once he'd left the room, Fiona blew out a breath, making a rude noise as she poured herself a cup of tea. "I think that means you both plan to behave in a shamefully reckless manner. And what is all this Mr. Hazelton and Lady Harleigh nonsense? I should think the two of you could be less formal around me." She took a deep sip from her cup, closing her eyes as she savored the brew.

I gave a toss of my head. "True, but one never knows who's listening. I'm not quite ready to explain my future plans to my mother just yet."

"Then perhaps you'll explain what escapades the two of you are up to this morning?"

"No escapades. We're just looking into the so-called accidents that have been happening around here lately."

Fiona set down her cup. "You mean your cousin Charles's mishap with the arrow yesterday?"

"Not exclusively, but since you brought it up, did you see anything?"

"I didn't see anyone shoot an arrow at him, if that's what you mean. I was chatting with Eliza

Durant at the time and never looked up until Mr. Evingdon let out a shriek. I assume that's when he was struck."

"At least that means I can take Eliza Durant off the list."

"Of suspects?" Fiona raised a brow. "You thought she might have shot the arrow?"

"Someone did. What makes Eliza less likely than anyone else?"

"Perhaps because she wasn't part of the competition? She never had a bow in her hand."

I glanced at her over the rim of my cup. "Well, there is that. But her husband is the one who started the rumor that Anne shot the arrow, which makes me wonder if he is covering for someone else."

"I hadn't heard that. You don't believe him?"

"He didn't actually say he saw her do it, only that it must be her. I don't find such an argument very convincing. Besides, Anne denies it."

"It amazes me that so many of us were about, yet none of us saw what happened."

I dabbed my lips with the napkin and dropped it on the table. "We'll come to the incident with Charles eventually. First, your brother is going to speak to the steward, and we expect someone from the constabulary to call and speak to the servants about Michael O'Brien. George asked me to take part in those interviews."

"Then you'd best make haste. Mrs. Ansel has

just escorted a Sergeant Fisk to the servants' hall."

Heavens, I was already making a mess of my investigation. If not for Fiona, I might have missed the police altogether.

I tracked Mrs. Ansel down in the kitchen, consulting with Mrs. Humphries, the cook. Neither of the women hid their surprise at my sudden appearance in their domain. The housekeeper, in particular, looked quite panicked. She rushed to my side and asked that I speak with her in the hall.

"I beg your pardon, my lady," she said, closing the swinging door to the kitchen. "Mrs. Humphries doesn't yet know the police are here, and I fear she'll succumb to hysterics again once she hears of it." She raised her brows. "I assume that's why you're here?"

I'd forgotten the cook had been blamed, at least initially, for O'Brien's poisoning. "I'm afraid she'll find out soon enough, Mrs. Ansel."

"Yes, but I was hoping to shield her from that news until after luncheon is prepared. Did you wish to speak to the police sergeant?"

"Yes, do you know where I'll find him?"

"He's in with Mr. Crocker. I can take you to his sitting room." She took a step toward a hallway, then stopped and turned back to me. "Do you know why they're here, my lady? I assume it's about Michael, but I thought the doctor decided he died accidentally."

Mrs. Ansel waited with a stoic expression and a straight-backed military bearing that reminded me of my Mrs. Thompson. Housekeepers would probably make excellent military officers if only they had the chance.

"Do you recall he took the jug of ginger beer we found in Michael O'Brien's room to test it for arsenic?"

She nodded.

"He did not find any."

The housekeeper folded her hands at her waist. "But he was convinced the boy died from arsenic poisoning."

"And his opinion has not changed. He still believes O'Brien managed to ingest arsenic. He just doesn't know how, so he notified the police."

"Heaven help us if they decide Mrs. Humphries had something to do with it. I don't know who we'd get to cook for everyone." Her face reddened when she caught my eye. "What I mean to say is she's a God-fearing soul. She'd never harm anyone."

"I understand your distress, Mrs. Ansel, but there's no reason to think she poisoned the boy. You all ate the same meal, and no one else even became ill. I'm certain they will question her, but Mrs. Humphries should not be uneasy."

She nodded, releasing a long breath.

"I would like to know if you've noticed anything missing that might contain arsenic, rat poison, for instance, or perhaps some cleaning powders that might include it as well."

Mrs. Ansel brought her hand to her mouth and widened her eyes.

"You've thought of something?"

She lowered her hands and clutched them together. "I'm not certain. I've recently noticed the rat poison isn't in the laundry, where we usually keep it, but I just thought someone misplaced it."

"A logical conclusion, Mrs. Ansel. And that may be the case. Regardless, I'd like you to start a search for it. Choose someone trustworthy, and if they find it, make sure they tell you precisely where it was. And the police, of course. You should tell them as well."

"Yes, my lady."

"In the meantime, can you show me to Mr. Crocker's sitting room?"

I followed her a few steps down the hallway where she turned and rapped sharply on a door then opened it to reveal a small sitting room. Mr. Crocker and another man sat at either end of a small, rectangular table. Both came to their feet as I stepped inside. Mrs. Ansel closed the door softly as she left.

"Lady Harleigh," Crocker said. "How can I be of assistance?"

"I understand a police sergeant is here about Michael O'Brien." I glanced at the other man;

youngish for a sergeant, perhaps thirty. He wore an older, but crisply pressed brown suit. He wore his light brown hair oiled and parted in the center, a bad decision for such a long face. But his mouth is what truly struck me, or rather the smirk he wore. I gave him a nod. "Would that be you, sir?"

"Indeed, my lady. Sergeant Fisk. There seems to be some question about this O'Brien chap's death. I'm here to interview the staff and see if we can answer those questions. Mr. C here was just giving me the lie of the land as it were."

Mr. C? Crocker wouldn't like that, and my guess is Fisk knew it. "And what have you determined so far?"

"Seems like the lad was an employee in good standing. Been here above a year and to hear Mr. C tell it, everyone loved him."

I raised a brow at the sarcasm and turned to Crocker whose face was turning just a bit red.

He nodded. "To the best of my knowledge, O'Brien conducted himself properly and got on with all the staff. I never heard of any trouble."

"That's about as far as we got," Fisk said.

"Excellent. Then I haven't missed much."

"You plan to stay?"

"I most certainly do. Have you another chair, Crocker?"

Crocker removed the officer's homburg from the third chair and pulled it out for me, a slight smile tilting his lips as Fisk stared and sputtered, clearly struggling with the change in authority.

"My lady, Mr. C is here to protect the rights of the staff. I don't believe you're needed and you must have more important things to do."

"This is definitely the most important thing I have to do, Sergeant Fisk. Please continue with your questions."

Fisk snapped open a small notebook and returned his attention to Crocker. "When was the lad's most recent day off? Do you know where he spent his free time?"

Crocker returned to his chair. "He had a half day on Sunday. His last full day was the previous Thursday. As to his activities away from Risings, on the first day of their employment, all the staff are told what is expected, and what will not be tolerated, as to their behavior. Unless I hear they are breaking any rules, I don't pry into their personal lives."

Gad, the man was stuffy. If I liked Fisk more, I might have felt sorry for him. "Do you recall what his duties were on the day he died?" The question popped out before I could remind myself this was not my investigation.

"His duties, my lady?"

"I'm trying to determine if he'd done anything that might have brought him into contact with arsenic. Did he perform any tasks that varied from his usual routine? Tackling a rodent problem for instance?"

Crocker nodded his understanding. "I shall have to check my schedule to be certain, but I believe he was performing his regular duties. Ben is the footman who usually worked with him. If Sergeant F is through with me, I'll bring him in at once."

At Fisk's nod, Crocker left to find the footman, very deliberately leaving the door open. I smiled. Perhaps Crocker and I had become allies of a sort.

"Stuffy bloke for a servant." Fisk shook his head as he scribbled notes in his book.

"Crocker is a highly skilled butler who runs this household. Service is not all bowing and scraping, Mr. Fisk. And if you find him stuffy, I'd advise you not to get on the wrong side of me."

The return of Crocker with a young, strapping man in footman's livery precluded an answer from the sergeant who merely flashed a curious glance my way.

Crocker introduced the young man as Ben, first footman. About eighteen to twenty, he had an open, earnest expression. While the butler remained standing, Ben took his seat at the table. His hands rested in his lap, his fingers clasped so tightly, the tips had turned white.

Fisk crossed his arms over his chest and leaned back in the chair. "I understand you worked closely with the deceased. Can you tell us what the two of you did on the day he died?"

The young man squirmed a bit, but I couldn't tell if it was Crocker or the sergeant who caused the nervous energy. "We were together most of the day. As there are guests, we both laid the table for breakfast and assured the chafing dishes and the coffee and teapots were full. After all the guests had eaten, we cleared away and brushed the room. Two of the gentlemen visitors didn't bring valets. I attended to Mr. Durant and Michael took care of Mr. Kendrick. They didn't need much, but from time to time, one of us would leave to answer one of their bells. We both cleared the earl's office after the gentlemen went in to dine and we both served at dinner."

While Fisk jotted down Ben's words, I probed further. "It sounds as though you were together all day unless you were attending one of the gentlemen. Is that right?"

He frowned. "Mostly, my lady. Mr. Kendrick rang once more an hour or so after dinner. I was in the common room and heard it. I knocked on Michael's door to tell him he had a bell. That's when he told me he felt unwell, so I went up to tend to Mr. Kendrick myself."

"You spoke to Michael through the door?"

"No, I opened the door a bit and looked inside. He was in bed and didn't look very well at all."

Fisk's head jerked up from his notes. "Did you not think to send for a doctor?"

"I asked him, sir, but he told me he'd just have some ginger beer and go to sleep."

"So you say," Fisk muttered.

"So we both say," Crocker added. "Ben informed me immediately that Michael was ill, and I checked on him myself. He was clearly unwell, so I relieved him of his duties and sent the under-butler to clear the dining room with Ben."

Fisk blew out a breath and focused on Ben. "Did you get on with Michael?"

He tipped his head to the side. "As well as anyone, I suppose."

"What about the rest of the staff? Did he rub along well with them?"

Ben's gaze moved to the side. Toward Mr. Crocker. Was he concerned about speaking freely before his superior? Or something else? The pause lasted long enough for the butler to clear his throat.

"All the staff got on. I've never heard any complaints or grievances about Michael." Crocker turned a determined eye on the footman. "Wouldn't you agree, Ben?"

Ben took his cue. "Yes, sir. No complaints at all."

Really? There wasn't much to say after that. I heartily wished Delaney were here instead of Fisk. For all his superiority, I saw no evidence he knew what he was doing.

It didn't sound as though Michael had done anything throughout the day to bring him in contact with arsenic, and with the rat poison missing, it surely seemed someone might have disliked him enough to slip a bit into his food. After all, the man had become ill just after dinner.

"Do either of you recall if Michael left the table once your meal had begun?"

Crocker frowned at the suggestion any of his staff would be rude enough to do such a thing. "He remained with us throughout, my lady."

"Mrs. Ansel says the rat poison stored in the laundry is missing. Have you any idea where that may be?" I hated to give Fisk more reason to suspect the servants, but I could hardly keep this to myself.

All three men turned to me in surprise. Ben shook his head. "No idea at all, ma'am."

Fisk gave him a nod. "If you think of anything further, I'll expect you to send word to the constabulary."

The butler turned to the young man as they both came to their feet. "Be certain to let me know as well."

Ben left to find, and send in, the next servant. The interview had left me disappointed. Though Fisk appeared to accept Ben's answers, it seemed to me that under Crocker's watchful eye, the young man would not speak freely. The following interviews were conducted in the same manner. Fisk asked everyone essentially the same questions. Almost all of them showed the same hesitation before answering, as Ben had done. But each one indicated they were one big, happy group. I couldn't say what Fisk learned from his morning's work, but I felt as though I knew no more than when we began.

When he finally gathered his belongings shortly before noon, I asked how he would proceed, and once again received his smug smile. "I'll be making some inquiries in the village, my lady, and reviewing my notes. Nothing for you to concern yourself with, though I would like to know if the rat poison turns up."

I left Crocker to show the man out through the kitchen and went in the opposite direction through the baize door that led to the gallery behind the great hall.

"Lady Harleigh."

I whipped about at the sharp whisper to see Ben, lurking suspiciously under the stairs to the bachelors' quarters. "Ben. You gave me quite a fright. Is something wrong?"

"Yes, my lady. Mr. Crocker would dismiss me on the spot if he knew I was talking to you, but I didn't tell the truth when that police bloke questioned me."

I'd hate to see the young man dismissed, but I needed to hear what he'd withheld. "Can you tell me quickly? Are we likely to be overheard here?"

I joined him in checking over my shoulder for any intruders.

I followed him as he drew back under the stairs. "The thing is, ma'am, none of the staff thought much of Michael. Maybe the grooms and the gardeners, and some of the young girls were taken in by him, but the household, in general, didn't trust him. He's trifled with the female servants, he drank, and things went missing when he'd been around."

I gaped at the young man who continued to glance around the gallery, while he spoke as quickly and quietly as possible. This was a far cry from what he'd told Fisk. "Why did you not mention this earlier?"

"Mr. Crocker, ma'am. He doesn't tolerate any nonsense from the staff. And he doesn't give warnings. He'd have turned the maids out as well as Michael, so they didn't bring him their complaints. As far as he knows, Michael always behaved just as he should. As for the stealing, like I said, things went missing when he was around, but I never had any proof he took them."

He shot another glance around when a clock chimed farther down the gallery. "Should be getting back to my duties, my lady."

Was he serious? "Ben, you need to tell Fisk what you just told me. Michael might have been murdered by someone in this house."

He held up his hands as if to hold me off. "No,

ma'am. I'm just saying no one on the staff would give tuppence for him, but I don't believe for a minute any of them would think of murdering him."

I was still reeling from his revelations. "If none of the staff cared for Michael, why on earth did you all cover up for him? I can understand the maids fearing the loss of their positions, but why didn't someone report his drinking?"

"I thought about it, ma'am. But we get quite a bit of liberty here, and I was afraid Mr. Crocker would just tighten the rules for all of us when it was only Michael who took advantage." He let out his breath in a huff. "When we cleaned up the office the other day, he finished off the drink from the gentlemen's glasses. And him still on duty." His teeth dug into his lip as he shook his head. "Michael was a bad one, he was, and I can't believe he behaved any better in the village than he did in this house. You might find someone there who'd want to kill him. The police should look there. Now, I really should get back to my work, ma'am."

I allowed him to return to the servants' hall, my head full of this new and shocking information. Yes, perhaps someone in the village did want to murder him, but he couldn't have gone to the village since Thursday. If Michael O'Brien didn't die accidentally, the murderer was in this house.

Chapter 13

～⌐

I resolved on two things as I made my way upstairs—I'd let George decide what to do about Ben's information, and I'd interview the maids again, this time in private. It would have to be later in the day though as Lily and Rose were having dress fittings and Lily had asked me to stop in. I'd just turned into the south hallway at the top of the stairs when I caught a glimpse of a man slipping out of one of the guest rooms. He closed the door carefully and quietly, then moved away from me to the servants' door midway down the hall. Behind it was a stairway to the gallery below. In only trousers and a shirt, his coat draped over his arm, I couldn't tell if he was a gentleman or a servant.

Odd though. All the gentlemen were still out in the field; at least they were supposed to be. And why would a guest use the servant's stairs? Stupid question. Because he didn't want to be seen, that's why. For some guests, the entire point of a house party was to carry on with someone other than one's spouse. But in this case, the guests were all family, or at least soon to become family. That led me to assume the man was likely a servant. But who was he visiting?

As usual, I had far too many tasks to juggle. I'd have to file this bit of information away for consideration at another time. With a tap on the door, I let myself into Lily's room.

"Frances! Please do come in." Though one glance told me Lily felt much better than she had this morning, her voice was strained, as if she were trying very hard to control some emotion. Whatever was wrong? I glanced around the large room, done up in white and rose. Sunlight streamed through the south-facing windows and glowed like a beacon on my mother. Perhaps what Lily was trying to control was her temper.

She stood on a footstool while the seamstress made some adjustments to her waistband. Rose and Mother were seated on the bench at the end of the bed, Rose smiling and swinging her legs, my mother, with brows lowered and lips pursed. Ah, yes, she did appear to be the source of Lily's distress.

I stepped forward. "Leo is going to love your gown, dear. You look absolutely breathtaking."

"Hmph! A waste if you ask me." Mother punctuated her opinion with a snort. A snort! Good heavens, what was wrong with her?

Lily turned around, causing the poor seamstress to scramble forward or risk tearing the dress. Clearly, I'd walked in on an argument.

I held out a hand to Rose who bounced off the

bench and with a sniffle, came to my side. "How was your ride this morning?"

She wrinkled her nose and sneezed. "We saw a ruined castle." She shrugged. "But the ride was fun."

I handed her a handkerchief. "Why the sniffing and sneezing, dear? Are you feeling well?" She nodded, and I put a hand to her forehead, which felt cool enough.

"All right then, your gown is in my dressing room. Why don't you go there and ask Bridget to help you find it?"

She looked back at Lily and Mother as if she might balk—this was rather juicy stuff for her. "Now?" she asked.

"Now would be best."

She shuffled so slowly to the door, one might think she was headed for the gallows. When I still hadn't stopped her by the time she turned the door handle, she sighed and left the room.

I turned to my mother. "Is it the gown you object to?"

She gave me a cold, hard glare. "The gown is divine. The groom is questionable."

I seated myself beside her. "I can't stop you from arguing with Lily about her choice of a husband, but my daughter sees this wedding as the most romantic thing she's ever experienced. And no matter what you say, Leo will very likely become her uncle Leo, so I do not want you disparaging him in her presence."

Her eyes widened to the point I worried they would pop. Then, something happened that I would later refer to as akin to a miracle. She backed down. My mother, the woman who always believed she was right, did not pick up the gauntlet. Instead, she dropped her gaze to her hands and sighed.

Then she patted my hand and uttered words I have never heard pass her lips.

"You are right, dear."

It was all I could do to keep from gaping.

"I should not have spoken out in front of Rose, but I do feel it's my duty as a mother to counsel Lily in choosing a husband. I'd assumed you or Hetty would have taken on that responsibility in my absence." She sighed and gave me a disappointed look, which put an end to my gaping. This was much more like the woman I recognized as my mother.

She squeezed my arm and continued. "Do you remember the fun we had during your come out? We made quite a splash in London society. Why, to think you had a prince ask for your hand."

"I don't believe he was truly a prince, Mother. I never found the principality he was supposedly from on any map. And he didn't actually ask for my hand." What he had asked for was so insulting, I'd slapped his face, thus putting an end to his pursuit.

Mother released my arm and swept hers in a dismissive wave. "Perhaps not, but the point is you and I worked so well together. You understood your debut was about improving our standing in society. Lily always drifted from wanting to find an aristocrat to wanting to fall in love. She had no focus."

"Lily is standing right here, you know." Lily scowled from her footstool and crossed her arms, which hiked up her hem and caused the seamstress to sigh. "I can hear every word you say."

Mother seemed lost in her memories. "I felt she might work better with you as her sponsor, but I'd expected you to guide her."

"Frances did guide me and so did Aunt Hetty. They are both pleased with my choice. You are the only dissenting voice."

"Is that so?" Mother gave me a look of inquiry. "Just what was your counsel, Frances? Find the only commoner among the aristocrats and marry him?"

I opened my mouth, but Lily was faster. "She told me to follow my heart."

Mother's nostrils flared. Her lips twitched as she forced a bitter smile. "Is that so?"

Not exactly.

"We investigated each of Lily's suitors carefully, Mother. I didn't want her to fall under the spell of some fortune hunter." Like that so-called

213

prince. "There were two such men chasing after her."

"I assume they were aristocrats?"

Another difficult question. I didn't want to go into detail about either gentleman's background; that could take hours to explain. Instead, I shrugged. Let her think what she will.

"You married an aristocrat. Didn't you consider your sister worthy of such a man?"

Lily raised her hands in a gesture of surrender and started speaking to the seamstress about her hem. I gave my mother a scowl. "Of course Lily is worthy of any aristocrat, but more importantly, she is worthy of a man who will love and care for her. Leo is that man. The two of them will have a happy marriage, unlike mine."

"Happiness." She batted the notion of happiness aside with a swipe of her hand. "Marriage does not make a woman happy. It gives her status, or money, or position."

"None of those things are worthwhile with a husband who makes you miserable."

She shook her head. "Don't be so dramatic. A woman can find happiness in her children or even society. Miserable indeed. With your father's money and your husband's title you had all of London at your feet."

It was my turn to sigh. My husband had left me at the family home in the country for the years of our marriage. I visited London once or twice a year and never did anyone fall at my feet. But my mother preferred her fairy-tale version of my life.

"I don't understand you, Frances. Lily has always been backward—"

A groan emanated from Lily's direction.

"—but you seemed to understand how marriage works in our circle." She gave me a searching look. "You are so changed now that I barely recognize you."

I had changed, and it wasn't just due to my failed marriage. It was falling in love with George. It turned my view of the world on its head and showed me I was worth more than just my dowry. Loving him was everything I didn't know I needed, and it occurred to me if my mother didn't recall her feelings for my father, she'd be very lonely once her children were all settled.

"All I'm saying is it isn't too late, perhaps, to postpone the wedding." She emphasized the word *postpone* with a fanning of her fingers. "That is all. There were two single men at dinner last night, both from aristocratic families, one of them heir to a title. Both of them were attractive, and one in particular was very interested in Lily."

Lily blushed at the allusion to Ernest Treadwell. I'd have to make sure to keep him far away from Mother over the next few days. Between the two of them, they might just devise a way of *postponing* the wedding. The other man I assumed was Percy Bradmore.

"Lily has made her choice, and with the wedding just a few days off, I do believe it is too late to call it off or postpone it."

"Nor do I want to," Lily added, glaring over her shoulder.

"I don't know what's happened to you, Frances. I can't find one drop of ambition between the two of you girls." Raising her chin, she glanced at me. "And what are your prospects? Have you considered a second marriage?"

My head reeled at the sudden change of subject. I hadn't expected such a direct attack. I felt my face flood with color and quickly turned to my sister for help. I could see she wanted to come to my aid, but her desire to protect me warred with her reluctance to engage our mother in yet another battle. Before I could form a suitable reply, Lily decided in favor of the battle.

"Frances still has to get me to the altar, Mother. At least wait until after my wedding before you pounce on her."

This set Mother into another tirade about ungrateful children and why fate hadn't blessed her with all sons. As she raged on, I caught Lily's eye in the mirror and mouthed the words *Thank you*.

I was so grateful for Lily's defense I convinced my mother to leave her in peace and join me for the picnic lunch Fiona had planned. We were to

216

be joined by the ladies from the Stafford estate where the gentlemen were shooting.

"I had no idea the British were such outdoorsy people," she said, wrinkling her nose and picking her way across the gravel drive to the open carriage. "What is the point of having such an enormous house if everyone spends all their time out of doors?"

"You've just spent all morning indoors, Mother. A little fresh air will do you good."

She released a heavy sigh but pasted on a bright smile for Fiona, who directed everyone to one carriage or the other. "Ah, Mrs. Price. We've saved a nice spot for you here." She turned my mother over to the groom who assisted her into the Staffords' carriage and settled her in next to Eliza Durant.

"The carriage appears to be full up now," Fiona said with feigned regret. "Why don't you come with me, Frances? A few of us are planning to walk to the site. If we cross through the meadows, it's not far."

The thought of a walk and the chance to avoid my mother's impertinent questions sounded perfect. Four of us set off on foot—Lottie, Anne, Fiona, and myself—first down the lane that wound past the maze and the steward's and gamekeeper's cottages, then through the open meadow where the cool breeze threatened to run off with our hats.

"How is Charles faring today, Lottie?"

"Well enough to chase me away," she replied with a twist of her lips. "I'm afraid I don't make a very competent nurse. He's propped up in bed with pillows to cushion him everywhere and keep him from rolling onto his wound. I adjusted his dinner tray last night then knocked it over when I sat on the bed." She winced. "We had to get him up to change the bedding. This morning I was bringing him a book when I stumbled over the carpet and landed on his injured—area."

This time I winced.

"He kept the book but sent me off. I'm hoping he'll be able to join us this evening after dinner. He says his pain has subsided quite a bit."

We all agreed it would be a pleasure to see Charles up and around again. Anne engaged Lottie in conversation, and Fiona and I allowed the younger ladies to outstrip us.

"I must bring you up to date about the rest of my morning," I said, quickly relaying the gist of the interviews and my subsequent conversation with Ben the footman.

"Yes, he must tell the police. But I'm not surprised as it coincides with the information I managed to pry from my maid," she replied.

"Your maid?"

She nodded. "I was devastated I couldn't sit in on the interviews with you, but it occurred to me Jonesy, my maid, might have overheard some talk below stairs since the footman passed away."

"Clever, Fiona. I shall have to talk with Bridget, too. I've already asked her what she knew of Michael, but never considered asking her opinion of the rest of the staff. What did Jonesy tell you?"

"It seems Michael O'Brien was quite the ladies' man, at least he thought so, and the younger girls were foolish enough to swoon over him. One of the housemaids told Jonesy of how he dallied with both the kitchen maid and a scullery maid at the same time." She shook her head. "It was inevitable that one would find out about the other. That gave rise to a row unlike anything the housemaid had seen before, and it took her and the cook to break it up and calm both girls down before Mrs. Ansel or Mr. Crocker found out about them."

I sucked in a breath. "None of that came out during Fisk's interviews. Either girl would have had access to the rat poison. Do you suppose they were angry enough for such an act?"

"Perhaps, but this happened a good six months ago. According to Jonesy, both girls decided he wasn't worth their jobs or their friendship. Particularly since they believed he'd taken up with someone in the village."

That sounded too convenient to me. "He played the two girls off one another, and neither of them bore a grudge? They were content to work together, and with him?"

Fiona shrugged. "Jonesy seems to think they've quite resolved their differences."

"And the object of their difference is now dead."

"You can't imagine one of them poisoned him?"

"Why not? Someone did. Why not them?" I worried the button at the top of my jacket as I considered the situation. Six months is a long time to plot retribution. "How did they react when Michael's body was discovered?"

"I have no idea, but I'll see what Jonesy can find out. Is Ben the only one you were able to speak with alone?"

I nodded. "He sought me out, and we had a very brief conversation. I thought he'd strain his neck watching over his shoulder for Crocker all the while. After that, I was stuck in Lily's dress fitting with my mother. No, that's not true." I latched on to her arm and glanced up to ensure the younger girls were well ahead of us. "On my way upstairs, I saw someone leaving one of the guest rooms two doors down from Lily. Do you recall whose room that is?"

Fiona furrowed her brow in thought. "Two doors down would be Eliza Durant. Her husband is in the connecting room to her right. Why?"

How interesting. I sidled closer to her. "A man, who I can definitely say wasn't Arthur Durant just based on his height, slipped out of her room in a very surreptitious manner."

She waved a dismissive hand. "Eliza's been carrying on with the under-butler almost from the moment she arrived here." She released a tiny *tsk*. "With Arthur gone every morning, she thinks no one will be the wiser. But I know. The staff knows. It won't be long before everyone knows."

"The staff knows?"

Fiona lifted a shoulder. "It was my maid who told me about it. She pretended outrage, but it was clear she could barely contain her excitement in telling me. It seems there's plenty of devilment going on in my brother's house, but the staff is careful to avoid detection from Mr. Crocker."

"I understand he wouldn't tolerate such goings-on if he knew about them. Ben told me they'd be dismissed on the spot, probably without a reference. I suppose I understand why they'd protect one another, but I've never seen a household where everyone seems to be up to something."

"I think it's because the earl is so rarely here. He's either in London or traveling. The staff is free to do as they please."

Fiona took my arm to steady me as I stumbled over a stump, buried in the tall grass. "About Eliza Durant. Why would she risk a liaison with a servant? She can't claim an absent husband. He's right here with her."

"You'd have to ask her. I know what she does;

I don't know why." She narrowed her eyes. "I
I remember correctly, her father encouraged the
match with Durant and she went along."

"Perhaps she has regrets."

"Wouldn't you?"

I grimaced. "He is not someone I'd care to
spend a lifetime with, no."

She caught my wrist and pulled me to a stop
staring into my face with widened eyes. "A
lifetime? Dinner or even tea would be too long
He doesn't even speak in complete sentences."

"Do you think she wants to end her marriage?"

"She may have regrets, but I daresay she'd
never leave the man. Her father holds him in high
regard. Henry Kendrick would be more likely
to keep his son-in-law and disown his daughter
if she ever considered divorce." She turned
her gaze on me. "I suppose that answers your
question. She regrets her marriage but can't leave
the man, so she has affairs and amuses herself
with servants. At least that's one theory."

"But as much as he loves his son-in-law, he
won't make him a partner. Maybe Durant will
leave Mr. Kendrick."

"But one assumes that was the reason he
married Eliza, to get a foot in the door of her
father's company."

I stopped in my tracks and grasped Fiona's
arm. "You said all the servants knew about Eliza
and the under-butler. What if O'Brien threatened

Eliza with revealing her affair to her husband?"

"Gad, Frances, you think she'd poison him?"

"I don't know. Would she?"

Fiona pondered the idea for a moment. "To be honest, I'd be surprised if Durant isn't well aware of her behavior." She shrugged. "As long as Eliza doesn't become notorious, I suspect he'll put up with her escapades."

"What a mess." My shoulders slumped as I considered the emptiness of the Durants' marriage.

Fiona touched my shoulder. "I see where your thoughts are going, and you must stop them. Not all marriages are doomed to fail. All you need do is look at my marriage for a shining example of wedded bliss."

I smiled. "Yes, but the two of you are that once-in-a-lifetime match. None of us mere mortals can aspire to such happiness."

She waved a hand. "Piffle. It's all down to me, you know. I must constantly remind Robert of the happiness and comfort I bring to his life. Though George is a bit like me." She pondered a moment. "He may take to reminding you. It makes no matter, I suppose. As long as you're both thinking about it, your marriage will be happy."

As we were approaching the picnic grounds, she stopped me with a hand on my arm. "My point, dear, is that you and my brother are marrying for love. This is not something your mother arranged. It will be nothing like your first marriage."

Dear Fi. I squeezed her hand and took a step toward the group when I recalled what I'd forgotten to ask my mother. "Do you know if George and my mother ever had some sort of disagreement?"

"Not that I'm aware of. Why do you ask?"

"Initially, because of the way my mother acted around him. First, she pretended not to remember him, and when she did recall, it seems as though she doesn't remember him fondly."

Fiona's eyes widened, her lips tightened, and she drew herself up to her full height. "That's curious. Has she been speaking ill of him? Your mother, the same woman who thought Reginald Wynn was the perfect match for you?"

"She thought his title the perfect match for the family. And you needn't take offense. It wasn't that she spoke ill of George, it was more that I spoke highly of him and she clearly didn't care to hear it."

"Perhaps she doesn't like you having your own opinions."

"She always listened to my opinions before."

Fiona gave me an assessing look.

"What?"

"When I first met you and Mrs. Price, your opinions were her opinions. You were so eager to please her."

I bristled at the implication. "I've always acted on my own judgment."

"You were always capable of doing so. Of that I'm certain. But for your first season, you deferred to her in everything, the style of your hair, your dress, what events you'd attend."

"I thought she knew best."

"Did she? Wasn't Reggie her choice?"

"Yes, but I can't blame my mother for my marriage. I didn't just go along with the idea, I thought it a good one."

"But you've since come to realize that isn't the best way to enter a marriage. You didn't allow Lily to choose a husband in such a manner."

"Of course not."

"I'm just saying you've changed over the years. Your mother hasn't."

I pondered this. "She did try to make Lily reconsider her choice."

"She didn't!"

I nodded. "You may be right. She may not be used to a daughter who knows her own mind. She might have been arguing with me about George just for the sake of arguing." Just as I took some comfort in the idea, I recalled my conversation with George and how he told me I'd have to ask my mother for an explanation. I relayed the conversation to Fiona.

"I can't imagine what type of disagreement they could have had, but if you want to know, I suggest you ask her." She nodded to the group of picnickers. "She's right there."

While I could hardly open such a conversation in the midst of a group of jolly picnickers, I did join my mother, Aunt Hetty, and Eliza Durant at their little table situated in the shade of a willow tree. I no sooner seated myself than the under-butler brought the teapot.

I nearly jumped from my seat and shot a glance at Eliza whose calm demeanor showed no embarrassment or any other reaction to her lover. The three other women turned to me with inquiring gazes. I smiled. "My chair was unsteady," I said, and made as if to adjust it. The under-butler stepped up behind me, almost making me jump again.

"If you'll allow me, my lady?" I stood while he settled the chair on the perfectly flat patch of earth. Reseating myself, I gave him a nod. "Much better, thank you."

Hetty kept an eye on me, but Mother returned to her conversation with Eliza. "I don't believe I understand you, my dear. Your husband is a baronet, but he is employed by your father?"

Eliza gave her a stiff smile. "My husband is heir to a baronetcy and is unlikely to come into the title for many years. His employment is due both to his interest in the world of business and a need to occupy himself."

"I see." Mother looked altogether baffled at the

226

thought of working for the purpose of occupying oneself.

"He's quite remarkable in his field. My father doesn't know what he'd do without Durant's guidance."

"Is there a reason to think Mr. Kendrick will lose Mr. Durant's guidance anytime soon?" Hetty was fond of Mr. Kendrick and clearly believed he'd survive the loss of Mr. Durant without losing sleep.

"One never knows," Eliza said airily. "As Durant gives so much of himself to the company, it would seem only reasonable that my father should make him a partner so he'd have ownership in the business. If he's exerting so much effort only to hand the reins over to Leo someday, what is the point? He may just move on to another company where he's appreciated."

Hetty's jaw tightened, my mother made an encouraging response, and I wondered about Durant's other options and if this was the extreme measure he'd mentioned. Yes, he could leave Mr. Kendrick's employ and take his skills elsewhere. But he'd married Eliza as a way to advance in the company. He could hardly do that a second time. There was another option, however. He could eliminate the one person who stood between him and his goals—Leo.

Durant had started the rumor it was Anne's errant shot that hit Charles and everyone seemed to accept that theory, much to poor Anne's chagrin. But Durant had been her partner for the competition. He'd stood next to her. In all the confusion, was it possible Durant made the shot with the intention of hitting Leo, but Charles stepped in the way at the last moment? If so, his accusation of Anne had been well timed. She would have been blamed, and he would have been made partner.

Chapter 14

W e lingered over our picnic far too long for my liking. Long enough for my mother to bring up the subject of the wedding. Between the shoot, the so-called accidents, and Michael O'Brien's possible murder, the wedding had been pushed farther to the back of my mind.

"I so had my heart set on seeing my daughter wed from St. Thomas's in New York," she said. "I still don't understand their desire for a such a small, country affair."

"Our mother is likely to be disappointed as well," Eliza added with a *tsk*. "Leo mentioned something about the timing of the wedding trip or some such reason. I should think the ceremony itself is at least as important as the trip. He could certainly let Durant take over whatever business is in the way and keep to the original plans. It is only a difference of a few weeks after all."

"It was closer to a difference of seven or eight weeks." Hetty stood as if to put an end to the conversation. "And the ceremony is important to them, which is why they chose something meaningful, with only close friends and family, over a showy production meant only to impress society at large. Besides, if changing the date allows for less disruption to Mr. Kendrick's business, all the better."

I silently gave thanks for Aunt Hetty's presence of mind in putting an end to any speculation about the change in wedding plans. So far there had been few questions, which suited me perfectly. If Eliza's sour expression was anything to go by, she felt quite put in her place and was not likely to mention the subject again. My mother was another story. She could never leave an issue alone while there might still be a chance of winning her point. With her lips pressed together and her eyes narrowed, I could see her working up an argument.

I came to my feet to join Hetty. "Perhaps it's time we should be heading back. The gentlemen have surely returned from the field by now, and it seems we may be in for a shower soon."

Fiona glanced at the clouds gathering overhead and seconded my suggestion. We all collected our belongings, and those who preferred to ride, headed for the carriage.

I had another reason for ending this gathering. Since George had forgone the fields this morning in favor of visiting his steward, I was eager to speak to him before losing him to some other task. Fortunately, as the four of us walked back to the manor, I spotted him leaving Mr. Winnie's cottage. The wood between us had thinned and would soon give way to the manicured lawn leading to the maze and on to the manor. He was dressed for a ramble in the country: a rough tweed coat over his white shirt, no tie, sturdy boots. He'd apparently forgotten his hat, so the wind had given his dark hair a casually tousled look that made my legs feel quite rubbery. A smile spread across my lips of its own accord.

It quickly faded as George, in an attempt to convey some message, enacted the most ridiculous pantomime I'd ever seen. He'd already caught my attention, so waving his arms in that wild manner was unnecessary. His depiction of walking was clear, but did he mean me, or him? And walk to where? He then crouched down, touched the ground in front of him, and wiggled his fingers in the air as he stood up.

The message completely escaped me.

"He wants you to meet him in the rose garden." Fiona had leaned into my side to enlighten me with a whisper. "Now, acknowledge him so he'll stop that nonsense."

With a nod and subtle motion of my hand, he ceased his activities and moved away from us around the other side of the maze. I glanced behind to see if the two younger ladies had noticed this exhibition, grateful their heads were together in conversation.

"How on earth did you know what he was saying?" I stared at Fiona in wonder.

"George has always been impossible at charades, but over the years I've learned to understand some of his pantomimes." A smile played at the corners of her mouth. "See, he does have some failings. Do you know where the rose garden is?"

I did not. Fiona provided directions and distracted Lottie and Anne long enough for me to slip away. I worked my way past the maze and over the lawn, to the back of the manor and the formal gardens. The rose gardens were just through an archway in a stand of conifers. As I walked through, George surprised me with a touch on my shoulder. I turned to find myself in his arms.

After a breathtaking kiss, he took a step back, resting his forearms on my shoulders, his fingers twisting a lock of my hair that had come loose from its pin. "If I ever wondered if you were the woman for me, the fact that you correctly interpreted my wild gestures and contortions, proves you are." His gaze sharpened. "Not that I ever wondered, of course. Not even for a moment."

"Not that I think you should wonder, but I confess I had no idea what you were trying to tell me. Fortunately, your sister did."

"I shall have to brush up on my skills," he said with a sigh. "Or we could devise signals."

I widened my eyes. "Or we could just speak to each other?"

"Well, if you insist on taking the easy route." He led me over to a wooden bench beneath an arbor where a climbing rose released a tart lemony scent. I leaned into the pink blossoms and breathed in their fragrance before sitting down with George beside me.

"Since you were so eager to see me, you must have some news," I said.

He took my hand and brushed his lips across my fingers. "I beg to differ with you, my dear. I am always eager to see you, especially as we are surrounded by guests and have had so little time alone."

"There does always seem to be someone about, doesn't there? I must say you've been very inventive in finding these secluded spots, but I'm going to be very unromantic now and ask if you visited Mr. Gibbs this morning."

"Unromantic to say the least." He *tsk*ed. "But yes, I did see him, and it does appear he ran into something narrow, and straight, which was much more likely to be the line you found than any branch. And as to that, I checked the path and found the fishing line, just as you described. It's quite possible Gibbs might have run into it, had it been stretched across the path." At my expression of satisfaction, he nodded. "But there's little reason to assume that's what happened. He can't think of anyone who'd want to harm him, or who would get up to such malicious mischief."

"I had similar results in talking with the staff. None of them could think of anyone in particular who'd want to harm Michael, but I did learn there is much more going on below stairs than Mr. Crocker knows." I told him what I'd learned about the footman's dalliances with the maids and the under-butler's tryst with Eliza Durant.

"From what I've been able to learn, Mr. Crocker is quite the tartar with the staff, so they are all eager to keep the knowledge of these goings-on from his attention. He sat in on Fisk's interviews with the staff, and while he was there, everyone spoke as if the household ran like clockwork and they were all the closest of friends."

He raised a brow. "How did you learn any different?"

"Fiona passed on a bit of gossip from her maid, and Ben, the first footman, caught up with me in the gallery so we were able to speak privately. Between the two of them, I've come to believe none of the staff thought well of Michael. Ben told me the man drank and stole from the household. At least he suspected that was the case. Things went missing when Michael was around, was how he put it. Still, he didn't think anyone on the staff was likely to murder him. He suggested it was someone in town."

"But you say the young man hadn't been in the village for a few days."

I nodded. "I understand why he didn't want to

speak ill of O'Brien in Crocker's presence, but I do think he should go to the constabulary and inform Fisk. As much as I hate the thought of the murderer being part of the staff, I hardly think an outsider could walk in and slip rat poison into O'Brien's food or drink."

"Rat poison?"

"Mrs. Ansel informed me it was missing from the shelf in the laundry. I've set her to the task of looking for it."

"Does Fisk know about that?"

"He does, but I have no idea what he makes of that information."

George blew out a breath. "So, what do we have? One member of Hart's staff was injured, and another possibly murdered." He held up a hand as I sputtered a protest. "There is still a possibility he accidentally ingested the arsenic."

I gave him a grudging nod. "But what of Charles? Did you learn anything from Tuttle or Winnie?"

"Tuttle looked at the maze and claims no animal could have made such a mess of the hedges. Winnie has learned the gardeners were trimming them yesterday, but none of them confessed to cutting the holes."

"Those holes didn't appear to be cut by accident."

He nodded. "Gibbs's injury looks deliberate as well, but his employment didn't bring him into contact with the footman. And I can't see a common thread other than their employment here. If you add Charles's injury to the mix, they have nothing in common."

"They were all injured or killed here, on your brother's estate. Does Hartfield have any enemies?"

"None that I'm aware of, but I've written to him about these incidents. We'll see what he has to say. Meanwhile, let's consider the scene of each accident."

"Mr. Gibbs first. Who was there?"

"We were at the stables. The usual grooms were working. Gibbs was giving instructions on the shoot to Treadwell, Durant, and Kendrick."

I tapped my finger against my lips. "I hadn't considered the grooms. Did you notice which ones? And what they were doing? If the trap was meant for Gibbs, one of them could be responsible. One of them could also have a grudge against Michael."

"I'm afraid I don't know them by name. One was saddling a horse for Kendrick; he was in a nearby box. I have no idea where the others were or what they were doing."

My heart thudded. "That's right. Leo was heading out for a ride."

I could see the realization dawn of George. "Anyone in the stables might have known that."

"Or anyone in the house. Michael would

236

have valeted him that day. If Leo wore riding gear, Michael would have drawn the obvious conclusion. He could have mentioned it to Mr. Durant."

"Durant?"

"Is one of the staff more likely to want to injure Leo? He might have told anyone he planned to ride. Unless he intended to ride across the field, he would naturally have ridden down that lane. It would be easy enough for someone to set that trap for him."

George came to his feet and paced a few steps back and forth, rubbing his hand over his chin. "Leo and I were standing by the targets when that arrow hit Charles. It could have been meant for Leo."

I nodded. "What about the footman and the arsenic? We don't know where the scene of that crime was." I cut myself short and clutched George's arm. "Maybe we do. Michael and the first footman cleared the earl's office after you gentlemen had your meeting there two days ago. Ben told me Michael drank the sherry left in the glasses."

I sprang to my feet as the realization came to me. "Leo didn't drink his sherry. The footman, Michael, drank the sherry meant for Leo."

"What do you mean, meant for Leo? We all had glasses of sherry. Are you suggesting someone managed to poison only Leo's?"

"I think I am," I said, horrified by the revelation. "Help me remember who was in the room."

We made a mental list of everyone. Aside from George and myself, there was Durant, Robert Nash, Leo, Treadwell, John Winnie, and Tuttle.

"Durant poured the sherry, Treadwell and Winnie passed out the glasses. It seemed random enough, but what if it wasn't? If Charles, Mr. Gibbs, and Michael O'Brien were all in the wrong place at the wrong time, Leo might be the real target of this attack."

George came slowly to his feet. "How well do Durant and Treadwell know each other?"

"I've no idea. Why?"

"Both men have some sort of motive. What if they're working together?"

"One poisoned the sherry, the other handed it to Leo?"

"We need to find out if that sherry was poisoned." He took my hand and led me back through the formal gardens and to the north wing. Pushing open the door, he escorted me inside and down the hallway to the earl's offices.

"If only Leo's glass was poisoned, the rest of the sherry would be fine. What do you expect to find?"

"Perhaps the missing rat poison?"

We set about searching the cabinet behind the massive desk where the earl kept his records, his cigars, and several bottles of sherry.

"Odd that your brother only stocks sherry." I moved the two dusty bottles aside only to find an empty cabinet behind them.

"It would be odd if that were the case." George tapped a mirrored panel at the back of the cabinet, and I watched in surprise as it popped open. "Just like my father, Hart leaves the wine out, but keeps the stronger stuff in here."

"Unless he also keeps arsenic in there, I don't see how that helps."

George bent to search through the small opening. "No, nothing but spirits." He backed away from the cabinet and leaned against the desk. "I suppose finding the rat poison was a bit of a long shot. Even an amateur wouldn't be foolish enough to leave it here."

I waved my hand at the cabinet. "We still have the decanter. What do we do with it?"

He blew out a breath. "Chances are there's no poison in it, but I'll take it to Woodrow, just the same. He might as well test it. While I'm in the village, I'll speak to that police sergeant and pass along the information the first footman gave you. Perhaps I'll be able to find out where he stands on the investigation."

"Will you tell him about the other accidents as well?"

"I suppose I should, though I wish I had more to tell him."

"Durant and Treadwell." I tapped a finger against my lips. "And I'd been leaning toward Bradmore."

George leaned back against the desk. "As was I."

"He's the perfect suspect save for one problem."

"He wasn't in this office when we drank our toast."

I nodded. "He couldn't have poisoned the sherry."

"Since we don't know for certain if the sherry was poisoned, I wouldn't count him out just yet."

"Then we should report our suspicions."

George held up a hand. "I'll report the accidents, but I'd rather know a little more about all our suspects before informing the police of our suspicions. You don't know how they work out here. I don't want them to arrest Leo's friend or brother-in-law until we have more evidence."

"How do we get more evidence?"

"We need to start questioning our suspects."

"Then we must start tonight. I don't like the idea of leaving Leo in danger. In fact, I think we should warn him. Then we'll find out what we can this evening and call in the police tomorrow."

"Agreed. And as I've invited Bradmore and a few other neighbors from the shoot to join us, we should have plenty of chances to make some inquiries."

"In that case, I agree." I laced my fingers with his. "This is all very unsettling. If Leo is the target, then one of our guests is a killer."

"Or, Leo is not a target and these are all accidents."

I let his comment stand, but for my part, I didn't think there was anything accidental happening here.

Rose's sniffles and sneezes increased throughout the day and by evening they were joined by a sore throat. I had to give her the bad news that she must stay in the nursery until her symptoms had passed. She required some convincing, and as a result I only joined the rest of our party as they processed into the dining room.

We had three extra guests to dinner this evening, in addition to Mr. Bradmore. The gentlemen had been shooting on a neighbor's property earlier this week, a Mr. Easton. He and his wife were invited to dine with us, and as his brother-in-law, Mr. Kraft, was visiting, he joined us as well. Both gentlemen were in their mid-forties and avid sportsmen, so Mrs. Easton, left to her own devices for the past week, was delighted for the company. Without Charles, who remained in his room, we were eighteen to dinner. As we seated ourselves, Clara Kendrick cleared her throat as if preparing for an announcement.

"I suggest the ladies join the gentlemen for the

last day of the shoot. That is, if they have a mind to do so."

Every head turned in her direction. Some nodded eagerly, others smiled indulgently but shook their heads, probably thinking the poor girl had lost her mind. Still more stared in abject horror at the suggestion of a lady invading the men's domain.

For my part, I was simply shocked the suggestion came from Clara. It was more in keeping with Anne's inclinations for women and men to work side by side. Clara seemed far too fashionable to don shooting gear and boots to tromp through the fields.

My brother, seated across the table from me, grinned. "I've no objection, but neither do I feel I have any say in the matter." He challenged George with a mischievous glint in his eye. "What say you, Hazelton? Are the ladies to accompany us on Friday?"

Before George could answer, Durant spoke up. "Ladies invading the field? Preposterous."

"And why ever would you want to, Clara?" Eliza angled a glare at her sister. "Can you find nothing better to do with your time? Lady Fiona has gone to great lengths to keep us amused in the daytime hours, and the gentlemen join us in the evening. I say leave them to their own pastimes."

"That may be your inclination, Mrs. Durant."

Treadwell tipped his head back and gazed down his nose at Eliza. "I for one would enjoy the company of the ladies as we trudge through the fields. Those who are brave enough to join us, that is."

"It is more than just an inclination, Mr. Treadwell. It's my belief that we should each keep to our own places and enjoy our own pursuits. Ladies and gentlemen need not always be together."

If they were, she would certainly have less time for the under-butler.

I glanced at Clara and noted a flush pinkened her cheeks. So that was it. The days were flying past, and she had not had enough time with the gentlemen. Was there one in particular who had sparked her interest? I hadn't paid her much attention these past few days.

Much to my surprise, and Clara's too, no doubt, Anne came to her defense. "As Clara said, it would be optional for the ladies. If a few of us have a mind to join the shoot, why shouldn't we? Ladies are included in fox hunting, why not shooting?"

"*Tally-ho,* I say." Alonzo beamed at Anne. "I would take up the challenge. Who's with me?"

I suppressed a groan. Under the present circumstances, I would prefer that the shooting part of this house party cease altogether. Too many people carrying firearms for my liking.

Of course, the Kendrick girls would pick this occasion to form a united front.

The room buzzed with voices both for and against the proposal. Finally George held up a hand. "We've had the fields to ourselves all week, gentlemen. None of us will shoot tomorrow, but if any ladies wish to join us Friday, I shall warmly welcome them."

A few groans arose to mix with the cheers from a few ladies. "I'd love to join you," Lottie said. "But only if Charles is recovered enough to shoot. He loves it so much, I'd feel terribly guilty going when he cannot."

Though I wished for a speedy recovery for poor Charles, I had to hope he'd not feel up to shooting Friday. The thought of Lottie toting a shotgun was far too frightening. I was pulled from my thoughts when Percy Bradmore addressed me.

"What of you, Lady Harleigh? Will you join the men or stay at home?"

George had left the table arrangements to Fiona this evening. She seated me between Mr. Bradmore and Mr. Durant knowing I'd wished to speak to both men. There must be something deeply wrong with me to be grateful she'd placed me between two suspected killers. Since poison had been one of the weapons, I should keep a close watch on my plate.

"I'm not entirely certain, Mr. Bradmore. I've

never done any sort of shooting before, and I should hate to be an obstruction."

"You can partner with me, Franny." Alonzo was still grinning. "I had no idea what I was doing as of yesterday. And today I am the great hunter. I'd be happy to take you in hand."

"Ah, yes. I think he may have killed a bird or two today," George said, his tone mocking, "while the rest of us had several braces."

Alonzo turned to him in feigned outrage. "A bird or two? Don't you believe him, dear sister. I'm sure I shot far more than he did."

"Shot at them, more like." From the head of the table, George looked past Bradmore to wink at me. "He missed far more than he hit. If you wish instruction, my lady, you should partner with me."

"After you sully the family honor by questioning my skill?"

"Alonzo, don't be nonsensical," Mother said. "Frances has no interest in such masculine pursuits."

Well, now I'd have to consider it.

Before I could respond, Fiona stood and raised her hands. Everyone left off the subject and turned their attention to her.

"As the gentlemen have been gone all day today, I believe they've had enough time to themselves, so I propose we all proceed to the drawing room together." Everyone murmured their agreement. "I've had card tables set up in the drawing room and the carpets removed from the blue salon. After some tea, I think a spot of dancing is in order—or cards, for those of you who wish it."

Fiona's announcement met with agreement from all, particularly the younger people. In fact, no one lingered long over tea. My mother, Aunt Hetty, and both Mr. and Mrs. Durant preferred a game of bridge, and cards were procured for them, as they placed themselves at the table in the drawing room. Fiona threw wide the doors between the drawing room and the blue salon, and the rest of us made our way into the adjoining room. Mrs. Easton was called upon to take a seat at the piano. She opened the set with a lively polka, and the dancers paired off.

Much to my relief, Mr. Treadwell allowed Leo to lead Lily out to the impromptu dance floor and chose Clara Kendrick for his partner. Mr. Bradmore drew Lottie out to the floor where she immediately trod on his foot. As the dance had yet to begin, I feared he was in for a painful experience. Fiona and Nash joined the group, followed by Mr. Kraft and Anne. I turned to George expectantly, but rather than offer his hand he joined me on the sofa.

I tried not to look disappointed and failed.

"What is wrong?" he asked.

"Wrong? Why, nothing. I thought you might ask me to dance."

He raised his brows. "Dancing with you would be lovely, but I was thinking of replacing your aunt at the card table."

"You prefer to be at a card table with my mother than dancing with me?"

"Both the Durants are playing, and it would be a good opportunity to discuss his role in the Kendrick business, don't you think?"

I saw my dance slipping away but had to admit it was a good idea. "What do you want me to do?"

"Find a way to speak with Treadwell and perhaps learn his thoughts about Kendrick and your sister. And if you can learn anything about Bradmore, I'll be thoroughly impressed with your skill."

"Divide and conquer, it is," I agreed. "I'll do my best."

"As will I." With that, he removed to the drawing room. Considering how much Hetty enjoyed bridge, I wouldn't place a wager on his success in gaining her seat at the table. On the other hand, George could be quite convincing. Well, that was his challenge. I glanced around at the dancers in the blue salon. Mine was in here.

Mrs. Easton ended the polka in a resounding flourish, and the dancers gave her an enthusiastic round of applause. I fell in behind Treadwell and Clara as they ambled off to the side of the room. She whispered something into his ear, causing him to jerk away like a startled deer. What was that misguided child up to now? Treadwell seemed quite relieved to find me at his side.

"Such a lively dance," Clara said, pulling him toward one of the love seats now arranged against the wall. "We should rest ourselves."

Rather than accompany her, Treadwell released her hand. "If you are fatigued, Miss Kendrick, perhaps Lady Harleigh would like to dance."

I couldn't miss the look of disappointment on her face, but neither could I miss my chance to speak with the young man. I gave him my hand. "I'd be delighted, Mr. Treadwell."

Mrs. Easton played a little trill of music, drawing our attention. "As there seems to be eight of you dancing, perhaps you'd like to form a quadrille for a gallop?"

The dancers met her suggestion with enthusiasm. For my part, I could have kissed her. A gallop was easily as energetic as a polka, which made it difficult to carry on a conversation. But as a quadrille, two pairs would dance in the center for several measures, while the other two stood aside, allowing for at least a bit of discussion.

Treadwell and I took our corner and waited while the first two couples danced. "Tell me, Treadwell, are you truly desirous of the ladies' presence in the fields or did you simply wish to argue with Mrs. Durant? You seemed to be enjoying yourself."

"I do enjoy an argument, Lady Harleigh, but I am always desirous of female companionship." His gaze was focused at a spot over my shoulder where I was quite certain Lily and Leo danced. "Certain females more than others, of course." His lips turned upward. "Sometimes a very specific one."

Before I could ask whom he meant, I found myself in his arms, making our first round of the floor. I'd thought his flirtation with Lily was odd considering his long-standing friendship with her fiancé, but wearing that smile, the man looked positively predatory. Was he actively trying to win Lily's affections away from his friend?

We returned to our corner and waited while Lily and Leo, and Alonzo and Anne, danced through the center. I had done little to mask my thoughts, and he must have read the confusion in my expression, for when his gaze returned to mine, he gave me a mischievous grin. "You think I'm speaking of your sister."

I drew back in surprise. "I certainly hope you are not speaking of her."

"Would it be so terrible if I were?"

Off we went again in a circle, rather like this conversation, which was getting me nowhere. This time when we returned to our corner, it was our turn to chasse across the center. Treadwell guided me effortlessly into a step-hop before our reverse.

"Ho! Look at the two of you." Nash, standing along the wall with Fiona, clapped his hands in time to the music. Indeed, Treadwell's expertise made me a better dancer as well. We performed our last step-hop, and once again all of the couples danced around the floor.

When we returned once more to our corner, it took a moment for me to recall where we left off. "Lily and Leo are in love and about to be married," I said. "Both their families approve of the match, and as his friend, I would hope you'd have nothing but good wishes for their happiness."

A frown pulled at his lips as he considered my words. Was this man playing with me?

"I was under the impression your mother did not entirely agree with her daughter's choice. That is to say . . ."

She didn't! My stomach seemed to turn in on itself. "You and Mrs. Price spoke about this? Whatever did she tell you?"

Off we went again. Gad! Would this wretched dance never end?

Treadwell smiled indulgently as we moved around the perimeter and I missed several steps. My steady glare kept him talking. "Well, only what I just said. That in her opinion, things were not completely settled. If I could win Lily's approval, I would have her mother's."

I dropped his hand as soon as we returned to

our corner. "Truly? My mother approves of you, does she? And this on an acquaintance of one day's standing."

"Your brother seems to like me as well. In fact, you seem to be the only one whose good opinion I cannot win." He glanced around. "Lady Harleigh, we ought to be dancing."

I refused to budge. "Let me assure you, my mother does not speak for my father and she most certainly does not speak for Lily. Their marriage is definitely a settled matter. If you wish to hear Lily's opinion on the matter, then you must speak to her, not our mother. I'd caution you, however, you are likely to cause her pain if you do reveal your feelings to her."

Treadwell took a step as if to leave, but I moved into his path and held fast to his arm. "I'll further caution you that I have my eye on you. If something should happen to Leo, I shall look to you first." Finally, I had the satisfaction of removing the smirk from his face.

As the music had ended, I left him, stunned and stammering, and strode over to Fiona who watched me in horror.

"Whatever have you done to that poor boy?"

"Nothing he didn't deserve." I looked around for my sister, wondering if anyone in the room had missed the heated conversation I'd just had with Treadwell, who, after straightening his cuffs, headed directly to the closest footman, took a drink from his tray, and slipped out of the room. I could use something bracing myself.

Lily sat blissfully at Leo's side in conversation with Anne and Alonzo. So there were at least four people in the room I hadn't just embarrassed. What had I been thinking? One does not have an argument in the middle of a dance, even in a private home. I should have better controlled my temper.

Hetty came to my side and pressed a short-stemmed glass into my hand. "It's about time someone set that young man straight. Though Lily should have done it herself."

"Bless you, Aunt Hetty. This is precisely what I needed." I took a healthy sip—and gasped, my throat aflame. "Why didn't you tell me it was whiskey? I thought it was wine."

"Ridiculous. Who would serve wine in such a glass?"

She reached for the glass, but I pulled it back. "I didn't say I didn't want it."

"What your sister needs is a good talking-to." Fiona gave me a cautious look. "I love her dearly, Frances, but I fear she's leading Treadwell on."

"I have spoken with her. She agreed to stop seeking his attentions, but I'm afraid that may not be enough. Apparently, my mother also needs a good talking-to. She encouraged Treadwell."

Hetty huffed. "Daisy never ceases to amaze me. They are to be married in a few days."

"Lily will simply have to make it clear to him that she is in love with Leo."

Hetty and I shared a glance. None of this would have happened if Lily hadn't been emotional and in need of Leo's attention. One would think love would be easier than this.

"Perhaps it will all blow over," Fiona said. "There's little more you can do." She brightened. "I meant to tell you I heard something of Lady Esther this morning."

Hetty gave me a little pat on the arm and moved on to speak to Alonzo. I gave my attention to Fiona. "Have you? Is she recovering?"

"From what I'm told, she was never ill." She nodded at my surprise. "I received a letter from Nash's sister in London, and she happened to mention Lady Esther was at Lady Grafton's salon Monday evening."

"In London?"

Fiona nodded.

"If Mr. Bradmore isn't nursing his aunt, just what is he doing at her home?"

Fiona raised her brows. "An excellent question."

Chapter 15

~⌒~

My chance to speak with Percy Bradmore appeared almost immediately. Clara Kendrick required Fiona's opinion on a millinery shop in the village, leaving me to my own devices. Mrs. Easton stood by the piano bench, stretching both her back and her fingers between songs. I joined her just as she reseated herself and I complimented her skill and good nature in playing for us rather than dancing herself.

She waved aside the praise and leaned toward me in a conspiratorial manner. "I am afraid I ate rather too well at dinner and am quite ready to burst." She chuckled and shook her head. "Dancing would be far too uncomfortable. Besides, I need the practice. Fortunately, country dances are simple enough, and people don't notice if I hit a sour note now and then, as long as I give them something lively to dance to."

Percy Bradmore joined us in time to contradict her. "I noticed nothing sour."

"Ah, Mr. Bradmore."

"You, sir, were in the other room," Mrs. Easton said. "You weren't likely to notice the music at all."

A footman stepped up to the piano and offered refreshments. We each took a glass of Fiona's special punch, and I returned the whiskey to his tray. "Do you play bridge, Mr. Bradmore?" I asked.

"Very poorly, I'm afraid."

"And your aunt?"

He blinked. "I beg your pardon?"

"Lady Esther is a notorious whist player, but I understand she's waiting to see if bridge catches on before she bothers to learn it."

Bradmore chuckled at Mrs. Easton's comment. "I suppose one doesn't want to rush into these things. After seven or eight years, it is only an upstart game, wouldn't you agree?"

It was Mrs. Easton's turn to laugh. "Your aunt is simply so good at whist, she's reluctant to give it up. I made the mistake of partnering her at a card party the last time she was in the country. She was appalled by my poor play." Mrs. Easton pressed her lips into a grimace. "I've been working on my strategy ever since."

I chuckled with her. "Perhaps you will have a chance to redeem yourself in the coming days. As one begins to recover from an illness, amusements are as necessary as any medicine."

Mrs. Easton tipped her head. "Do you mean to say Lady Esther is in residence?" She turned from me to Bradmore.

"Yes, of course. Has he not mentioned it?" I

frowned at the man. "For shame, Mr. Bradmore, you are depriving your aunt of valuable company during her retirement in the country. And just what did you say was ailing her?"

"Just a touch of gout," he said with a dismissive air. "It does seem as though she's beginning to rally and might be up to visitors soon."

Gout? Though I wasn't particularly familiar with that malady, I'd always attributed it to rich food and drink. Lady Esther was both painfully thin and a teetotaler.

"I am at liberty tomorrow," I said. "Perhaps Lady Fiona and I could call on her in the afternoon."

Bradmore drew his brows up but otherwise maintained his patience. "Allow me to inquire of her and send you word. I'd hate for you to waste the trip."

"It's a trip of less than a mile."

Mrs. Easton sighed. "Sadly, I'm engaged tomorrow afternoon, or I'd join you, but I could call on her the following day."

Bradmore gave her a tight smile. "I'm certain she'll be delighted to receive you then." He turned and gave me a nod. "I shall send word tomorrow morning to apprise you as to whether or not she's up to a visit."

With that, he stepped away to speak with Mr. Easton, and Mrs. Easton returned to her piano. I still didn't know what Bradmore was playing at, but I felt certain I'd receive a missive tomorrow advising me not to call.

As I had no further suspects to question, and the dancers were already paired, I decided to step into the drawing room and check on the card players. My mother and George were partners against Mr. and Mrs. Durant. They had just taken a trick as I walked in and Mother rewarded George with a delighted laugh. Though her lips puckered as she considered which card to play next, she looked relaxed and happy, and many years younger. It was difficult to reconcile this pleasant woman with a mother who would attempt to upset her daughter's wedding plans.

She caught sight of me as I approached the table. "Mind you don't disturb our concentration, dear."

"That's not my intention, Mother. I just came in to see how the game is progressing."

"They are beating us soundly," Durant muttered, throwing down a card. "Haven't taken a hand since the first." He threw me a glance. "Please disturb their concentration. Might help our chances."

"The games have all been close, Durant." George's voice was quiet and assured. "You are making us work hard for our wins."

My mother gave a little toss of her head as if she knew better. I stationed myself between her and Durant, giving me a clear view of George.

I enjoyed watching as he pushed his lips out then twisted them to the left, then right, as he considered his play. They took the next trick, and I watched him repeat the process.

"Frances, you are making me nervous." Mother threw out a card. "Why don't you go back to the young people and dance with that nice Mr. Bradmore?"

I repressed a sigh. The woman just couldn't stop herself. Yes, why don't I go dance with Mr. Bradmore, the murder suspect?

George threw out his final card to win the hand. "It appears she's brought us luck, Mrs. Price. I quite like having her here." I rewarded him with a warm smile.

"As if you needed luck." Durant looked at the tally. "Right. That's the game. Think I've been trounced quite enough for one evening. What say you, Eliza?"

"Quite," she said, coming to her feet. "A little music perhaps, then I'm for bed. It's been a long day."

Perhaps longer than her husband knew, I thought, recalling her tryst with the under-butler this morning.

Durant guided his wife into the other room while George retrieved and stacked the cards. My mother stood up with a sigh. "I think it's time I found my bed as well."

I wondered if I should mention Treadwell

and her interference but decided that was a conversation best held in private. I gave her a kiss on the cheek as she passed by me. "Good night, Mother."

George came to his feet as well. "Thank you for the game, Mrs. Price. Your skills are impressive."

At the doorway, she turned, narrowing her eyes. "You may be a good partner, young man, and I must admit I've enjoyed the last hour in your company, but that does not mean I'll allow you to linger here alone with my daughter." She jerked her head toward the other room. "Both of you, come join the other guests."

I nearly gawked at the impertinence of her statement and opened my mouth to tell her, in no uncertain terms, I'd make my own decisions. George stopped me with a hand on my arm. "We are right behind you, ma'am."

She sniffed and continued on her way. "Be sure that you are."

George and I shared a look that sent us both into spasms of laughter, which we choked back as best we could. "Honestly, you would think I were eighteen again."

"You've been out of her life that long, Frances. It may well be how she still sees you."

I scoffed. "She clearly considered you a naughty schoolboy."

"She always has."

"Why is she so standoffish toward you?"

He gave me an impish smile. "I told you, you will have to ask her that question. I won't come between a mother and daughter." He laughed at my scowl. "It's nothing I hold against her, Frances. At least, not any longer. Ignore it and set your mind to our investigation. Have you learned anything this evening?"

I told him about my mortifying argument with Mr. Treadwell on the dance floor, and the mysterious appearance of Lady Esther at a London salon. "I expect a note from Bradmore tomorrow telling me his aunt is unable to receive me."

"Strange that he'd invent a ruse so easy to disprove."

I shrugged. "We can't exactly disprove it without seeing her empty bedchamber. No matter how many reports we have of Lady Esther in London, he can keep denying it."

"Still, it only buys him a little time. Perhaps a week at most before someone informs the lady that some rogue is staying at her home."

"Then whatever purpose has sent him here, he expects to accomplish it in short order. Though I can't find a connection to him and the poisoned sherry, he is the most suspicious to my mind."

He lifted a brow. "We don't know for certain the arsenic was in the sherry."

"There's not much we do know for certain. However, I think it's time we warn Leo."

"Agreed. Let's see if he's still in the salon."

Almost no one was left in the salon when we entered. Mr. and Mrs. Easton and Mr. Kraft had taken their leave of Fiona and gone home. With the music over, nearly everyone else had gone up to their rooms. Only Fiona, Nash, Durant, and Mr. Bradmore were still about.

"I shall go and look for Lily."

George nodded and moved to speak with Bradmore while I bid the others good night. Rather than return to the drawing room, I left through a side hallway and stepped outside to the formal gardens, situated in something of a courtyard between the two wings. A lovely spot for a romantic rendezvous, but I saw no sign of Lily and Leo as I crossed the cobbled path. It was possible they'd retired for the night. As I was closer to the north wing, I decided to enter the house that way.

Once inside, it took a moment to get my bearings. This house was entirely too large. I'd have to return to the gallery, take it back to the south wing, then up to the first floor to tap on Lily's door. I'd just about reached the gallery, when I saw Lily waiting at the foot of the stairs to the bachelors' quarters. She leaned against the wall, her eyelids drooping.

"Are you waiting for Leo?"

She snapped around at my words. "Frances, you startled me. Yes, I am waiting for him. He's looking for a coat of some sort for me so we can walk out in the gardens for a bit. I didn't want to fetch one from my room or Mother might hear me, or see me. Then, of course, she'd demand my attention for something, and I'd lose my time alone with Leo." She huffed in exasperation. "It seems we're either parted all day or in company with a dozen other people. I had no idea how little we'd see of each other once we came here. I begin to wish we'd eloped after all."

"Only three days stand between you and your wedding." I placed an arm around her shoulders. "You'll be glad you avoided the scandal of eloping—and Mother's wrath. She would have been horrified if you'd just run off and married."

"Mother seems to be trying to come between me and my wedding as well. What is wrong with her? Why does she dislike Leo so? You came in at the tail end of her tirade this morning. You should have heard the things she said."

"Mother means well. She just has a different view of marriage than we do." I paused. "By the way, you may have to have another conversation with Mr. Treadwell and make sure he understands you want to marry Leo. I'm afraid Mother's encouraged him."

Lily rolled her eyes, but I held firm. "You did your part to encourage him, too. Now you have to tell the poor man the truth." Though I said the words, I had a difficult time seeing Treadwell as an unfortunate bystander. It seemed more as if he felt entitled to Lily's affections. And he might be trying to murder his best friend. Perhaps I should have let them elope.

"I wonder what's taking Leo so long?" Lily mused.

"There's a back stairway," I said, remembering my tour of the house a few days ago. "It's closer to his room. Let's see if he's gone that way, shall we?"

Lily threw me a glance as we walked down the hall. "Please tell me you plan to excuse yourself when Leo does arrive. I really would like to spend some time alone with my fiancé."

"I won't keep you long," I said, uncertain how to tell her I had some rather upsetting news to impart. Before I could form the words, a scream rent the silence, followed by a series of thumps.

We froze for an instant before racing to the back staircase. I gasped when we arrived to see Clara Kendrick's limp body sprawled half on the carpeted stairs and half on the stone floor of the hall.

Her chest heaved as she struggled to take in the breath that had been knocked out from the fall. Thank heaven, she was alive. As I rushed to her side, I noticed her arm lay twisted at an unnatural angle.

"Don't move, dear," I said, stooping to the floor next to her. "I'm afraid your arm is broken.

Any movement could make it worse." I swept the chestnut hair from her eyes to examine the pupils through her tears. They did not appear to be irregular. I glanced up at Lily. "Find Mr. Hazelton and send him here. Then ask the butler or housekeeper to call Dr. Woodrow. We need him immediately."

She hastened up the hallway, and I turned my attention back to Clara, who struggled to right herself until a stab of pain made her gasp.

"I know it hurts, dear. Try to be still. We'll have help for you right away. Would you like me to call for one of your sisters?"

The wail she sent up was enough of an answer for me. Fine. No sisters. Instead, I worked my arm under her neck and cradled her as best I could without moving her arm. Her tears gave way to a quiet whimper as she tried to keep still in this awkward position. I needed to distract her from her pain until help arrived. I glanced up the stairs, wondering what was keeping Leo, which reminded me exactly where we were.

"How did you come to be in the bachelors' quarters?" I asked.

She muttered something I couldn't make out, then said, "I lost my way."

I wondered if she knew how true that statement was. She had to be visiting one of the young men. It could only be Treadwell or Alonzo, and so help me, if one of them had encouraged her, he'd have to answer to me. I should have taken responsibility for this young lady from the start. She was only seventeen after all. Her mother was absent, and neither sister seemed to care what she did.

I was trying to decide which gentleman I would have to throttle when Leo stepped down from the landing.

"Take care," I called to him. "Your sister has just fallen down those stairs. You had best watch your step."

He'd paused when I first spoke, then, completely disregarding my warning, skittered down the stairs as fast as he could, leaping over Clara's legs to the floor.

"Clara, my heavens. What are you doing here? Are you all right?"

I went directly to his second question. "No, she has a broken arm at least. We cannot move her until we can do so without damaging it further. Mr. Hazelton is on his way, and the doctor has been called."

His mouth gaping open, he took in the scene of his youngest sister spread out on the stairs and at least half cradled in my arms. "Thank goodness for your quick thinking, Lady Harleigh. My mother would have my head if Clara came to any harm."

I sighed, sharing both his guilt and concern. Patricia Kendrick would see her daughter wearing a cast on her arm when she arrived in two days. She might well have both our heads.

"Frances!"

"We're here," I called back upon hearing George's voice.

He rushed to the stairs, Lily trailing down the hall behind him. After giving Clara a more thorough going-over than I had, he and Leo lifted her, while Lily guarded her arm. Making a face, she held it at the wrist and elbow, not allowing it to move. In this manner, they carried her back to her own room. Rather than follow, I headed upstairs in a blind fury. Perhaps I'd been remiss in chaperoning the girl, but I wasn't entirely to blame. Someone had some explaining to do.

I rounded the landing and stepped into a hallway that contained six doors. George had told me his and Leo's rooms were closest to these stairs, on either side of the hall. I didn't know who'd been placed next door to Leo, but I knocked anyway. Alonzo, in shirtsleeves, with the ends of his tie trailing from his collar, opened the door.

"Franny. What are you doing here?" He stepped back and opened the door wide, allowing me entry. I strode in and whipped around to face him, but before I could ask any questions, I picked up a scent in the air. Roses? No, attar of roses. Clara's preferred scent. My mouth sagged open as I stared at him.

"Alonzo, how could you?"

The look on his face was almost comical as he shook his head in confusion and backed away from me. "How could I what?"

"Clara Kendrick was in your room."

"Good Lord, Frances! How did you know that?" On noting the anger in my eyes, he raised his hands in a defensive move. "Franny, I swear I didn't invite her, if that's what you're thinking. She came here of her own accord, and I sent her away immediately."

I narrowed my eyes.

"Stop glaring at me. I didn't invite her, nor did I give her any undue attention that would lead her to think she'd be welcome." He ran a shaky hand through his already-mussed hair, making clumps of it stand on end. "My God, what did she tell you?"

"Nothing." I drew a deep breath and let it out slowly, studying his face. Alonzo looked not only terrified but sincere. Had the girl come up here to throw herself at my brother? If so, I didn't envy her mother. Patricia had her work cut out for her.

Alonzo stared in confusion. "If she told you nothing, how did you know she was here?"

"I didn't until I smelled her perfume. Was she upset when she left you? Were you harsh when you rebuffed her?"

"First you are angry because you think I seduced her. Now you are angry because I may have dismissed her too harshly? How am I to win with you, Franny?"

I slipped into a chair by the washstand and rested my head in my palm. "I suspect she rushed away from your room to the stairs, where she tripped and tumbled down the length of them. The poor girl broke her arm."

He looked stricken. "I pushed her away from my door and told her to return to her room." He ran a hand through his hair. "She looked surprised, but she was not upset, crying, or hysterical. She left quietly." He made a supplicating gesture. "I'm very sorry she was injured, but I don't believe I caused her accident."

It was that final word that drew me from my musing. Accident. Yet another one. There had been far too many of them happening around here lately.

A knock sounded at the door. Alonzo raised his brows. "Another caller?" Stepping over to the door he opened it to reveal George on the other side.

"Hazelton?"

George nodded toward me. "I was looking for your sister."

I gave him a little finger wave and wearily raised myself from the chair. "Has the doctor arrived?"

"He's with her now." He glanced from me to Alonzo. "Was she up here visiting you?"

"Not at his invitation," I replied before Alonzo could speak.

George raised his eyes heavenward. "Thank God, she's not my daughter. If you're through here, may I escort you back downstairs?"

Alonzo stopped us at the door. "If there's any way you can keep this from getting to her sister, I'd be obliged." His cheeks flamed as I gave him a curious look. "I'd hate for the elder Miss Kendrick to think I was trifling with the younger."

George and I exchanged a glance. Revealing the truth of Miss Kendrick's whereabouts would serve no one. "I'm sure we can come up with a suitable story," I said.

Alonzo gave us a sheepish smile and closed the door. George and I headed for the stairs. He heaved a sigh. "Thank heaven she's not my daughter."

I glanced up at him. "That's the second time you've given thanks in as many minutes. You realize you will have a daughter when we marry."

He took my hand. "Rose is only eight, and already she has more sense than Miss Kendrick. I am not worried."

I hated to tell him that sometimes sensible eight-year-olds became quite empty-headed when they turned seventeen. We'd both find out what that would be like—eventually.

When we reached the stairs, George took my

arm. "Watch your step going down," he said. "She tripped over something."

My eyes were already trained on the wooden steps. "It might have just been her hem, but I had the very same thought. In fact, what's this?"

He followed the line of my gaze. Taking a few steps farther down, he turned and reached out for a curled strand of something attached to the side of the riser. I watched as he twisted and turned it and finally pulled it free.

"It's a piece of line." He held it up for my inspection. "Looks like the one you found tangled in the tree, doesn't it?" He brushed my skirts aside to reveal the rest of the stair. "And here's where it was attached to the other side. It came loose from the nailhead. Someone fastened it across the step as a trip line."

I didn't want to believe the evidence before my eyes. "She could have been killed had she hit the floor headfirst. Who would do such a thing?"

George stood back up and, taking my hand, guided me down the stairs. "It wasn't Bradmore. I showed him out just as Lily came to fetch me."

"Durant?"

"He and Mrs. Durant were just going up to their chambers."

"No one would have expected Miss Kendrick to visit this section of the house this evening. This was another trap, meant to hurt or kill someone. Considering you and Leo are situated closest to this staircase, I expect it was meant for one of you."

"I left Kendrick with his sister. In all the excitement, I forgot about our plans to warn him."

We'd come to the foot of the stairs. I leaned against the banister and gazed up at him. "And what of the rest of us? I actually find myself grateful Rose is in bed with a cold, so I don't have to worry about her stepping into one of these traps. None of us is safe."

"That's why we need to set a trap of our own."

Chapter 16

George's idea of setting a trap was not high on my list of proper ways to deal with a murderer. I proposed a far less risky option—we should all just leave. He thought no more of my idea than I did of his.

"Consider it, Frances. Are we to put Leo on a train with Treadwell and Durant when one or both of them might be plotting to murder him?"

"What if it's Bradmore or someone we haven't even considered yet?"

"There's nothing to stop Bradmore from following Leo back to London, where he'd have even greater access. Whoever is doing this wants Leo's death to look like an accident. I'd say it's someone close to him. Someone with a grudge."

We were heading up to the nursery as I had a sudden need to check on Rose. I put my finger over George's lips as I turned the knob and pushed open the door to the large, airy room. We tiptoed past shelves of books and toys to the bedroom Rose occupied. I slowly opened the door and peeked inside. Nanny had retired to her room next door, and Rose was sleeping peacefully, her long dark braid draped over the covers. No sniffles, sneezes, or coughs. Was it horrible of me to hope she'd require another day in bed? At least then I could be certain she'd be safe.

We backed out of the room and padded silently to the hall where I pulled George aside, under the light of a sconce. "We'll speak with Leo in the morning. If he's agreeable, we'll work on this trap you have in mind. I want to catch this murderer before anyone else is hurt."

The following morning, I opened the door to the breakfast room and took a step back in surprise. It was full of guests. I'd forgotten there was no shooting today, so nearly all the gentlemen, except for George, were seated around the table. Nash, the angel, manned the coffeepot, so I handed him an empty cup and found a seat next to Leo, who was digging into a large helping of kippers. Treadwell and Durant were farther down the table by Hetty, working on their own breakfasts.

Alonzo, seated across the table from me, brightened as Anne Kendrick entered the room. He jumped to his feet and pulled out the chair next to his. She blushed, smiled, and glided over to his side.

"How is your sister?" Durant asked from his end of the table. "Eliza said she had some sort of accident. Injured herself."

I wondered how Eliza, a late sleeper herself, had learned of her sister's accident.

Anne nodded. "Yes. Didn't Leo tell you about it?" She glanced over at Leo who barely looked up from his plate and made a rolling motion with his hand, indicating she should continue. "I only learned of it this morning, but it seems she slid on something in the hall by the entrance to the gardens."

She made as if to stand, but Alonzo gestured her back to her seat. "Please continue your story, Miss Kendrick. I'll fill a plate for you."

She smiled and let her gaze follow him as he moved to the breakfront. "Actually, Lady Harleigh might be able to tell the story better. Clara says you found her in the hallway and sent for help."

"The poor dear," I said. "It was clear she'd broken her arm and I didn't want her to move on her own. Your brother and Mr. Hazelton helped her back to her room, and the doctor arrived shortly afterward."

Durant frowned. "Strange she took that route. Only leads to the kitchens and the bachelors' wing."

"Nothing strange about it," Leo protested with a hint of anger in his voice. "She left the salon into the formal gardens. Once outside, she took the wrong entrance back in. Easy to become turned around in the gardens. What's so strange about it?"

"Actually, I did the same thing," I lied, wondering how one could become disoriented in a square garden with straight lines and paths, and plantings no taller than four feet. "It was fortunate for Clara that I did or who knows when she'd have been found?"

"Right." Durant returned to his food clearly confused, but not interested enough to pursue the subject. Of course, he might not need to pursue it if he knew the story was false. Had Durant fastened that wire across the stair? George said he'd been in the drawing room at the time Clara stumbled into it, but who knows when it had been placed?

I pushed the frustrating question aside and addressed Leo. "Mr. Hazelton and I would like to discuss some details of the wedding with you and Lily. She should be up by now. Can you collect her and meet us in his office in half an hour?"

Leo stopped his fork halfway to his mouth. "There are more details to settle?"

I raised my brows.

"Of course, we can meet you."

"Does that mean you won't be riding with Rose this morning?" Anne asked.

"I'm encouraging Rose to stay in bed one more day." At least I would be doing so. "She'll want to be completely recovered for the wedding."

"What a shame. I'll stop in and visit with her this morning."

An odd sort of flush heated my skin and set my ears ringing. I didn't put so much as one ounce of credence in Arthur Durant's claim that Anne had shot her arrow at Charles. Even if he were to be believed, nothing would convince me she'd done it deliberately. So I couldn't explain the panic that caused my hands to shake at the mere thought of Anne in the same room with Rose. I let my gaze travel the length of the table, from face to face. George was right; we didn't know these people and we couldn't guess at their motives. Any one, or none of them, might be the killer.

Anne smiled and leaned back from the table as Alonzo set a plate before her with such a flourish, one would think he was presenting the crown jewels.

Lon! He was my answer. "Actually, Lon was speaking of riding this morning."

Lon glanced up with a blank stare.

Ask her, I mouthed, shifting my eyes once more to Anne.

Ask her what? he mouthed back. Did he never pay attention?

"Perhaps you and Miss Kendrick might enjoy a ride together," I said.

Finally, understanding dawned on Lon's face. "A ride, yes. Would you care to accompany me, Miss Kendrick?"

As she accepted his offer, I was hit with another wave of panic. Was I placing my brother in the company of a killer? Heavens, I must stop suspecting everyone.

"Since we are riding this morning," Anne said, "I'll plan to visit with Rose this afternoon."

Not if I could prevent it. I popped the last piece of toast in my mouth before excusing myself. Once outside the room, with the door closed behind me, I leaned against the wall to recover myself.

"How was breakfast?"

I glanced up to see Fiona approaching. I sighed. "Tense. Frightening. Exhausting."

She gave my shoulder a pat. "I completely understand. That's why I only ever have tea. You ought to consider switching from coffee."

I pushed myself from the wall and headed up to the nursery, coming to a complete stop when I saw Rose and George, heads together, leaning over a puzzle on the table. Rose smiled when she spotted me.

"Look what Mr. Hazelton found, Mummy. It was his when he was a boy."

"How kind of you to share your toys, Mr. Hazelton." I stepped up to the table and gave him a grin.

"It was part of our bargain."

"The two of you made a bargain?"

Rose passed one of the small wooden pieces from hand to hand. "I wanted to go riding today, but Mr. Hazelton said if I'd stay in my room to recover one more day, he'd bring me something to do."

"An excellent idea." Looking around the room, I noticed we were alone. "Where is Nanny?"

"Seeing to the breakfast tray."

"Herself?"

"Yes, well, I asked her to do so. A footman will help her bring it up, of course." He gave me a sheepish smile, and I realized he was just as concerned for Rose's safety as I. When Nanny did return with the footman and the tray, we managed to restrain ourselves from testing the food first, but did give her instructions not to allow anyone to visit with Rose alone.

Having thoroughly frightened the woman, we left for our meeting with Leo and Lily.

"I rode into the village first thing this morning and spoke to Sergeant Fisk," George said as we descended the stairs to the first floor. "They've contacted O'Brien's family and interviewed some of the villagers about his activities. I passed on the information the first footman gave you concerning the staff's true feelings about O'Brien, and I mentioned the accidents we've experienced lately."

We'd reached the gallery and turned right, toward the north wing. "What was his reaction?"

"That they were likely just accidents, but he'd keep them in mind as the case progressed."

"I've been thinking about the line across the

stair," I said. "Though we exonerated the two men who were still in the salon, the truth is, almost anyone might have placed it. They needed only to excuse themselves for a moment, slip through the garden to the north wing, and place the line."

We'd reached the estate office, and George held the door open while I preceded him into the room. "I considered that as well, but Treadwell is housed in the bachelors' quarters. He had the best access."

I took a seat in front of the desk as George moved around it. "He would also have known you and Leo were closest to the staircase."

"Though all Durant had to do was ask a servant where Leo's room was located."

I *tsk*ed. "I hate dismissing Bradmore. The man definitely seems to be up to something, but I don't know how he could be responsible for this accident. That leaves us with Treadwell or Durant. Or Treadwell and Durant in partnership? We considered that possibility earlier."

"Consider one more. Miss Kendrick's fall down the stairs brought to mind the luggage cart that fell down the stairs at the train station."

I raised my hand to my throat. "You and Leo were at the bottom of those stairs. How could I have forgotten?"

"There's been a bit of excitement since that accident." He cocked his head. "But what if it wasn't an accident? Neither Treadwell nor Durant were near that cart or the stairs."

"Bradmore? He arrived in the country that day."

"It might have been an unrelated accident, but I intend to find out where Bradmore was at the time."

A knock sounded at the door, followed by Lily and Leo stepping into the room.

"Good morning," Lily called out, seemingly in good health and spirits. I feared we were about to ruin the latter.

George stood up from behind the desk and waved an arm toward a worktable in the center of the room. A collection of books littered its surface, and he pushed them aside. Once we were all seated, he and I exchanged a look.

"Where to begin?" George mused.

"We think Leo's life may be in danger," I said, letting the words come out in a rush.

Both of them jerked back as if struck. George glanced at me, his chin resting on his fist. "I probably wouldn't have started with that."

"Apologies," I said. "I thought it best to get right to the point."

"And the point is Leo is in danger?" Lily looked incredulous. "Why? What makes you think such a thing?"

Leo took hold of her hand and held it in both of his. "I think we misunderstood your sister."

"No, there's no misunderstanding. Four people have been injured in what appear to be accidents, but they all seem to be happening very near to you. That leads us to wonder if these so-called accidents might have been planned—and meant for you."

With George's help, I walked them through each situation, from the steward's fall from his horse, to the footman's poisoning, Charles's injury, and Clara's fall down the stairs.

Leo put up a hand to stop me. "I don't understand. How could someone poison the footman, thinking it was me?"

"That's the one incident we are the least clear about because we can't say where he came by the poison. We do know he drank the sherry you left in this office the other day." I shrugged. "He died that night, so it's possible the sherry held the arsenic."

He frowned. "I follow your logic, but why me? Hazelton didn't drink his either."

I felt as if I'd been slapped. I turned to George, staring in disbelief as he reddened. How could he not tell me that? He dropped his gaze to his hands, confirmation that what Leo said was true. My fingers dug into the arms of my chair.

"How many times have we spoken of this, Mr. Hazelton? Did it never occur to you to tell me you also left your glass untouched?"

Lily muttered something to Leo, but I heard only the word *trouble*. She certainly had that right. I remained silent, waiting for an explanation from George.

He finally looked at me. Ran a hand through his hair. Smiled innocently.

"For heaven's sake, just tell me."

"You've been agonizing about Kendrick for days. I knew telling you I didn't drink the sherry either would only increase your concern."

Lily's head jerked up. "Agonizing for days? How long have you two known about this? And why didn't you tell us?"

I bit my lip and peered across the table at her. It was my turn to face the fury of one of the Price women. I shared a glance with George, and we both began to babble.

"He's exaggerating. We haven't known that long."

"We really don't know anything for certain."

Our comments were met with two cold stares.

Lily rose to her feet in a fluid, dangerous motion, her eyes chips of blue ice. "How long is not very long, and what do you mean you don't know for certain?"

I chewed on my lower lip and turned to George.

He raised his brows in amazement. "Now you defer to me?"

"You can explain it much better than I."

He released a huff of breath. "We don't know

if the arsenic that killed the footman was in the sherry. The rat poison went missing from the laundry and has yet to be found. That means anyone could have poisoned the young man. It wasn't until the past day or so that we put all these incidents together and began wondering if, in fact, they were not accidents at all, but deliberate acts. That led us to ask ourselves, who was in the vicinity when the victims were brought down? We realized Leo was nearby in each case, except the death of the footman. At that point, your sister began speculating that the arsenic might have been in the sherry."

I clapped my hands together. "I'd say that sums everything up quite well. Except that now I realize you were also in the vicinity when each of these incidents took place." I turned a glaring eye on George.

"Are you saying you believe someone is trying to murder either Mr. Hazelton or Leo?" Lily asked. "Who?"

"Naturally, we have a few suspects." I glanced at George who lifted his shoulder in a shrug, which I took as a sign to go ahead. I directed my attention to Leo. "Have you ever met Mr. Bradmore before?"

"Bradmore? The chap who was here last night? Lady Esther's nephew? No, not that I can recall. From what I understand, he's spent most of his time on the continent, and I haven't left England for years. Can't imagine how we'd have crossed paths."

To my mind, that didn't exonerate Bradmore, but though I wasn't ready to let him go as a suspect, I couldn't see a line of questioning to pursue right now.

I took a deep breath before my next question. "How do you get on with your brother-in-law?"

Leo's eyes rounded. "Durant? You think Durant wants to murder me?"

"Really, Frances. I know Durant wants Leo's position, but he's hardly likely to murder his wife's brother in order to obtain it."

Leo reeled back in his chair. "He wants my position? In the company?"

Lily sighed. "You are a wonderful businessman, but you must start paying more attention to the people around you, and how they feel about things."

I wondered if she was still talking about Durant but pushed the thought aside. We'd get to Lily's feelings soon enough.

"From what I understand, both your sister and brother-in-law feel some resentment that you are a partner in the company and he is not."

"Eliza is constantly telling me how much effort Durant puts into your father's company," Lily said.

"That's an indisputable fact," Leo said. "The man is full of ideas and the will to put them into action. He's a great asset to the company, but Father fully expects him to leave us the moment he inherits the title."

So we were back to that little detail. "Does your father realize he may not inherit for twenty or more years? Why not allow the man the status suitable to his contribution to the company?"

"I've no objection. It's my father who must be convinced."

"Well, surely you could—"

"Might we return to the matter at hand?" At George's tone, we turned as one back to him. "The threat on Kendrick's life?"

"Come, my dear man, Durant may be frustrated with his situation, but do you really imagine he'd try to kill me?"

"Hazelton and I have only a passing acquaintance with your relations. And your friends," I couldn't help adding. "We must consider anyone with a motive." I raised a brow. "Can you think of anyone with a stronger one?"

He gave me a blank look.

"What about your friend, Treadwell?" I was relieved George had asked the question, but it was still hard to see Lily blanch.

Leo chuckled. "Now you really are barking up the wrong tree. Treadwell? We've been the best of mates for years. Why, he'd sooner do himself a harm than me."

Lily gasped. "Do you honestly think he would harm himself?"

I could not recall a more awkward conversation. If we pushed further ahead on the subject of Treadwell, his marked attention to Lily was bound to come out, and we might just put an end to the wedding. I was beginning to think warning Leo was a terrible idea. He still didn't take the threat seriously, and only one of these men was guilty—maybe—but we might be damaging his relationship with both his brother-in-law and his best friend. Not to mention Lily. Perhaps we should just drop this subject.

"Are you aware of his feelings for Miss Price?"

Unfortunately, George had failed to read my mind.

Leo came to his feet so quickly, he toppled the chair. "That blackguard!"

He stomped out of the room, leaving Lily in tears. Lifting her skirts, she scurried to the door. "You've ruined everything!" She sent me a deadly glare before rushing after him.

George leaned back in his chair. "I'll take that as a no."

"Definitely no." I crossed my arms over my chest. "What do you think he's going to do to Treadwell?"

"Give him the thrashing he deserves."

I nodded. "Then I suppose he and Lily will

need to have a talk. I hope we haven't ruined everything, as she said."

"They'll work it out, Frances. Talking is the best thing they can do."

He was right, of course. George and I had some talking to do as well. But first I had to consider my reaction when Leo told me George never drank his sherry either—the fear and dread that coursed through me when I realized he might be the target of a killer rather than Leo.

Before I could bring it up, there was another knock at the door. Crocker.

"I have a note for Lady Harleigh, sir," he said, presenting it to George on a silver tray. George took the note and handed it off to me. Breaking the seal, I looked up to see him watching me. He indicated the card in my hand. "Who sent the note?"

I gave him an ironic smile. "Bradmore." I read the two lines it contained. "Surprise, surprise. Lady Esther is unable to receive us today." I handed the note to George. "When Leo is through with Treadwell, we still need to discuss that trap you spoke of. To my mind, Bradmore is still a good suspect."

Chapter 17

I thought it best to keep my distance from Lily while she was still angry with me. I was certain George was right; she and Leo would work through the problem of Treadwell as George and I would work through the issue of his secrecy. But for the moment, I thought it best to keep my distance from him as well. At least until some of my anger had subsided.

In an effort to distract myself, I visited with Rose again. We set her puzzle aside in favor of her geography lessons. Rose had been progressing quite well in her studies with her cousin's tutor, but it might soon be time to send her to school. While I contemplated the pain of that separation, someone knocked at the door and Nanny opened it to George.

He gave me a tentative smile. "Crocker inquired as to whether you'd like luncheon and where you'd like it served."

"Why is he asking me rather than your sister?"

"It seems she and the other guests have gone off for a ride and are taking their meal in the village."

There was a glint in George's eye that made me think he was up to something. "Well, then, yes, I would like luncheon, and the dining room would be just fine."

"Excellent." George presented his hand, and I placed mine in it automatically. "Let's inform him."

I glanced between him and Rose, who watched us with a rather indulgent expression. "Now? Must we both inform him?"

He brought me up to my feet. "I think that would be best."

Still suspicious of his motives, I gave Rose instructions to carry on with her geography book and followed him out the door. He flashed me a grin as soon as it shut behind us.

"We may be about to get our first lucky break, my dear."

"How so? Why do you look so suspicious?"

"All the guests are gone, and they won't be back until after lunch."

"Yes. I suppose Alonzo and Miss Kendrick's ride grew to larger proportions. What of it?"

"Everyone is away for at least another two hours, leaving us the perfect opportunity to search the house."

I felt a rush of excitement, followed by confusion. "Looking for what?"

"Arsenic, for one thing. If there's anything else to be found, I hope we'll recognize it when we see it." He held up Mrs. Ansel's keys and gave them a jingle.

This man surely knew the way to my heart. We nearly skipped down the stairs to the guest rooms, stopping first at Arthur Durant's. George found the right key and pushed the door open, revealing a room as sterile as the man himself. Clothing neatly stored in the dressing room, brushes and comb laid out on the dresser, shaving kit by the washbasin. Paperwork, his own notes, and letters of business were scattered on a small table near the four-poster bed. A pitcher of water and an empty glass stood beside them. Nothing under the bed or mattress, no notes in his coat pockets, and no conveniently hidden package of rat poison.

I waited while George finished with the drawers in the chest. "I suppose I understand why you didn't tell me you hadn't finished your sherry, but weren't you worried you might be the target of some assassin?"

"We don't even know for certain if the arsenic was in the sherry and no, I wasn't worried."

"Why not? You could be in danger."

"Hardly."

"Think of your line of work, George. You are something of a spy."

He gave me a hard look. "Investigator."

"If you prefer, but you must have been responsible for interfering with the criminal activity of several people. Have you never had to provide evidence in court? Has no one threatened you before?"

He pushed close the bottom drawer and came to his feet. Leaning a hand against the surface, he faced me. "Most of my activities have been covert. No one knows of my involvement."

"Most?"

He sighed. "Rarely, and only early in my career, did I have to come into the light and give evidence. And yes, I have been threatened by the guilty parties before—on two occasions, and both men are serving long prison terms. They can threaten all they want, but there's nothing they can do to me from behind bars."

"Now that I've mentioned the word *assassin,* I can't get it out of my mind. What if they hired someone to hunt you down? Treadwell? We don't know much about him. Or Bradmore, of whom we know even less."

He held up his hands in a conciliatory gesture. "An actual assassin would not be so clumsy. I would most definitely be dead."

"If you are trying to reassure me, you're going about it all wrong."

He gave me a sheepish grin. "Forgive me. All I mean to say is if a single person is creating all these accidents in an attempt to murder Leo, or me, he is definitely an amateur of the worst kind. And if we continue the assumption that the arsenic was conveyed to the footman through the sherry, your favorite suspect, Bradmore, was not around to poison it." He heaved a sigh. "I still don't know if all the incidents are connected. They appear to be, but if so, the culprit is someone who has no idea what he's doing."

"That reassures me. I'm glad to hear there's no one from your past who could come after you."

He tossed his head as if shaking off a bad memory. "And I'm glad it's in the past, that I don't do that type of operation any longer."

"What type?"

"Where I insinuate myself into the criminal's life, find out what he's doing and how, collect evidence, and turn it over to my superiors."

"And you dislike it because of the danger it puts you in?"

"Because there are always other people in the criminal's life. A wife, children. There was one case where I became very friendly with my target's family." He shook his head. "The man was a police sergeant running a ring of thieves."

"Good heavens! What was your role in bringing him to justice?"

"I became a police officer, placed in Sergeant Bracken's division."

I must have heard wrong. "You were a police officer?"

"Not a real one. It was just a ploy. They needed someone to work with Bracken and find out what he was about." A shadow of regret clouded his eyes.

"It took about a month before I reported to a call with him. Prior to that, he'd been testing me. I gave every impression I would be his willing pawn, and eventually, he rewarded me by taking me on a call with him. I kept my mouth shut when he didn't bother to go through the proper motions of an investigation. After we left the house, he pulled me aside and asked me point-blank if I was with him or not."

George shuddered. "He would have killed me then and there if I'd said no. Fortunately, my orders were to pledge myself to whatever plan he suggested, so I did." He leaned against the wall, arms crossed over his chest. "As it turned out, he wasn't just looking the other way when one of these break-ins happened, he was scheduling them."

"What do you mean by *scheduling them?*"

"The constables who walked the streets were friendly and chatty with the residents. They'd let him know when a home was vulnerable. The thieves would pose in all manner of jobs. Sometimes they'd get themselves hired on to the staff, but most of the time it was as a deliveryman. Coal, milk, produce, whatever could get them into the house long enough to unlock a window."

"That's where you learned that trick. With so

many people involved in this enterprise, you must be proud to have put an end to it."

He frowned. "When he was imprisoned, his family were left with nothing and no means of support."

I placed my hand on his shoulder. "But you had to stop him."

He gave me a sad smile. "We did, but it gave me no pleasure, no satisfaction. His family didn't ask for such a life." He pushed away from the wall and put his hand over mine. "Enough of that. It's in the past. Suffice it to say, I don't think anyone is trying to kill me."

I nodded. "All right. That will do for now."

We let ourselves out of the room into the hallway where George produced the ring of keys from his pocket and relocked the door.

"One down," I said, trying to sound cheerful. "Eliza's room is just here." I turned the door handle, and finding it unlocked, stepped inside. I felt George's hand sweep past my arm, but I'd moved too quickly for him to stop me.

"Can I help you, my lady?"

Eliza's lady's maid stood before a highboy, a stack of clothing in her arm and a look of surprise on her face. That's why the door was unlocked. Bother! I gave her a bright smile. "Ah, there you are."

She blinked. "You were looking for me, ma'am?"

"Well, no, not I, but I understand my maid has been." I stepped forward and took the shirtwaists from her arm and laid them on top of an open drawer. "My dear, you work far too hard. Bridget, my maid, and Mrs. Ansel have a lovely tea laid out in her sitting room. Bridget had hoped you'd join them."

The young maid's hands fluttered to her chest. "Why, how very kind of her." Her glowing face transformed to an expression of confusion. "Were you looking for me on your maid's behalf?"

I released a little tinkle of laughter, placed a hand on her shoulder, and guided her to the door. I assumed George had taken himself somewhere out of sight. "No, I was just passing by when I heard you in the room." I waved my hand. "A happy coincidence."

"You heard me folding clothes from the hallway?"

"I have excellent hearing. Now your mistress should be gone for another hour or so. You ought to take advantage of this rare time off-duty."

She gave me a careful look, along with a curtsy, and headed down the hall to the servants' passage. She cast a single glance over her shoulder, but when I nodded encouragement, she pushed through the door and was gone.

I released a sigh and stepped back into Eliza's room. I'd no sooner reached the bed when George popped his head around the door. "That was the most ridiculous story I've ever heard," he said, closing the door behind him and heading to the highboy.

"What was I to do? Back out and pretend I'd walked into the wrong room? I don't keep a list of falsehoods at the ready for such occasions, but if we were to search this room, we had to get her out of here on some pretext or other."

I glared while he struggled to hold back a snicker. "I'm sure you could have done better, but I didn't see you coming forward with a story of your own."

"Well, I wouldn't have sent her below stairs to some fictitious tea. What happens when Bridget tells her she has no idea what the girl is talking about?"

"Bridget will always back me up no matter what I tell someone. And as for the tea, it is not a fiction. Bridget told me about it this morning." I sniffed. "They should have invited the girl in the first place. Then I would not have had to fib."

He raised his hands in surrender. "Then all I can say is, well done." He nodded. "I'll also remember Bridget will lie for you."

I'd slipped to my knees to search under the bed. "You needn't worry, George. I've always told you the truth." Leaning my elbows against the bed I frowned, wondering if that were true. "At least I think I have."

He released a bark of laughter as I glanced

under the bed. Perfectly clear. Now for the mattress. While I ran my hand under the fluffy ticking, he pulled open drawers from the highboy. "Should I put away these shirtwaists, do you think?"

"Please do. I'd hate to give Eliza a reason to chastise the girl." Having found nothing, I came to my feet and headed for the dressing room next to George.

"What do we have here?"

I glanced at him as he unfolded a sheet of expensive vellum. He perused the note, let out a little sound of disbelief, and handed it to me.

Taking it from his fingers, I noted the upright script and the closing—*Yours, Ernest*—before reading the message. There could be no interpretation other than one of affection and intimacy between Eliza and the writer.

I let my hand fall to my side, still holding the note. "This is truly astonishing. I was under the impression they could barely tolerate one another."

"I'd say there is a good deal of tolerance involved, but it's all on Durant's side."

"Do you suppose he knows his wife is in love with another man?"

George tipped his head and narrowed one eye. "I don't know that love has anything to do with it."

I held the letter aloft. "He refers to Eliza as the

sunlight in his otherwise dreary day. A man only says words like that when he's in love."

"Or when he hopes to convince the lady to share his bed."

"Hmm, all right then. Do you suppose he knows Eliza is involved with Treadwell? They made such a display of their antagonism, I suppose it was to mask their relationship." I let out a groan. "His attentions to Lily. Do you think that was just a ruse as well?"

"Either that, or he used Lily to make Eliza jealous."

I leaned back against the wall, considering their actions over the past few days. "That might be it. Eliza was able to ignore Treadwell until he became attentive to Lily. That's when she'd snap at her sisters or make some waspish comment to him. She was jealous. Perhaps her rendezvous with the under-butler was an attempt to pay him back."

"I think we can say your sister is safe from Treadwell. By the way, do you know if Kendrick caught up with him this morning?"

"Indeed he did, and he gave him the thrashing you spoke of. Bridget told me she saw them out by the maze, and after a bout of fisticuffs, they limped back to the house like two old friends. Apparently, all is well between them again." I shook my head. "I still say he deserved it—playing with Lily's affections and dallying with Leo's sister."

George positioned himself beside me and crossed his arms. "So, Treadwell's a cad. How does that signify in this case?"

I pressed two fingers against my temples to stop the dull throbbing. "If the man would have an affair with Leo's married sister and romance his fiancée at the same time, he has an extraordinary idea of friendship. To me, that makes him rather despicable, and a likely candidate for a would-be assassin."

"Despicable or not, what would be his motive for murdering Leo? Their friendship gives him an excuse for at least occasional contact with Eliza. Given what we've just learned, I'd think he'd prefer Leo stay alive."

"And they do appear to be on good terms again. What about Durant?"

George rubbed a hand across his chin. "That's a bit more complicated. Is he aware of his wife's escapades?"

"Does he care? He and Eliza married because Mr. Kendrick favored the match. Durant thought that would gain him a partnership in the company." I shrugged. "I've no idea why Eliza agreed."

"If Durant sees Leo as standing in his way, he still has a motive. His wife's infidelity plays no role."

"Before we dismiss Treadwell, I suggest we check his room while we still can."

Treadwell's room produced nothing of any significance. If he received any notes from Eliza, he wisely chose not to keep them or at least he'd hid them better. As the rest of our party were set to return at any moment, we decided to end our search efforts for the afternoon. We separated at the door—George to meet with the gamekeeper to see about tomorrow's shoot, and me to my room, where Bridget was waiting to take me to task for involving her in yet another subterfuge.

I pled necessity, and before long she was chuckling about the incident. As it turned out she found Eliza's maid, Cora, to be a delightful girl, and I was right, they should have invited her in the first place.

With that settled, and my hair put back in place, I headed downstairs to see if anyone was about. I found my mother, Lily, and Mr. Bradmore in the drawing room. I bid them a good afternoon and asked if they had enjoyed their outing.

My mother, comfortably ensconced in the corner of the sofa, set down her embroidery and glanced up over the rims of her spectacles. "There you are, Frances. We had a lovely time in the village and came across Mr. Bradmore while we were about it."

I nodded to Bradmore and seated myself beside Lily, placing her between me and my mother. Bradmore sat across from us.

"You should have come along with us," Mother

continued. "I can't imagine what Hazelton needed you for. You are a guest here; you should be enjoying yourself. Isn't that right, Mr. Bradmore?"

Bradmore looked confused at being asked to weigh in. "I think Lady Harleigh never shirks her responsibilities yet finds time to enjoy herself."

Which meant the man was a coward and preferred not to take sides.

"Just what are your responsibilities, Mr. Bradmore?" Lily asked. "You are staying with Lady Esther now, but do you have a household of your own? In what part of the country do you reside?"

Coming from one as young as Lily, the questions were impertinent, but as I, and apparently my mother, were just as interested in the answers, neither of us reproached her. Instead, we turned our inquiring gazes his way.

He looked for all the world like a trapped animal. "I have rooms in London," he began hesitantly.

Lily pounced. "But I understand you are rarely in London. Where do you make your home?"

"I spend much of my time on the continent."

She gave him a cold smile. "Where, exactly?"

"Lily, have I not taught you better manners than this?" My mother was every bit as curious as her daughter. Bradmore was an unattached gentleman after all, and one who would be coming into

301

a title someday. Even though Lily was about to be married, Mother currently had two single daughters, and she'd love nothing more than to find out if he could be a potential son-in-law. While out loud she questioned Lily's manners, what she really meant was, hadn't she taught her daughter more artful interrogation techniques?

She didn't know Lily's motivation was of an entirely different nature. This man might be out to hurt Leo, and she would use any means to draw him out and put a stop to his plans.

Bradmore looked decidedly uncomfortable. "France?"

"Indeed? Where in France would that be? The Kendricks have a manufacturing facility somewhere around Strasbourg. Have you ever been there?"

"No. I have a cousin in Provence. We've been close since childhood, and I spend a great deal of time at his home with his family. I also have rooms in Paris where I go when I wish to take in the art or theater."

"Is that where you were before coming to the country?" I asked.

"No, I came up from London."

"On Sunday? I wonder if you were on our train."

He smiled politely. "My train arrived quite early Sunday morning. I understand yours was a few hours later."

Mother didn't chide me for my questions. She might be losing interest in Bradmore. Heir to a title or not, if he had no estate at which to settle down, and he spent his life wandering about the world, he would simply not do in her opinion. It did seem he had no plans to marry and start a family anytime soon. Men were inequitably lucky in that way. Unless they had to work for a living or run an estate, they were free to do as they wished. His life reminded me a bit of George's.

Except, of course, Bradmore might be a killer.

Chapter 18

⁓

A s it turned out, poor Clara, who'd started the whole ruckus about the ladies joining the shoot, was herself unable to participate, owing to her injury. So, bright and early the following morning, only three of us ladies gathered in the drive with the gentlemen. Lily had conquered her morning queasiness by sheer force of will in order to be at Leo's side and ward off any possible danger involved in the so-called trap to catch our killer.

"I must say, this is the most ridiculous plan I've ever heard. I have no idea why we're going along with it."

I gave my sister a "buck up" pat on the shoulder. Since last night, this was only the sixth or seventh time I've heard her opinion on the matter. While I shared the sentiment, the fact was, George and Leo were the principals in this scheme, and they considered it a lovely idea.

It took the better part of an hour last night for George to convince Leo someone might want to murder him, and it wasn't until George conceded that he might actually be the killer's target, that Leo agreed to participate. Today's shoot would take place on the Risings estate where at some point moorland, woodland, and pond converged. George and Leo would enter the woods on the pretext of cutting across to the other side of the pond in search of more coveys. George expected the killer to follow, and there, they and Tuttle would lay in wait for him.

That was the plan in its entirety—isolate the two men and hope the killer came after them. No wonder he hadn't told me about it sooner.

"It's not perfect, of course," George had said. "But we must try something to flush the killer out. I'm hoping he won't be able to resist a chance to take a shot at Leo. Or me," he amended when Lily shot him a glare.

I wasn't convinced. "It's nowhere close to perfect. What is to keep him from shooting you during the event? With birds flying, and gentlemen shooting, would anyone even notice until after you've been hit? You should call off the shoot and find some other way to flush this man out."

The four of us had debated the subject well into the evening, with George and Leo insisting the shoot must continue. Canceling would let the killer know we're suspicious. George also thought it a way to make the culprit show his hand, and now that he and Leo were on guard, they might very well catch the fiend.

"It's because we're women," Lily said, folding her arms in front of her, "that our logic is falling on deaf ears. If Hazelton told Leo the plan was ill-conceived, Leo would change his mind immediately, and vice versa."

"I'm not so sure about vice versa. I believe George is so stubbornly determined to shoot, he isn't about to let anyone stop him." Such determination was admirable, but it might also be one of those flaws Fiona had mentioned.

"I need coffee," Lily said, and wandered off toward one of the footmen attending the group gathered on the front drive.

George's boots scuffed the gravel as he approached. He looked even less rested than I at this early hour. "Have I mentioned I'd rather you not join the shoot?" He wore an expression of concern.

"Not in the last five minutes. I admire your restraint."

Another matter of contention between us was that George wanted me to stay at the house and out of danger. But on that point, I prevailed. That is if this was to be considered prevailing—out of my bed by six o'clock and dressed in sturdy boots, tweed walking skirt and jacket—almost, but not quite enough protection against the damp morning chill. Boisterous and eager gentlemen surrounded me, wearing tweeds and gaiters, and brandishing shotguns.

George held his under his arm. And he looked quite fetching in tweeds and gaiters. "If you are out there and shadowing Bradmore," he said, "I shall only worry about you."

"We settled this last night. You can't keep an eye on Bradmore, Durant, Treadwell, and Leo. You need me out there to take at least one of them off your hands. I choose Bradmore."

"I'm beginning to see you are very stubborn."

"All you have to do to dissuade me is call off the shoot. Even if someone weren't trying to harm Leo, or you, I don't know how this can be considered a safe pastime."

"Ah, but that's where you're wrong." His eyes took on a glow of excitement, and I knew I'd already lost the argument. "A shooting party is carefully orchestrated, my dear," he said. "With safety as the main concern. Guns are inspected, the men have all been instructed by Tuttle, which by the way, the ladies will have to go through as well. We walk through the fields side by side, send the dogs out to flush the birds, and shoot up at them as they fly away. It's drilled into us to honor the man beside us, or lady if the case may be. We shoot straight ahead or at least no more than forty-five degrees to either side." He raised his hands. "And there you have it. It's actually quite rare anyone is shot."

"That's very interesting, and I'm sure all of you will observe every possible precaution, but I am less worried about a stray shot than a deliberate one, aimed at Leo or you."

He nodded in concession. "That is a problem, I'll admit, but the probability is low. Should Durant, for instance, take a shot at Leo, everyone would be witness to it."

"Need I remind you we were all in attendance at the archery match, and no one saw a thing?"

"We don't have many options, Frances. I sent a letter to the Home Office explaining our situation, but as this seems to be a personal matter, I have no idea if they'd be willing or able to provide their assistance." He scrubbed his hands down his face. "In any event, I want to take action as soon as possible. I'll do my best to keep Leo safe."

"I want you safe too, which is why I'll keep an eye on Bradmore."

George raised his hands in surrender just as Tuttle, dressed in muddy boots and tattered hat, stepped up, carrying three guns. "If you'll be shooting today, my lady, I'll be giving you some instruction on the rules of the shoot and the handling of the gun."

"Thank you, Tuttle. I won't be shooting today, but those ladies will." I nodded toward Lily and Anne, just a few feet away.

He pushed his soft cap aside to scratch his head, exposing a patch of thinning gray hair and a broad expanse of scalp. "You'll be missing all the fun if you don't mind my saying."

I laughed as George made a show of clearing his throat while he threw the older man a glare.

"I do plan to join you. I just won't be shooting."

He nodded and stepped off to collect Lily and Anne for their instruction. I turned to George. "Apparently, Tuttle has no problem with women joining the shoot."

"Neither do I, under normal circumstances. Actually, I am surprised you aren't shooting."

"I considered it, but feared my skills wouldn't be up to snuff, and my suspicions might cause me to shoot one of our suspects in the event they made any sudden moves." I ended with a casual shrug. "As a result, I thought it safer not to carry a gun."

George shook his head, still frustrated with me, but as he was called away to attend to some other matter, he could offer no further protest.

"Franny!" I turned to find Alonzo at my side, looking quite the sportsman in his hunting gear. "I'm delighted you've decided to join us. This has been great fun. I love these country gatherings. Don't you? I spend almost all my time in the city, so this is quite a treat for me." He gave me a wink. "I, for one, am delighted Lily changed the venue for her wedding."

He did look quite delighted. In fact, right now he reminded me a great deal of Leo, unabashedly thrilled to be tromping around in the countryside for a change. Well, Lily had said she hoped to find a man like our father or brother. It seemed that's just what she found.

"I'm glad you're enjoying yourself, Lon. Perhaps you'll consider extending your stay."

He sighed. "I don't think that will be possible. But another visit, and soon, could be in order. By the way, would you like to join Miss Kendrick and me?" He glanced around at the crowd. "Have you seen her?"

I nodded toward the edge of the drive. "Here they come now."

The gamekeeper had apparently approved Lily and Anne for shooting, and the trio was coming to join our group. Lily was dressed similarly to me, but Anne had surpassed us in style. Unlike the men's soft caps, her dark hair was topped with a small, very chic wool fedora in a herringbone pattern, which matched her jacket and waistcoat. And instead of a heavy skirt, she wore wool bloomers with gaiters covering her lower legs. Indeed, she looked the perfect advertisement for the sporting countrywoman. I chuckled as Alonzo's jaw dropped.

He finally closed his mouth as she joined us. "Miss Kendrick, it looks as though you always planned to join the hunt," I said, as my brother was clearly speechless. "You have outdone us all."

A smile lit her brown eyes. "Let's just say I had hopes, and I thought it best to come prepared."

Tuttle brought us to attention, announcing the arrival of the carts. Heavens, this was quite

310

rustic. George stepped up to assist me in climbing aboard.

As I took his arm, he bent close to speak to me. "Bradmore will be in this cart. You should join him. Since you'll all arrive together, you're more likely to be shooting near each other."

Well, that almost sounded like a vote of confidence. Perhaps he thought I'd be of some assistance after all. "Thank you, George. I promise not to do anything reckless. I know I can't expect the same from you, but please try not to make me worry."

"I'll do my best. And though I appreciate your promise, it won't stop me from worrying about you." He leaned in to whisper in my ear. "Just be careful."

Alonzo and Anne squeezed in beside me, with Nash and Bradmore seated across. Soon we were bumping along the rutted track out to the farthest fields on the estate. Anne leaned around Alonzo to catch my attention.

"Lady Harleigh, I haven't had much of a chance to speak with you about this, but I do hope you don't believe Durant's talk that it was my arrow that felled Mr. Evingdon."

My gaze darted to Mr. Bradmore, to see how he reacted to this bit of information, but his expression gave nothing away. I smiled at Anne. "I never did believe that rumor, Miss Kendrick, if it ever was a rumor. Mr. Durant was most likely jealous of your skill with the bow and arrow and simply teasing you."

"If it was teasing," Alonzo said, "it certainly grew out of hand. No one who saw you hit the bull's-eye so accurately could think you'd let fly an errant shot."

"And we all know you wouldn't have done it intentionally." Nash's eyes were sparkling with amusement.

"Of course not," I said. "No one would think *you'd* hit Mr. Evingdon intentionally." Again, I cast a pointed look at Bradmore. He'd been in the maze after all, where the arrow had been shot.

He leaned back when I'd placed emphasis on the word *you*. He wore a look of confusion then squared his jaw and crossed his arms over his chest as if affronted.

Anne chuckled. "I just wanted to make sure you all felt safe with me since today I am carrying a shotgun."

As our cart mates laughed, Bradmore and I carried on our silent confrontation. I hoped he knew I'd be watching him. We scowled at one another as we continued the short bumpy ride. We reached the edge of the wood, alighting from the cart in the short grass, which grew taller as the field stretched out before us. Now I understood why the sport of shooting took up half a day. The area was vast, stretching out to a pond far in the distance.

As George anticipated, we paired off and met up with our loaders. I stayed with Alonzo and Anne, while Nash and Bradmore, along with their loaders, were stationed just a few yards away. Farther to my left, the group from the other cart filled in the space between us and the woods, with Leo, Lily, and George at the farthest end.

Even with my concerns, I couldn't help but enjoy this moment, and I could see why the gentlemen loved this so much. In the early-morning chill, a mist floated above the pond and worked its way into the trees and brush, only clearing perhaps a hundred yards around the group of us. A few workers from the estate drove up in yet another cart with a small pack of dogs.

Alonzo leaned toward me. "Some of the dogs will stand on point when they find the grouse. Others jump into the grass and flush them out." He shrugged. "I haven't been able to figure out which are which, as sometimes they just run around and bark. I suppose it's part of the tradition."

He let out a laugh as the dogs jumped out of the cart and gamboled into the grass.

"If the dogs don't flush out the birds, what do you do?"

"We just walk forward, into the tall grass. That stirs them up, and as they fly off, we try to shoot them, with the emphasis on *try*. Grouse are small and fast. I'm not sure I've actually hit any yet. I'm too enthralled by the sight of it all."

He was correct. The birds, which were quite small, but very noisy, took flight the moment we stepped into the field of scrubby grasses and heather. Mr. Tuttle had certainly done his job as, between dog and man, every few yards we advanced sent half a dozen of the creatures shooting skyward. The silence of the morning gave way to the flapping of wings, shrill chirping, and gunshots. As the day warmed and the mist dissipated, loaders scrambled to keep up with the shooters as we moved steadily forward toward the pond. More birds took flight, and round after round was fired, until all that remained was the echo of gunfire, gray wisps of smoke, and the smell of gunpowder.

About fifty yards from the pond, Tuttle called for a halt while the dogs and their handlers retrieved the birds, and the shooters clapped one another on the back. The activity was exhilarating, exciting, and absolutely horrifying. Those poor birds. Though I could see an overwhelming majority of them managed to escape, I didn't think I could ever bring myself to eat grouse again. Unfortunately, considering how many were shot, I was quite certain it would be on the menu this evening.

I shook off the thought and looked around for my quarry. Bradmore. I spotted him in the group of gentlemen to my left, drinking from their flasks and debating who was the best shot. Throughout the morning, I'd kept an eye on Bradmore, and though he'd fired his gun a few times, he seemed more preoccupied with watching the proceedings. I'd even caught his eye once or twice. He'd given me a nod and returned to his observations. What was he about?

Lily slipped up to my side. "There's not much more ground to cover before we reach the pond. Should we make one more attempt to talk them out of their plan?"

I put an arm around her shoulder and gave her a squeeze. "I'm sorry Lily, but at this point, I suppose we have to trust them."

Tuttle called us back to order, and we moved forward once more. We cleared the final yards in no time at all, and the dogs were set on the pond to retrieve their master's kill. Amid their barks and splashing, and the huzzahs of the gentlemen, another shot rang out, startling us into silence.

A shriek rent the stillness of the air. I jerked around toward the woods to see Lily drop to her knees as Leo collapsed onto the ground, clutching his arm. A look of shock and pain contorted his expression.

Dear Lord! It wasn't supposed to happen this way. From the corner of my eye, I caught a flash of movement. Bradmore, running toward the woods.

Chapter 19

~~~

George left Leo in Lily's care and ran after Bradmore. I hesitated only a moment, but as the men in our party ran toward Leo, I clutched Alonzo by the arm. "Come, we have to follow George."

The mist had long since lifted but the men we trailed, in their gray and brown tweeds, were difficult to spot among the trees. Fortunately, the racket they made crashing through the woods made them easier to follow. I gave thanks for the sturdy boots I'd put on this morning. Another silent message of gratitude went out to my brother who at first followed me without question, then pushed ahead, guiding me and making way through the brush.

I heard a grunt and a thud up ahead just before we stumbled into a small clearing. George pushed himself up from the ground, his hand wrapped firmly around Bradmore's ankle. Bradmore himself thrashed about, facedown in the brush with only his kicking legs in the clearing.

He managed to twist himself around enough to shout over his shoulder, "Turn me loose, you dolt! He's getting away."

Alonzo pushed past me to help George subdue the scrapping man. Between the two of them, they pulled Bradmore from the grass and undergrowth, and dropped him on the damp leaves in the clearing. Alonzo knelt behind him to take hold of his arms while George leaned an arm against a tree to catch his breath.

"What the hell's the matter with you, Hazelton?" Bradmore's face, red and scratched from the brush, was the picture of impotent rage.

I emerged into the clearing. "He said someone is getting away, George."

"A ploy, Frances." He straightened and glared at the man. "You're the only one I saw running, Bradmore."

"Yes, running after the shooter."

George shook his head, ignoring the man. "Frances, go back and find Tuttle. He should have some rope on one of the carts. Have him bring it back here."

Bradmore shook his head in disgust. "You're an idiot, Hazelton."

I took a step away and turned back, battling with indecision. It had seemed as if the shot had come from the woods and Bradmore had definitely been in the field at the time.

"Frances, hurry."

Somehow this felt very wrong, but I didn't think now was the time to question George's judgment. He knew what he was doing. I left the three men in the clearing and stumbled through the path of broken limbs and trampled brush to make my way back to the field. Tuttle had managed to bring the chaos into some sort of order. Leo had been loaded onto one of the carts with Lily seated next to him, pressing a bloodied cloth against his shoulder. He appeared pale and shaken, but relief washed through me to see him alive and sitting up, though leaning heavily against my sister.

I spotted Mr. Tuttle across the field, shouting orders to the estate workers as they rounded up the dogs and herded the gentlemen to the various conveyances. By the time I reached him, Leo's cart was already heading back to the manor.

He pulled his cap from his head and wrung it in his hands. "My lady, did Mr. Hazelton catch the shooter?"

Breathless, I nodded. "He needs a length of rope to secure him, and we should leave one of these carts for conveying him back to the manor."

"Are Mr. Price and Mr. Hazelton all right?"

I turned to see Anne behind me. "They are both unharmed, but I must hurry. Miss Kendrick, if you can arrange to clear one of the carts for them and try to get everyone out of here and back to the manor, I would be in your debt. And Mr. Tuttle, if you can find that rope, I must take you to them."

Within minutes Tuttle and I were crashing back through the woods to the clearing.

With the gamekeeper's assistance, they bound the protesting Bradmore's hands and walked him back to the field. As they dragged him into the cart, I couldn't help thinking we were missing something. By no means did I trust Bradmore, but I didn't believe he fired the shot.

Bradmore remained silent on the short ride back to the manor. George directed Tuttle to drive the cart up to a door in the north wing. He unloaded Bradmore from the cart and pulled him through the door that led to the estate offices. Once inside, Alonzo offered to fetch the authorities.

With a shove from George, Bradmore fell into one of the guest chairs near the desk. "Not just yet." He offered Alonzo his hand and slapped him on the shoulder. "Thank you for your assistance back there. I'll send word to the constabulary shortly, but I have a few questions for the man first."

Hoping George would forget about my presence, I slipped into a chair by the bookshelves, as far away from Bradmore as the room would allow. George walked Alonzo to the door. He held it open as he looked around the room. Spotting me, he raised an eyebrow and gestured to the door. "Frances?"

"No. I can't allow you to question this man on your own. If you are not sending for the police, I shall stay here with you as a witness."

"He is bound, Frances. He can't harm me."

I came to my feet. "Then he can't harm me either. Besides, I am more concerned that in your anger, you may do something you will come to regret."

"Ha!" Bradmore's laugh was mirthless. "Thank you, Lady Harleigh. I too think Hazelton will come to regret his actions."

"This is not a matter for debate." George's voice was more of a growl.

"Good, because I'm not debating. I'm staying here, and that's final."

Bradmore tossed his head in a show of bravado. "Let her stay, Hazelton. Unless, of course, you plan to bring out the thumbscrews." He cast an ironic glance at me. "That would be a sight you'd rather not see, I'll wager."

George closed the door with an impatient shove and crossed the room in three strides. "Who are you? And just what is your quarrel with Kendrick?"

Bradmore released a long sigh. "I have no quarrel with Kendrick or anyone else in your party. My name is indeed Bradmore, and I am here at Her Majesty's behest."

I glanced at George to see this had taken him by surprise. Bradmore noted our reactions with a mocking grin. "I'm in the queen's service, and I'm given to understand you are as well." He tipped his head and narrowed one eye. "In a roundabout way, that is."

George crossed his arms over his chest, watching Bradmore with a wary eye. "Do go on."

"The order didn't come directly from her of course, but the Home Office."

"What has the Home Office to do with my brother's estate?"

"*You* are on your brother's estate, and I understand you recently received a threatening letter. While you chose to ignore it, the Home Office did not. I am here to keep a watch over you. Make sure no one follows through on that threat."

While Bradmore explained himself as if remarking on the weather, I groped for the chair beside me—something to lean against as a cold hand squeezed the breath from my lungs. Leo wasn't the target. It was George. *My* George. Bradmore's words barely penetrated the fog in my head, but I heard and latched on to one. "Recently?" My voice rose to a shrill note. "The threat you mentioned was one you received recently? You told me it was in the past."

George ignored me and stepped closer to Bradmore. "Why should I believe that? You could be in league with Bracken. How do I know he didn't hire you to kill me?"

Good Lord, this just kept getting worse.

"Well, there's the letter I have from your superior at the Home Office, giving me this assignment." He raised his arms. "It's in the inside pocket of my coat."

George studied Bradmore a bit longer, then stepped over to the man and reached inside his coat. I bit my lip when he pulled out a folded sheet of paper. Heavens, was the man finally telling us the truth after lying about himself for days?

"Is Lady Esther even your aunt?" I asked. "Does she know you are here?"

"She is, and she does, though she has no knowledge of my assignment. I imagine that's the reason I was chosen. I could visit her home with no questions asked." He released a snort of a laugh, reconsidering his statement. "At least not many questions. I take it you've learned Lady Esther is in London."

I couldn't look at the man and turned to George who was still studying the letter. Finally, he looked up and cast a glance my way. "It's legitimate," he said. "Bradmore works for the Crown and was sent here to see to my welfare." Folding the page, he reached into the desk drawer and pulled out a pocket knife. He swiftly cut the rope binding Bradmore's hands. "Sorry, old man."

"Understandable, considering the circumstances." Bradmore rubbed his wrists.

"There is nothing understandable about this at all," I said. How could they be so calm? "Why did you not speak to us about your assignment earlier? You've been coming here for several days now."

Bradmore shook his head. "It's in the letter. My instructions were to make contact, join your party, and keep an eye out for any possible threats. As to why they didn't want Hazelton in on this mission?" He raised his newly unbound wrists. "I'm just pulling this from the top of my head of course, but perhaps they feared he'd take matters into his own hands."

George winced as the barb hit home.

Bradmore turned his attention to George. "At any rate, that business at the archery competition prompted me to send in a report about all those accidents, which were beginning to look less like accidents. I decided you and your guests were definitely in danger, and I should take you into my confidence. Their answer arrived today. I planned to speak to you after the shoot, when I could get you alone, but obviously, you had other plans."

I'd heard enough. Cold resolve stiffened my spine. All this time I'd been worried about Leo, and it turned out someone was trying to murder George. He owed me some answers.

"Who threatened you, George?"

He heaved a sigh. "The threat came from a man named Bracken. About seven years ago I was part of an investigation into his criminal activities. I told you about this. It was one of my first assignments."

"But you said it was in the past. You told me he's in prison."

George looked at Bradmore. "I thought he was."

"He's still in prison, all right," Bradmore said. "We checked up on him."

"You did?"

My head was spinning. "Stop. The two of you clearly understand one another, but I'm part of this conversation as well. Please back up and explain yourselves." I looked at Bradmore. "How do you know Mr. Hazelton received a threat?"

"Because he reported it."

"I'm required to do so," George said. "But I didn't expect them to take any action."

I gasped. "That's where you were headed just before you left town. The letter you dropped. It was from Newgate Prison. How could you have told me it was nothing?"

George held out his hand in a placating gesture. At least he knew how angry I was. "I wasn't trying to mislead you, Frances. I really didn't think it amounted to anything."

"The Office disagreed," Bradmore said. "Sent me to Newgate to speak to the old man. A cagey sort, but smug enough to make me suspicious. I thought the threat serious. By the way, do you recall he had a son?"

George stilled as if he'd stopped breathing for a moment. Finally, he nodded. "Jamie, a gangly, tow-headed lad. I'd say he suffered more punishment than his father. As a consequence of the man's imprisonment, the family was ruined. They lost not only his ill-gotten gains but his legitimate earnings."

"Neat little operation, from what I understand." Bradmore had relaxed by now and leaned back in his chair. "It's not unusual when a police officer is called to a burglary that he eventually files his report as 'lost goods.'"

"Lost, as opposed to stolen goods?"

"Exactly," George said. "Petty thieves, pick-pockets, and crime rings abound in London. The police could search for stolen goods for years and never find them. When something is stolen from a wealthy household, it's even more difficult because the culprit could be a family member or a servant with light fingers."

"But Bracken had a massive number of cases that were filed immediately as lost goods, with no investigation at all. It might have gone on longer if he hadn't run one of his sham investigations for the wrong person. Someone working for Special Branch called Bracken's division after a break-in. The victim knew the general procedure, so when Bracken and his constable didn't bother to interview the staff or the other members of the household, he knew something was wrong."

George took up the story. "The officer from Special Branch notified Bracken's superiors and caused quite a stir. That's when they looked through his cases. Bracken had been with the Metropolitan Police for fifteen years and had distinguished himself enough to gain his promotion. They suspected this wasn't just a case of poor police work. Something was up."

"That's where Hazelton came in."

I turned to George. "This was the case where you acted as a police officer. You must be quite an actor, George. What made him think he could trust you?"

"I was young and willing, still wet behind the ears as far as he could tell. Remember, I didn't know he was at the head of this crime ring. I assumed some crime boss had him in his power. He was a likable man. I was a new recruit. He invited me home for meals. I became part of the family."

"And you became close with his son." I could see it all now.

"Jamie was about twelve. Wanted to be part of everything, and his father involved him far more than he should have. In fact, it was Jamie who provided the last piece of evidence I needed to prove the case."

"And now he wants to kill you," Bradmore said dryly.

George came to his feet and rounded the desk to open the hidden panel and retrieve the decanter of brandy. Bradmore brightened at the sight. "Happy to join you in that, old man."

I stepped over to join the two men. "You may as well pour one for me as well."

He filled the glasses to the break and handed them round. Taking a deep drink, he leaned back against the desk and gestured to Bradmore with his glass.

"Just what makes you so certain young Jamie wants to kill me?"

"Newgate keeps a close eye on the prisoners and their visitors. Jamie, who by the way isn't so young any longer, used to visit his father three or four times a year. Those visits came to an end about six months ago, to be replaced by letters. When you reported the threat, we asked the guards about his correspondence. Sure enough, Jamie and his father mentioned a chap named Hazelton. The letters would have been read as a matter of course, and the prisoners know that, so there was nothing overt marking you for death, but combined with the threat you received—" He waved a hand. "Well, the department likes to watch out for their own."

"If the guards read the prisoners' letters, how was he able to send a threatening letter to Mr. Hazelton?"

Bradmore gave me a shrug. "Guards aren't impervious to bribery."

George pushed away from the desk. "I have a difficult time seeing the lad as a killer. And I doubt he sees himself that way. I expect he's after revenge. Maybe he even calls it justice. I'm sure he considers me as some sort of traitor. Bracken's partners in crime worried he would give them away to the authorities and threatened the family. If I remember correctly, they left London immediately."

Bradmore nodded. "Moved to Birmingham to live with the wife's relations. But they definitely came down in the world. It's his father's own fault, but I can see why a twelve-year-old might blame you."

"And now he wants to settle the score with me."

"Whatever his motives may be, his intent is murder. And he's hiding somewhere in the village or even right here on the estate."

"Damn!" George shook his head. "Everything does seem to point to Jamie, right down to the amateur execution of the accidents. At least we have that in our favor. He's clearly no professional."

The young man's lack of professionalism gave me no comfort. "I'd say he's gaining experience by the day, George. I wouldn't count on his ineptitude to keep you alive. If he's responsible for all the accidents—Michael O'Brien, Gibbs, Evingdon, Clara, and Leo—that means he's been in the house. He's either very stealthy or someone we'd expect to see here. Heavens, he may even have been at the train station." I turned to Bradmore. "Do you know what he looks like? How long he's been in the area? Where he's likely to be hiding?"

"No to all three. That's why I've basically been shadowing Hazelton, hoping to be on hand when he strikes. I suspect he's holing up somewhere on the estate, but all I can tell you with any certainty is that he was in those woods today. I caught a glimpse of a man in the woods, and might have had him if you hadn't tackled me."

George made a noise of disgust. "If the Home Office had alerted me, I wouldn't have had to tackle you."

"You know how they like secrecy."

I took a healthy sip of my brandy. "What do we do now?"

"I'd prefer you do nothing until after I stop by the constabulary and tell them what's what. Once I have, I'd like to return here and make this my base of operation. I'll need to keep a close eye on you."

George nodded. "We should have no problem finding a room for you as everyone else will be leaving."

"Leaving?"

He faced me, his expression drawn, eyes filled with regret.

"I've already risked the lives of everyone here, Frances. We must send them away to safety."

Chapter 20

C an't blame yourself, Hazelton." Bradmore
came to his feet and slapped George on the
shoulder in a show of male camaraderie. "How
were you to know the threat was serious?"

I gaped at the man. Was he joking? "I'd
have thought you'd take any threat to your life
seriously."

Bradmore swung around to face me, his hands
raised, palms out. "Don't be too hard on him,
Lady Harleigh. The letter did come from a man
in prison after all."

George held up a hand to stop the other man.
"Don't defend me. Frances is right. It wasn't
hindsight I needed but some foresight. I should
have considered Bracken might be behind the
accidents. Now look what's happened. Because
of me, one man is dead, and several more are
injured."

Goodness, both men had completely misunderstood me. "I'm not saying you're to blame for
young Mr. Bracken's mayhem."

"Perhaps not, but it's true, nonetheless. If I'd
paid more attention to the threat, all of those
people would be fine right now."

"Stop it." I stepped to his side and took his arm. "Your life is precious to me. When someone threatens you, you cannot simply shrug it off. Nor will you ever again hide such a threat from me. I shan't allow it. Perhaps I am a bit hysterical at the moment, but all I can think of right now is what I'd have done if the man had killed you."

"Instead he managed to hurt others. That's my fault."

"You're wrong. As much as I want to throttle you right now for lying to me about that letter, even I can see this is not your fault."

He blinked. "I don't recall lying to you about the letter."

"You used your customary evasiveness, saying you couldn't tell me about it, but we can discuss that later." I dropped his arm and jabbed a finger at his chest. "Right now, I want you to understand that you are not the one to blame for Jamie Bracken's actions, George. Both he and his father made their own choices."

Bradmore stood apart, one hand stroking his chin. "Frances and George, hmm? Like that, is it? You two have been very sly."

We both ignored the remark. I gazed into George's eyes and felt his pain. "You cannot exonerate me from all guilt, Frances, though I love you for trying. This was a mistake, one with tragic consequences. But the tragedy stops here. I want all innocent bystanders removed to safety at once. And that includes you."

"If you think I'm leaving you now, you had best think again. Someone needs to be here to make sure you have a care for your own life."

"Ahem."

We both turned to Bradmore. "That's all very well and good, but in the matter of who stays and who goes, moving everyone out of the house might pose some problems. At least one or two of your guests are injured."

"Heavens, that's right. I've forgotten all about Leo's injury. We don't even know how badly he's been hurt."

George was once again all business. "The doctor must have come and gone by now. If his injury is serious and we must make some other provision for his safety, so be it, but everyone who can leave should do so. We don't know where this man is, what he looks like, or where he'll attack next."

Bradford consulted his pocket watch. "I need to check in with the constabulary but I'll return this afternoon to see your guests safely to the station."

George nodded. "I'll see to organizing their transport."

"I suppose I'll go check on Leo and let everyone know they must leave at once."

"That includes you, Frances."

I made no reply as he followed me to the door. We could argue about this later, but with his life in danger, I was not about to run away to safety.

Since the guests would have to depart as soon as possible, George left to check with Mr. Crocker and Mr. Winnie to ensure everyone's belongings would be packed up, a train schedule consulted, and both guests and bags transported to the station in time to depart.

I headed up to Leo's room in the bachelors' quarters. For all I knew his life may have been hanging in the balance all this time, while the three of us had been downstairs, arguing over who was to blame for this tragedy. Anne answered my tap on Leo's door and beckoned me inside. The doctor had already left. Lily looked up from her station by Leo's bed. His chest rose and fell in a reassuring rhythm under the coverlet, but his skin looked as white as parchment against his dark hair. His lashes rested against dark circles beneath his eyes.

He didn't stir when Lily released his hand and, placing a finger against her lips, drew me to the opposite side of the room. I nearly wept to see my sister's eyes rimmed with red and shining with unshed tears. This was worse than I'd anticipated.

She shook her head, noting my anxiety and took my hand. "The doctor's given him laudanum for the pain, but he's likely to be fine, though he'll have a rather nasty dent in his shoulder."

"His shoulder?"

At my look of confusion, she continued. "Where the doctor removed the bullet. It caught him right in the muscle just below his shoulder." She tapped her own arm to show me the location.

"To think it almost missed him." She released a little huff of frustration and dabbed her nose with a handkerchief. "Though I suppose if it had, it just would have hit whoever was behind him." She raised her hands to her cheeks. "That might have been me."

"A bullet, you say? Not shot?"

"Not shot, so it wasn't Bradmore or any of the other gentlemen on the shoot."

I didn't bother pointing out any of the other gentlemen could have concealed a pistol in a coat pocket or somewhere else on their person. It just didn't signify at this point. We knew the shooter was Bracken's son, and though we had no idea what he looked like, he couldn't be Durant or Treadwell, and certainly not Bradmore.

"George and Bradmore are convinced the shot came from the woods, not the field. Bradmore was certain he saw someone running away."

Lily's forehead furrowed in confusion. "I take it Bradmore is no longer a suspect?"

What to tell her? "As it happens, he is out here hunting for the very man causing all this trouble.

We now know he isn't any of our party but he is on the loose somewhere on the estate, and George and I feel it's safest if everyone returns to London as soon as possible."

Anne had heard the last part of the conversation and joined us. "Are you saying some lunatic has been attacking the guests here? Is that what happened to Mr. Evingdon and Leo? What about Clara? Did she really slip in the hallway?"

Why did I never settle on a story before being confronted with questions? Especially now when I wondered how the young Mr. Bracken had managed to enter the house to set the trap that caught Clara—and poison the sherry. Did we have a second assassin? I dare not even begin to consider that possibility. Bracken must have found a way inside the house. Could he be posing as a servant? After interviewing the staff with Sergeant Fisk, I knew most of them had been here for years. O'Brien had been the most recent addition to the household staff. Ben was roughly the same age as Jamie Bracken, but he grew up in the village and had been employed at the house for years.

While my mind wandered, Anne still waited for an answer. Surely it wasn't necessary to tell the truth about Clara's accident and reveal she'd been visiting Alonzo? What happened to Leo and Charles should be enough to send everyone packing.

"I can't see how Clara's accident had anything

to do with this man," I said. "We believe he shot the arrow at Mr. Evingdon and took a shot at Leo. It's possible he caused Mr. Gibbs's accident and perhaps poisoned the footman. He's unidentified as yet and clearly unstable. I really think it's safer for all of you to return home, and Mr. Hazelton insists upon it."

Lily let out a groan as I turned to her. "I'm afraid you must make other plans for your wedding."

I read in her eyes what she couldn't say in front of Anne and pulled her into a hug. "I'm sorry, dear, but it's just too dangerous to stay here."

"All this planning for nothing," she said. Pushing away from me, she blotted her eyes and took a breath. "There's nothing to be done for it, I suppose. But what about the lunatic? Have the authorities been notified?"

"Bradmore is on his way to the constabulary as we speak. Mr. Hazelton is consulting with his steward to make sure everyone and their belongings make it to the station safely."

"I'll have my maid start packing, but I won't leave until Leo's able to travel. He'll likely sleep for the next couple of hours. We'll see how he feels then."

"Of course. We'd like to get everyone to safety as soon as possible, but I wouldn't dream of putting Leo on a train if it will cause him more harm."

"Is there something I can do to help?" Anne asked.

"Would you inform your sisters? Is Clara able to travel?"

"I believe she is, and yes, I'll get everyone packing." She gave me an encouraging smile and left to see about her task.

I turned back to Lily. "You stay with Leo, dear. I'll tell your maid the two of you will be leaving in the morning if not sooner."

"Will you tell Mother?"

I felt my entire body sag. "I'd forgotten about her. Yes, I'll tell her. With any luck, Aunt Hetty will be with her. I can't imagine her reaction to another change to your wedding plans."

"Well, just don't let her know you left me unchaperoned in Leo's room. She insisted Anne stay with me as it's unseemly for me to be here alone with my unconscious fiancé, you know."

"I'll try to distract her with the fact of a killer running wild on the estate. Will that do?"

It was good to see my sister smile again, even if it was rather sardonic. I left her with Leo and made my way through the gallery to the south wing, all the while thinking of the lunatic, as Lily had called him. Might he have slipped into the house to set the trip wire on the stairs? Was he so stealthy, or had he managed to steal a set of livery? Was he in the house now?

The thought sent chills down my spine and

quickened my steps. With a few backward glances, I arrived at my mother's room within minutes only to learn from her maid that she was in the drawing room with Lady Fiona. I would have preferred Aunt Hetty, but any buffer was better than none.

Back down the stairs, I arrived at the drawing room door just as my mother's plaintive voice rang out. "But how did the boy get shot? Didn't they all shoot into the air? You must explain yourself better, my dear."

To my surprise it was Hetty's voice I heard in reply. "A hunter didn't shoot him, Daisy. And it wasn't an accident."

"Of course, it was an accident, Hetty. You're speaking nonsense. People in the upper classes don't go around shooting at each other. They are far above the petty grievances that would cause such a thing."

Clearly, my mother hadn't paid much attention when meeting the members of the upper classes on her previous visit. I pushed through the door and took in the scene inside. Fiona appeared to be inching her way off the sofa as if waiting for any excuse to leave the room. My mother sat beside her, puffed up in her anger. Aunt Hetty, with her hands on her hips, loomed over Mother, ready to deliver a lecture.

I saved her the trouble. "Aunt Hetty's correct, Mother. It wasn't an accident."

Hetty released a little humph of satisfaction. "I'd wager the shooter was that Mr. Bradmore. Lily tells me Hazelton ran after him as if he were going to tear the man limb from limb."

Fiona's brows shot up. "Was it Bradmore, Frances?"

"No. In fact, Mr. Bradmore saw the shooter in the woods and gave chase. That's why Mr. Hazelton ran after him."

Mother sputtered in outrage. "What kind of gathering is this where the guests are shooting at each other?"

"Daisy, you are being deliberately obtuse." Hetty turned back to me. "Are you certain it wasn't Bradmore? He looked rather shifty to me."

"It wasn't a guest, and it wasn't Bradmore. In fact, Bradmore is actually here to find the culprit. That's what brought him to the country in the first place."

"Then he isn't Lady Esther's nephew!" Fiona was glowing with satisfaction. She did love being right.

"He is indeed her nephew, but he was never here to visit her."

"Is he some sort of police officer, like someone else we know?" Hetty gave me a wink. She was aware George did some sort of work for the Crown though she didn't know it all.

"Now you are being obtuse, Hetty." Mother

waved her arm as she spoke. "The man is a gentleman and will one day be a lord. He wouldn't lower himself to working with the police."

I felt a certain satisfaction in contradicting her. "As he came here on the hunt for this man, he must have something to do with the police."

"Don't be silly, dear. That can't be true." At my nod she drew back in her seat, head tipped to the side in a puppylike manner. "Frances, you just keep ruining all of my notions of the British aristocracy."

I thought it rather time someone ruined those notions, but I had more pressing business at the moment. "You are all straying from the subject, which is rather urgent, I might add. If you'll stop asking me questions, I'll attempt to explain everything I know."

Hetty joined Mother and Fiona on the sofa, and I revealed as much of the story as I felt I could. Rather than naming George as the target I characterized Bracken as being something of a murderous lunatic, prepared to kill anyone in his path.

"Which is why you must all leave as soon as possible before someone else is hurt."

They'd been so quiet and attentive up to this point, I'd hoped it would last, and the three ladies would calmly head to their chambers and see to their packing. Instead, they exploded into a heated argument, each talking at once, the words pelting me like pebbles.

Hetty cocked her head to the side, hands on her hips. "Surely we must hold the wedding first."

"I shall not let a lunatic chase me from my family home," Fiona declared.

"Leave? How ridiculous. Why don't they just catch the man?"

"That's right, Frances. If Bradmore is consulting with the police, why not just bring them to Risings and flush this man out?"

"Yes!"

"Exactly!"

My mother, aunt, and friend, each such different women, all wore the same expectant expression, waiting for me to work some magic and make this happen.

"I'm sure they plan to do something of that nature, but this man has been all over the property. He's even been able to access the house and kitchen. Mr. Hazelton is concerned for your safety. He is not asking, but telling you to leave."

"Why, I have never been so insulted." Mother rose to her feet and crossed her arms over her bosom. "This house party has been a disaster from the beginning. Hazelton should be ashamed of himself."

Fiona turned on her before I could say a word. "I beg your pardon." The words sounded as though they'd been chipped from a block of ice. She rose slowly to her feet and drew herself up until she'd stretched every aristocratic inch of herself, fairly towering over my diminutive mother.

"Just what do you mean by that? My brother has done nothing but graciously host your daughter's wedding party."

I considered intervening, but if my mother was too foolish to back down, then let them battle it out.

"He is simply trying to get into Frances's good graces," she said. "I shall have to give him another set down."

Hetty's head shot up. "Don't tell me you insulted the man while staying under his roof?"

Mother bristled at the suggestion. "It's not his roof but his brother's. And no, I've been nothing but polite to him. My set down was delivered years ago when he'd hoped to pay court to Frances."

An eerie silence reigned for the space of a heartbeat while each of us took this in.

We all found our voices at once. Hetty merely gasped, and Fiona railed something I didn't hear, for I was focused on one thing only.

"George wanted to court me? Back when I first arrived in London?"

"Can you believe it? A third or fourth son." Her smile grew smug. "I told him in no uncertain

342

terms you'd settle for nothing less than an earl." She tossed her head. "After all, there were no dukes available at the time."

"You turned away a man who was interested in me, who liked me, or at least was attracted to me, in favor of Reggie, whose only interest was in my dowry?"

Fiona and Hetty, who had the good sense to back away a few steps, watched us warily. Mother cast them a furtive glance. I didn't think Hetty could bring herself to side with Mother, and she'd burned the bridge to Fiona's sympathy just a few moments ago.

She took a step back and plopped onto the sofa. "Frances, dear, you make that sound like a bad thing. That was our plan, after all, to get you a title. And we succeeded. You became Countess of Harleigh. Why on earth are you turning on me now?"

I faltered. She was right that had been our plan. Well, it had been hers, but I'd jumped on board. I'd been so young and such an outsider in New York that my mother had been almost my only companion. I'd have fallen in with any plan she suggested.

"You must admit Hazelton has proven his unworthiness this week. The man can't even manage a house party. People are getting shot with arrows and with guns. Now we must call off the wedding and run away from a murderer.

What kind of life would you have had with such a man? You would never have been happy."

"May I remind you Hazelton is my brother and your host?" Fiona's face was so red, I feared an explosion from her.

I turned to my mother. "He is also your future son-in-law."

She huffed and slapped her hand against the arm of the sofa in frustration. "Frances, no! I could see the two of you had become friendly, but while I've given up on your sister, I'd have expected you to be more sensible. What could such a union bring you? You could do so much better."

Better? Gad, was she plotting again? "Don't even think about finding me another match. I'm not the young girl you married off ten years ago. I've grown up and have different ideas of marriage now. George is the man I love, and I believe he suits me perfectly."

"You're being emotional."

"Suitably so. It turns out Lily is the more sensible of your daughters. She followed her heart, and now I'll do the same. I've grown in the last years. I can think for myself and I know my worth—and I know Mr. Hazelton's worth. You are mistaken when you undervalue him. He is not the model of perfection I've often tried to imagine him, but he is the best of men, and I want nothing more than to share a life with him."

"Bravo!" Fiona brought her hands together as if she'd like to applaud.

Mother turned to Hetty. "Surely you agree with me."

"Not at all, Daisy. You have chosen the wrong audience. The three of us have a high regard for Hazelton, and when you rail against him, you offend us all."

"And you wrong him," I said. "He is intelligent and inventive, a kind man and master. Even his own brother's servants look up to him."

I smiled when I thought of how different George was from the usual lord of the manor. Rather than bark out orders, he asked the servants their opinions, relying on their expertise. He'd even shared a toast with Tuttle and Winnie. Tuttle clearly appreciated George's easy manner, though young Mr. Winnie seemed rather suspicious of it.

The argument continued around me, but I couldn't draw my thoughts away from that moment at the steward's cottage the other day when Mr. Winnie hesitated when George offered his hand, then only grudgingly shook it. George had noted it, but I'd thought it was just the reserve of a servant with his master. After all, it was a rare master who would offer his hand to a servant, and Winnie hadn't been employed at the house very long. He'd only just attained his current position and he was quite young.

Regardless, he'd worked dutifully for George.

He'd been very helpful, always on hand when disaster struck.

Always on hand.

He'd even been in the meeting several days ago. When George and Leo took, but didn't drink, their glasses of sherry. I pictured the scene. Durant had poured, but Winnie had helped Treadwell distribute the sherry.

A rush of fear made me unsteady, and I dropped into the nearest chair. Could John Winnie be Bracken's son? The young boy whose hate and resentment turned him into a twisted adult, seeking revenge? It couldn't be him, could it? Surely, George would have recognized him. But it had been seven years ago. Jamie had just been a boy. A towheaded lad, George had said. I thought of Winnie's attempt at a beard and the hair pomade he used. Could it make his hair darker?

I reviewed the scene of each accident in my mind. Winnie had been running from his cottage when Charles had been hit. His cottage directly behind the maze. When the steward had fallen, Winnie was right there. As an upper servant conducting business with the master, he'd have run of the public rooms of the house. It would be no difficulty for him to place the fishing line on the stairs to the bachelors' quarters. I remembered the servants I'd seen at the station, loading our bags. Winnie had been the man supervising.

I looked up to see the ladies gathered around me in concern. "Dearest," Hetty said. "Are you all right? You look so pale."

I came to my feet in a rush, not certain which way to turn. "No. I'm not all right. It's not all right. I must get to George."

"Not right now, dear." She gently pushed me back into the sofa and took a seat beside me. "I don't think you're well."

"I'll be fine, Aunt Hetty, but I must see George immediately." Before I could even come to my feet. I heard a fearful shout.

"Fire!"

Chapter 21

"Fire?"

All four of us shot up as one. Fiona, with a flustered waving of her arms, started first toward one exit, then turned and rushed back to the other, finally stopping in her tracks. She raised her hands helplessly. "Where? What is on fire?"

"The call came from outside," I said. My need to get to George became overwhelming. I feared I knew exactly where the fire was.

"Is there to be no end to the disasters befalling us at this godforsaken house party?"

Mother's expression turned to one of shock when I clutched her arm. "It's not in the house, I'm certain of that. All the same, go up to the nursery and make sure Rose is safe."

"Of course, but where are you going?"

Ignoring her, I rushed to the double doors that led out to the courtyard, hoping it was the fastest route.

"Frances, you cannot go running into a fire."

"She knows what she's doing, Daisy."

That was the last I heard before the door banged shut behind me. The soles of my boots bounced off the soft earthen path as I fairly flew through the rose garden. I rounded the north wing but didn't see the smoke until I turned onto the lawn. It wasn't thick or dark, but it was definitely smoke, and it billowed into the sky on the far side of the maze.

The steward's cottage. It had to be.

I tripped over a stone and fell against the evergreen boughs of the maze. The branches pulled at my hair and clothes as I righted myself and moved forward. Finally, as I reached the far corner of the maze, the cottage came into view. Smoke seeped through the cracks between the stones, up the chimney, and between the shuttered windows. Thin streams of smoke converged above the thatched roof and formed a cloud. The roof was smoldering, but I saw no flames. The fire must be inside as I knew George would be.

The cottage seemed to shimmer as I struggled to catch my breath. I clenched my fingers into fists and ran forward. This was not the time to falter. Mr. Tuttle called to me just as I reached the door. Ready to throw my weight against the heavy structure, I grasped the metal handle and shrieked as the heat radiated through my skin.

Blast! I shook my hand in the air only to find it captured by Mr. Tuttle who gave it a quick glance. "You'll be fine," he said. "Either the fire's not by the door, or it's not burning strong yet."

"Enough of me." I yanked my hand free of

his grip. "We have to get inside and the door's bolted. We need an ax or something to break it down."

Tuttle nodded and started jogging back to his own cottage. "Hurry," I called. "Mr. Hazelton is inside."

He turned long enough for me to see the horror on his face, then ran for his cottage at full speed. I couldn't stand here and wait for him. Every moment was precious. I tried to open the shuttered window by the door to no avail and moved along the wall to the next window, panic rising as precious seconds ticked by. I could hear the commotion in the distance, help coming from the house and the stables. I approached the window on the side of the cottage and this time luck was with me. The shutters were closed, but thankfully not latched. I pulled them open, releasing a wave of smoke and heat. Once it subsided, I stuck my head inside.

I'd found the fire. The desk which sat diagonally in the far corner of the room, was in flames that reached upward and flirted with the account and record books lining the wall behind it. A spark must have fallen to the carpet that ran the length of the room. Flames skittered across the rug and tickled the base of the door. Smoke blurred the entire room, but the worst of it rose like a thick fog lining the ceiling.

I finally looked down and spotted George on the floor directly below me, blood on his face and matting his hair.

My boots sought purchase on the stone walls, and I scrambled through the window. At least that was my intent. At the last second, something caught my ankle so tightly it had to be a hand. I kicked out and tried to flip myself over, but whoever had hold of me, was relentless.

"Frances, are you insane? Come out of there right now."

Relief washed over me. It was Lon. "Turn me loose," I shouted. "Hazelton is in here."

I must have startled him, and as he loosened his grip, I slipped through the window and slithered to the floor. My booted foot scraped down the wall as I used my hands to walk across the floor until I could flip myself over to see Lon's face in the window.

"What the hell is Hazelton doing in here?"

Thwack!

Heavens! Something nearly shook the little cottage off its foundation. Tuttle must have found the ax. *Thwack!*

Alonzo jumped at the noise. "What in thunder is that?"

"Tuttle is breaking down the door. Go help him."

The last bit came out amid a rush of hacking on my part. I was wasting precious air on this conversation. I gave my brother a glare and jerked my head toward the door.

"But, Frances—"

"Just go!"

With a mumbled curse he left the window, and I turned my attention to George. His heart beat against my palm. I leaned forward to feel his breath against my cheek. Pulling the handkerchief from my sleeve, I applied it to his face. With the blood cleared I found no cuts or gashes on his face. The injury must be to the back of his head.

"My poor darling."

Thwack!

Again, the walls shook with the force of the ax, bringing me back to my senses. I was inside. There was no need to break down the door. Gad, that's likely what Alonzo had tried to tell me.

I scrambled to my feet, trying not to breathe the hot, smoke-filled air. The desk and the shelves behind it were in flames. The fire had jumped to the carpet and sizzled across my path to the door, frighteningly close. It would seem they'd have to break through after all, but perhaps I could do something about the fire. The room opened to a small kitchen just off to my left. A wooden counter ran along one wall and on it stood a washbasin full of soapy water, a dishtowel, and a jug of lemonade. Beggars couldn't be choosers, I supposed. It was wet and not fuel; I'd try it.

When I stepped back into the main room, the

entire carpet was ablaze and heading toward George. I flung the contents of the dishpan at the flames, crockery, cutlery, and all. It made a hideous sizzle as blazing carpet diminished to smoldering carpet. The stench burned my nostrils and throat, but I now had a clear path to the door. Back in the kitchen, I took the remaining items. Covering my nose and mouth with the towel, I dumped most of the lemonade in front of me to ensure safe passage and poured the rest on the door. My boots squelched as if I were walking through a bog.

Thwack!

"Stop," I shouted through the louvers in the shutters. "I can unbolt the door." As they muttered some acknowledgment, I wrapped the wet dish towel around the heavy bolt and pulled it back. The door collapsed into itself with my touch. Tuttle and Alonzo drew back as the timbers crashed around them, then pushed their way inside.

I directed them past me. "See to George. I can get myself out."

Wracked with coughs, I stumbled down the steps and past a line of servants handing buckets of water up to the door, while Durant worked with a footman to connect a hose to an old pump.

"Lady Harleigh."

Anne hurried to my side. "Let me help you," she said, taking my arm.

"No." My throat was raw. "I want to make sure—" Another round of coughs ended my explanation. I pointed to the door where Alonzo and Tuttle carried George away from the cottage, now billowing smoke, though the buckets of water made their way inside.

Anne kept hold of my arm and helped me over to George's side, where he now lay on the ground, safely away from running servants and fire. Tuttle nudged me aside as he checked for a pulse, then turned George's head to the side to assess the wound.

"It's stopped bleeding," I said. "Is that a good sign?"

"He's had a good crack, all right, but I think what he needs most right now is air." The older man gave us all a look and tossed his head, indicating we should back away.

"Did Hazelton have a fall?" Alonzo tugged on my arm, pulling me away. "How did the fire start? What the devil happened, Frances?"

"That's what I'd like to know." The demanding voice behind me could belong to only one person.

I turned to face her. "Mother?" The word came out in a croak. In reaction, her expression changed from outrage to, well, outrage mixed with a bit of concern.

"What on earth happened to you? Look at your clothes. Look at your face. Look at your hands." Grasping my wrists, she held up my hands.

"Those are not the hands of a lady, Frances. What have you done?"

"You're supposed to be with Rose." My voice was now a gravelly whisper. "Why are you out here?"

She produced a handkerchief and proceeded to wipe at my face in a way she hadn't done since I was a toddler. "I sent Lady Fiona to the nursery. When my daughter runs headlong into danger, my place is with her." She waved the now-blackened handkerchief at a groom hauling a bucket of water to the cottage.

"You there! Bring that over here."

Startled, the young man complied, sloshing water as he hurried over. Mother dipped the now gray square of fabric into the bucket and returned to her ministrations. "Now, are you ever going to answer the question? What happened?"

"Yes," Alonzo prodded. "Did someone strike Hazelton?"

"Mr. Winnie must have." Heavens, I'd forgotten all about Winnie. What was I doing lingering here while he made his escape? I pushed my mother's hands away. "Have you seen Mr. Winnie since the fire started?"

I'd meant to shout the question out to the crowd, but only those nearby could hear my feeble rasping.

"You'll strain your voice, Frances. Take this." Mother opened a small tin and placed a lemon drop in my hand. She caught my stare as she secreted the tin away in her pocket. "I enjoy a sweet now and then. What of it?"

The drop eased the rawness enough to help me speak. "Alonzo, we must find Winnie. Go and ask around." He ran off as if pleased to have something to do.

"Begging your pardon, my lady, but I've seen him." It was the groom with the bucket of water, still standing by my mother's side, waiting for another order. "Saw him in the stables when I left to help with the fire."

Of course. He thought his work of revenge was complete. What better time to make his escape than while everyone tended to the fire?

I pushed away from my mother's support and glanced around to orient myself. There, the gamekeeper's cottage. The stables were directly behind it.

"Frances, surely you're not foolish enough to go after this man."

"You give me far too much credit, Mother."

I ran as fast as my boots, the terrain, my burning lungs, and my corset would allow, which was to say, not as quickly as I'd have liked. By God, if I made it through this crisis, I'd never wear a corset again. A crunch of gravel sounded behind me, and I threw a quick glance over my shoulder. My mother followed me at a much faster pace than I would ever have thought her capable. She had a handful of the groom's jacket and dragged him along behind. He still clutched the sloshing bucket.

We all reached the stables at the same time. Mother's chest heaved from her exertions. "Now what?" she asked.

An excellent question. Would Winnie have already made his escape? Time had seemed to stand still when I was in the steward's cottage with George, but in reality, I had no idea how much had passed. I leaned closer to the groom so I could whisper, "How long ago did you see him here?"

"Ten minutes. Maybe more?"

"Where?"

He nodded to our right. "Headed toward the loose boxes."

The stables were a long rectangle. We'd entered on the north side by the office and tack room. Farther down were the boxes for the horses and two doors suitable for driving a cart or carriage through. The near door stood open, the farther one, closed. We were likely too late, but we might just as well look.

The groom near my shoulder must have read my thoughts. "He'd have to saddle a horse, my lady, and collect the saddle and tack himself. Everyone's at the fire, so no one's here to help him."

We still had a chance. "Let's go then."

We scurried down the short hall and out into the open. At least a dozen horse boxes lined the wall to our left, a daunting number. Winnie could be in any one of them, or he might already have fled. A few horses pushed their heads over the half doors in curiosity as we scurried past the open door to our right. I heard Winnie before I saw him.

"Come on, you beast. We've a ride ahead of us."

A horse snorted in response. The groom tapped me on the arm and nodded to an empty box. I gestured to my mother, and we squeezed ourselves inside and out of sight. Though it didn't contain a horse, the box wasn't empty. We found it full of well-used straw and a pitchfork. I hadn't thought I'd ever smell anything but smoke again, but this refuse from the horse boxes proved me wrong.

The groom seemed remarkably unaffected by the stench surrounding us. He leaned close to whisper to me, "He'll have to pass by us or go to the trouble of opening the other doors." The clump of hooves on the wooden floor told me Winnie was leading the horse from his box.

"Steady, steady." Through the wall I just picked up the sound of leather stretching. Winnie, tightening the girth? He'd be mounting in a moment, then what? Would I let him ride right past us? The horse blew out a breath of air. The jingle of a harness rang out as he tossed his head. There was no time to wait.

I snatched up the pitchfork and strode out to the aisleway. And gasped at the sight I beheld. Winnie sat atop the largest horse I'd ever seen. Big enough to trample me without even taking notice.

"Frances, get back here." Mother hissed from her hiding place. But it was too late. Not only had Winnie seen me, but fear seemed to have frozen me in place. I couldn't move if I'd wanted to. There I stood like a statue of Poseidon, trident and all.

Winnie jerked in surprise at my sudden appearance and set the horse skittering to the side. "Don't block my exit, Lady Harleigh," he said, struggling to get the great beast under control. "I've done my job, and I'm getting out of here. I'll go right over you if I have to."

How had I ever thought him a nice young man? Anger helped me focus on him rather than the frightful horse. "He's not dead, Mr. Winnie. You've failed once again."

His brows drew together in a thunderous rage.

"I don't think you really want to kill him. Either you're not cut out to be a killer. Or you don't really believe Mr. Hazelton deserves your vengeance."

"Oh, he deserves it all right. He pretended to be my friend. Led me to trust him, then he betrayed my father and ruined our lives. He deserves to rot in hell for what he did." The giant horse became restless and skittered forward. Winnie took that as a signal to move. "He may not be dead, but I did my best, and I'm not waiting around for the constables to drag me off to jail."

He held up a finger. "I'm giving you one more warning. You'd best move out of my way."

Winnie gave the horse his heels at the same time my mother had heard enough. She snatched the bucket the groom had abandoned and, with a battle cry that would have done any ancient Scotts warrior proud, leaped out of the stall and flung the water into Winnie's path.

Her scream set the horse's ears back, and when the water struck him, he reared up on his hind legs, causing bile to rise in my throat as those hooves waved frighteningly close. Winnie fought for balance as the horse came back on all fours and danced around in the close confines. In a panic, the beast turned back to his box, I lunged forward and swiped at the young man with the pitchfork. I heard and felt a sickening thunk as the handle met with his head. Winnie lost his balance at the same time the horse twisted, sending the man spiraling off his back and into the wall. Sliding down, he landed in a heap on the wooden floor.

I rushed over to Winnie, my mother ran to my side, and the groom ran to the horse, snatching up the reins and making soothing noises to the frantic animal.

Winnie was just as frantic. While crashing into the wall had subdued him momentarily, he'd already scrambled to his feet. After all this trouble, I was not about to let him get away. I called on any remaining reserves, and by pure determination alone, I threw myself at him, quite literally.

We both crashed to the ground, but Winnie broke my fall, his rib giving way under my elbow. As I struggled to rise, his breath rushed out with a groan of pain.

"In here." Mother pulled open the door of a box, and we shoved John Winnie a few feet across the floor into the straw as a horse sidled away. Mother closed the door behind him.

Exhausted, we both sank down to the floor with our backs against the door, and spent the next few minutes breathing heavily until the groom, in a rage, stomped back into the walkway.

"That brute scared the wits out of poor Hector," he said.

It took a moment to realize Hector was the enormous horse, and the brute was Winnie. "He took a few years off my life as well."

The groom glanced up and down the stable. "Where is he?"

Mother jerked her thumb behind us.

The boy's eyes rounded. "You put him in with Satan?"

A gurgle of insane laughter bubbled up through my throat and emerged as a snort. "You had best go and summon assistance."

He gave me a nod and trotted off, back to the cottage, I assumed. "Perhaps Mr. Bradmore has arrived with the local authorities by now."

Mother heaved a sigh. "Mr. Bradmore. And just look at you. Your hair, your clothes, and I hate to say it, dear, but you have picked up a rather unpleasant odor from the floor. I suppose it's just as well you're not interested in Mr. Bradmore."

This time I did laugh, enough to make Satan snort and fidget.

"Stop that, dear, or there'll be nothing left of that man behind us to turn over to the authorities, and I do so want to see him brought to justice. You may laugh at me all you wish at some other time." She lifted her chin. "I've always tried to do my best for you children and I don't know why you all find that so endlessly humorous. I'm just trying to be a good mother."

"I'm not sure managing your adult children's lives is part and parcel of motherhood."

She tossed her head, causing another lock of hair to fall from her coiffure. "Well, then, I don't know what is."

I turned to her with a weary smile and placed my hand on her leg, palm up. She slipped hers on top, and I closed my fingers around it. "You came after me when I was in danger. You saved me from a charging horse and a madman at the same time." I squeezed her fingers. "You shared your hidden cache of lemon drops. You are not a good mother," I croaked. "You are the best."

Chapter 22

⟜ᔆᗡ

Bradmore returned, but without the constables we'd hoped for. Nonetheless, as the only person officially on the case, he wrote down our account of the incident for the local authorities. He then engaged the services of one of the larger grooms and dragged Winnie from the box where Satan had been as docile as any angel. Bradmore bound the young man and took him to the local constabulary in the village.

By the time Mother and I emerged from the stables, not only was the fire extinguished, but the groundskeepers were cleaning out the debris from the cottage. George had been carried on a makeshift stretcher back to the manor, though by all accounts he'd been conscious and grumbling all the while that he could walk on his own. Alonzo and Durant had countermanded his orders, insisting he'd walk when the doctor said it was safe to do so.

Mother and I parted at the door to her chambers. With her hairpins lost somewhere in the stables, her hair was half up, half down, and with the advantage of five inches in height, I could see all the streaks of silver mixed in with her golden waves. Her bodice was torn along the side seam from her exertions, and I picked away a few stray pieces of straw clinging to her arm. Still, her eyes were bright and her brow, for once, unmarred by disapproval.

"If I didn't know better, I'd say you enjoyed confronting a murderer. You are positively glowing."

She raised her brows and lifted her chin. "And just what makes you think you know better?"

With a pat on my cheek, she stepped into her room, turning back to me before closing the door. "I suggest you clean up a bit before checking on Hazelton, dear."

Hmm. Judging from her appearance, I could assume I looked—and smelled—even worse. It might be wise to at least bathe before visiting George, but frankly, I couldn't wait that long. Fiona told me he'd been taken to a room in the family wing just down the hall. The stairs to the bachelors' quarters had been deemed too difficult a climb for those carrying him. The doctor was still with him, and I hoped to hear from him personally as to George's condition. I knew George would pooh-pooh any cautions or restrictions Woodrow might advise.

His new room was right at the turning of the hallway. I gave the door a light rap with my knuckles before walking in. He lay in bed, his sooty clothing replaced with a robe, the sheet pulled up to his chest. He gave me a weak smile before Dr. Woodrow stepped between us, red-faced and blustering.

"Lady Harleigh, I beg you to remove yourself. Mr. Hazelton is in no state to receive visitors."

A movement in the bed caught my eye, and I peeked around the man blocking my way. George composed his face into an expression of misery, like a child pleading for a treat. I stiffened my spine.

"I am hardly a visitor, Dr. Woodrow. I am Mr. Hazelton's fiancée. Though I realize that is not the same as a wife, it's simply a matter of unfortunate timing. His care will be my responsibility, and I wish to gain an understanding of his state from your lips, sir." I glanced at George who now wore a boyish grin. "I'm not certain I can trust his version."

The doctor's lips twitched. He cast a glance at George who gave him a nod. "Well, then, Mr. Hazelton is to be congratulated not only on his impending nuptials but on the thickness of his skull."

"I've always considered it one of my best features," George added. His voice was surprisingly clear, with just a suggestion of the rawness I felt.

"That sounds rather like good news, Doctor. Please don't keep me in suspense."

"It is cautiously good news. One can never

tell with a blow to the head if there is internal bleeding or swelling, but at this point, everything looks good." Woodrow retrieved his bag from a chair beside the bed. "I'll want him to stay in bed this evening. I'll check back in the morning." He leveled a warning look at George. "If you continue without symptoms until then, you'll be free to do as you wish."

Woodrow gestured to me. "Lady Harleigh, if you please." He jerked his head toward the lamp. "I'd like to examine your throat."

I reluctantly moved into the glow of the lamp and obediently opened my mouth. After a minute or so of Woodrow turning my chin from one side to the other, he proclaimed I'd be fine in a day or two.

"Use a saltwater rinse," he advised. "And of course, send for me if you experience any pain."

I would have seen Dr. Woodrow to the door, but George called me back. "Frances, please stay."

I glanced at him over my shoulder. He wore such a beseeching expression that I could not deny him, and I must admit my heart tripped a beat or two at the thought that he couldn't bear for me to leave him. With a shake of his head, the doctor left, and I pulled a chair next to the bed. Seating myself, I took George's extended hand.

"Thank you for staying with me," he said. "Woodrow could tell me nothing of what happened, and while I recall some of it, there are far too many blank spaces."

So much for my romantic musings. I disengaged our hands and rose to loom over him. "Blank spaces? You poor dear. It must be terrible to be left in the dark when so much is going on." I poured myself a glass of water from the pitcher on the bedside table and took a few sips to ease my throat.

"Indeed." He looked somewhat bemused. "Will you tell me what happened?"

"Just exactly how would you like me to explain everything, George? In the same way you informed me you'd received a threat from a man you'd put in prison? Or maybe the way you told me you'd just shrugged off his threat? Shall I fill in your blanks in that manner?"

The corners of his lips inched downward. "You're angry."

"Well, aren't you a first-rate detective? Yes, I'm angry. We are partners. Yet you kept valuable information from me, and it almost cost us your life."

He at least had the sense to look sheepish. "Ah, yes. About that."

"Yes, George. Tell me all about that." I sat back down and folded my hands in my lap. Waiting.

"It was wrong of me. In many ways. I didn't take the threat seriously. Bracken was still in prison, so his note struck me as nothing more than impotent bluster. I still saw Jamie as an innocent, young boy. It never crossed my mind he'd come after me. As far as I knew, either the accidents were truly accidents, or Leo was the target. I didn't deliberately mislead you. I really couldn't credit that anyone wanted to harm me."

"Well, I suppose I could fill in your blanks." I gave him an offhand shrug, which brought the crooked smile I loved so much to his face.

"Please do. I'm eager to hear how you determined John Winnie was actually Jamie Bracken?"

I told him about my logic and that the answer had come just as someone alerted us to the fire. "I thought my heart would stop, George. I knew you were with him and felt certain he'd left you in that fire."

"Whacked me over the head the moment I turned my back on him. Since we were finally taking action, he must have seen this as his last chance." He frowned. "If the cottage was on fire, how did you get to me?"

I told him about climbing through the window after sending Tuttle for an ax to chop through the door.

He choked back a laugh. "Seriously, once inside you didn't think to unlatch the door?"

I straightened my back. "Things were moving rather quickly. I needed to assure myself you were alive, and need I remind you there was a fire closing in on us? I thought of it eventually."

By then he was laughing wholeheartedly, and I'll admit I was pleased to see him in this mood.

"I shall forever have an image of you wriggling through the window," he said. "And putting the fire out with dishwater and lemonade."

"It was wet and available. And it didn't put the fire out, just bought us a little time." I huffed in exasperation. "Are you truly going to criticize my methods?"

He brought my hand to his cheek. "You very likely saved my life. I shall never question your methods or your resources. I should have told you about the letter when I received it, and from this moment on, I shall trust you with my life."

Well. That brought on a warm glow.

"All right, I suppose I'll forgive you this once. But I want it understood this is never to happen again. I've already experienced a marriage in which husband and wife led separate lives. I won't do that again. You are never to keep things from me in the name of protecting me."

"You have my word."

"Then I'll marry you."

He sat up in alarm. "I thought that was already a settled matter. Was there still some question in your mind?"

"Not a question, exactly."

His brow furrowed. "Then what, exactly?"

Hmm, my turn for a confession. "I was a little worried that as your wife, you'd shut me out of your investigations—that you'd bid me to stay quietly at home."

He gave me a skeptical look. "I am under no illusion that I could bid you to do anything and expect you to comply. However, I may be forced to ban you from further investigations if you continue to outshine me as you did on this one."

I let out a huff. "My concern was in keeping you alive, not competing with you."

"Now you say you can best me without even trying." He paused, waving a hand toward me. "And you laugh at my plight."

Indeed, I was laughing—and coughing.

He reached out and took my hand. "I'll always want to keep you out of danger, but I'll also want you by my side. Surely we can find some middle ground that will satisfy your sense of adventure without giving me palpitations." His expression was so hopeful I had to smile.

"I believe we can. In fact, after this week, I see that you need me to keep you on your toes. If that's not reason enough to marry, I have yet another."

"I'll take every reason you have to offer."

"I've told my mother."

He pulled back, sucking air in between gritted teeth. "I can't imagine she approved."

"It doesn't matter if she does." I pressed his hand. "She told me she discouraged you from courting me all those years ago."

"Ha! That's quite an understatement. She made it clear I was not in contention for your affections."

"But why did you believe her? Why didn't you ask me?"

"I didn't know you then. I thought she spoke for you, and if she objected to me, would you have had the fortitude to defy her?"

A fair question. "I hate to admit it, but I'm not sure. Fortunately, I've grown up enough to think for myself."

"Dare I bring out the ring again?"

"You have it with you?"

He shrugged. "I carry it in my pocket. Woodrow put it in that drawer."

I opened the drawer in the bedside table and handed him the ring. He slid it on my finger and glanced up at me. "Are you certain? I can wait until we've had a chance to speak with your mother if you like."

"She already knows I intend to marry you, and while she objected at first, she seemed to be more amenable to the idea by the time I left her at her room just now."

"What changed her mind?"

I told him about the way we apprehended Jamie Bracken, which sent him into peals of laughter. "I think she realized I am every bit as determined as she is."

"You and your mother stopped a criminal with

a pitchfork and a bucket of water. The two of you are even more formidable than I thought."

I smiled. "And now it appears you have both of us on your side. Aren't you the lucky one?"

Bridget had a bath ready for me when I finally returned to my room. If only I could just lie in the hot water and have a good soak, but there was still so much to do. Yes, Mr. Winnie, or rather Mr. Bracken, had been taken into police custody, thus the threat had been removed, but did everyone know that? Not to mention the fire may have been the last straw for some of the guests. Had anyone already left? The only way to find out was to climb out of the tub.

Within half an hour, refreshed and dressed, I ventured out of my room to see what had happened with the rest of the guests. Crocker awaited me at the foot of the stairs to inform me that the guests were all still in residence, Mr. Kendrick was awake and planned to come down for dinner, and Mr. Bradmore had called and was waiting in the blue salon.

"Not the drawing room?"

"Mrs. and Miss Price are using the drawing room at present." His pursed lips told me they were likely using it for another of their arguments. I decided to see to Bradmore first.

"Lady Harleigh," he said, coming to his feet as I entered the salon. "May I congratulate you on a successful apprehension? I must say I'm impressed with the way you took charge."

"Considering you did your best to keep us out of it, I'm rather impressed myself."

He gave me a helpless gesture. "That wasn't my decision to make, and I had no idea you were conducting an investigation of your own."

"Didn't you?" I scoffed. "Even after I questioned you about your aunt? My, my, Mr. Bradmore, perhaps your detecting skills are lacking."

He grinned. "They are sharp enough for me to observe you and Hazelton are ready to make your intentions known." He looked pointedly at my ring. "I'm pleased to have the chance to wish you well before I leave. I'll be accompanying the prisoner back to London."

"Has he confessed then? All the accidents he orchestrated, were they meant for Mr. Hazelton?"

Bradmore cocked his head. "Not all of them. If he wanted to get close enough to Hazelton to cause a fatal accident, he had to eliminate the steward first."

"Of course. With Mr. Gibbs supervising him, he'd never have been able to set his traps. He'd have no reason to be in the house either." I heaved a sigh at the thought of the mayhem the man had caused. "How did he manage to poison the sherry?"

"A packet of the stuff in his coat pocket."

"And none of us noticed."

"From my understanding of the situation, it was a celebratory moment. You had no reason to be on your guard."

"I don't suppose he mentioned anything about a luggage cart at the train station."

He lowered his brows. "No. Should he have done?"

"That might have been an accident. We may never know." I blew out a breath. "What a misguided young man."

Bradmore nodded. "He's been stewing about his father's arrest for years now. And every time he visited Bracken in prison, the man would stir the pot some more."

"I've been wondering why Winnie, I mean Bracken, didn't pursue Mr. Hazelton in London. Wouldn't that have been easier?"

Bradmore shook his head. "The old man left a great many enemies in London. Cohorts who'd been sacked but not arrested, and others still on the force. Some of them would have been more than happy to take some revenge on his son. Bracken didn't want his boy anywhere near London."

"I see. Yet coming to the earl's estate meant playing quite a waiting game."

"The man was in prison. He was willing to wait for his revenge. It was the elder Bracken's idea for the boy to take a job here. He even forged a letter of reference, assuming Hazelton would visit at some point."

"As it turned out, he didn't have to wait very long."

"No." Bradmore consulted his pocket watch. "Speaking of time, I ought to be going. It was a pleasure meeting you, my lady. Hazelton is a lucky man."

I walked him to the door and headed to the drawing room where Ben, the first footman, waited outside the door.

"Mr. and Mrs. Kendrick have arrived, my lady."

Lovely. Bracing myself, I entered the room to find the Kendricks, my mother, Lily, and Leo, who looked pale and drawn, but much improved from the last time I saw him.

I greeted Leo's parents and joined my mother and Lily on the sofa. Between the four of us, we managed a modified and brief explanation of the past several days and how two of their children had come to be injured.

"Well, that settles it," Mr. Kendrick stated. "Patricia, we are not purchasing a house in the country. It is far too dangerous. And here we thought you were all having a jolly time of it."

"Some of it was lovely," Lily said, smiling sweetly at Leo.

"And the wedding is still planned for tomorrow, isn't it?" Leo asked.

Mother watched the interplay of glances

between the two of them. "I suppose since we have endured so much in the effort of organizing it, we might as well carry on as planned."

"I find it terribly romantic," Mrs. Kendrick agreed, gazing fondly at Lily and Leo.

If one could dismiss a depraved murderer wreaking havoc on one's wedding party, I supposed she was right; it actually was rather romantic.

Chapter 23

$\backsim$

A t last the wedding day had arrived. And a lovely day it was considering we were well into October. The sun shone brightly, the air was crisp, and the little village church had never looked prettier. Lily and her attendants, Anne and Clara, waited in the vestry with Alonzo, who stood ready to walk his sister down the aisle. I felt a twinge of regret on my mother's behalf. Father should have been here. Lily and Alonzo barely noted his absence, but I knew Mother felt it. No wonder she spent so much energy trying to organize her children's lives. I shook off the doldrums. This was a joyous occasion and his loss for missing it. As everything seemed in order, I stepped outside to watch for the rest of our party.

The first to arrive were the Kendricks and the Durants. After a warm greeting, I invited them to take their seats in the church. Patricia Kendrick waved the group inside and took hold of my arm, drawing me away from the door. She wore the look of a woman on a mission, which caused me no little alarm.

"Is something wrong?" I asked.

She glanced around to assure we were quite alone before facing me. "I've had no opportunity to speak with you or Lily privately since we arrived, and this may be my last chance before they go off on their wedding trip." She paused and took a breath. "Forgive me for coming straight to the point, but I must know. Is Lily expecting?"

Dear heavens! How did she know? I parted my lips. Then clamped them shut. I had no idea what to tell her.

She nodded, then patted my arm. "You needn't say a word. I have my answer." She pressed her lips together and lowered her head while I cursed myself for being the worst liar in the world. Or at least the slowest. Why could I never think fast enough?

I stared at the confection of ribbons and flowers nested atop her hair until she raised her head, her eyes shining with tears. Her compressed lips burst open with a gurgle of laughter, ending with a brilliant smile. "I'll be a grandmother," she said in a whisper.

It took a moment for my brain to catch up. "You are happy about this?"

She dashed a tear away with her gloved fingertips. "Well, of course, I'd rather they'd waited, but we haven't had a child in the house for fifteen years. I must admit when we received Leo's note about changing the wedding plans, I wondered if this was the reason."

Perhaps it was due to relief, or just pure joy, but I couldn't stop myself. I pulled her into a hug and laughed along with her.

"We will have to keep this from Mr. Kendrick, of course. When they return from their wedding trip, perhaps we can devise a reason to send them from town on some business or other."

"I'm sure Mr. Durant will be happy to step in for Leo while he's away."

"Yes, that will do very well."

I glanced back at the church to see more guests arriving. "We had best go, or we may miss the wedding."

We arrived at the door just as George walked up the path with my mother and Aunt Hetty. The ladies turned him over to my custody and went inside with Mrs. Kendrick. Hetty turned back to give me a wink.

"I believe Aunt Hetty is delighted with our engagement," I said. "And Mother seems to be coming around, too." George and I had discussed our plans to marry with Rose last night. She was quite happy with the idea and as expected, she did not keep the news to herself.

George tipped his head toward me, revealing the bandage his homburg didn't quite cover. "I assume once this wedding is over, nothing stands in our way?"

"Not a thing." I smiled. "We can begin making plans at the wedding breakfast if you like."

"Plans?" He looked concerned. "Are you thinking of a large affair?"

"Definitely not. I was referring to our future life together—where will we live and just how large a role will I play in your future assignments?"

"Ah. Those plans I'll be happy to discuss, but we had better go inside and get this wedding out of the way first."

We took seats in the front pew. George might have been better off remaining in bed—his head was still wrapped in bandages, and he allowed himself to lean, just a little, on my arm. But I was delighted he insisted on attending.

The organist struck the first chords, and we all came to our feet. Leo, his arm in a sling, stepped out from the sacristy and took his place before the altar. His best man, Treadwell, stood beside him, the blackened eye Leo gave him, now a purplish green.

Rose was the first to come down the aisle, dropping flower petals in her wake. I turned to the door as the bridesmaids approached and caught a glimpse of Charles in the pew behind us, balancing partly on a crutch and partly on Lottie. Anne smiled as she passed by. Clara came next, her arm in a plaster cast.

My mother blotted her eyes as Lily, wholly

unscathed and radiant, floated down the aisle on Alonzo's arm. I watched the scene unfold through a haze of happy tears. This was my family, and George would soon be a most beloved member.

Life couldn't possibly get any better.

Acknowledgments

Heartfelt thanks to the following people for helping to make this book a reality: To my writer friends; Mary Keliikoa, Heather Redmond, Bea Conti, and Clarissa Harwood, who, as beta readers and CPs, assist in untangling twisted plot threads, keep me from making historical errors, and push me to write better.

Many thanks to Christine Hounshell and Mark Fleszar for their technical support in medicine and sports. To J.W.—you know what you did. And to Bud Elonzae, you old romantic you!

There would be no book without my agent, Melissa Edwards, my editor, John Scognamiglio, and the team at Kensington Books, especially Larissa Ackerman, Robin Cook, and Pearl Saban. You are all amazing.

I owe a special debt of gratitude to the librarians and booksellers who have championed the Countess of Harleigh series, and to the readers who have enjoyed it.

Lastly, thanks to my husband, Dan, who lets me read full manuscripts out loud to him, provides endless love and support, and tells everyone he meets about my books!

Books are produced in the United States using U.S.-based materials

Books are printed using a revolutionary new process called THINKtech™ that lowers energy usage by 70% and increases overall quality

Books are durable and flexible because of Smyth-sewing

Paper is sourced using environmentally responsible foresting methods and the paper is acid-free

Center Point Large Print
600 Brooks Road / PO Box 1
Thorndike, ME 04986-0001 USA

(207) 568-3717

US & Canada:
1 800 929-9108
www.centerpointlargeprint.com